Praise for Danielle Steel

"One of the things that keeps Danielle Steel fresh is her bent for timely storylines. . . . The combination of Steel's comprehensive research and her skill at creating credible characters makes for a gripping read." —*Newark Star-Ledger*

"Danielle Steel has again uplifted her readers while skillfully communicating some of life's bittersweet verities. Who could ask for a finer gift than that?" —*The Philadelphia Inquirer*

"A literary phenomenon . . . and not to be pigeonholed as one who produces a predictable kind of book." —*The Detroit News*

"Steel knows how to wring the emotion out of the briefest scene." —*People*

"The world's most popular author tells a good, well-paced story and explores some important issues. . . . Steel affirm[s] life while admitting its turbulence, melodramas, and misfiring passions." —*Booklist*

"Steel is one of the best!" —*Los Angeles Times*

"Steel pulls out all the emotional stops. . . . She delivers." —*Publishers Weekly*

"Magical." —*Library Journal*

"What counts for the reader is the ring of authenticity." —*San Francisco Chronicle*

"Danielle Steel writes boldly and with practiced vividness about tragedy—both national and personal . . . with insight and power." —*Nashville Banner*

"There is something in Steel's work that readers cling to—that makes them identify with characters." —*The Washington Post*

"Steel is almost as much a part of the beach as sunscreen." —*New York Post*

"There is a smooth reading style to her writings which makes it easy to forget the time and to keep flipping the pages." —*The Pittsburgh Press*

"Steel deftly stages heartstring-tugging moments." —*Publishers Weekly*

"A veteran novelist who never coasts is Danielle Steel. . . . She likes her characters and gives them every chance to develop strength and decency; along with her creative storytelling it makes for very satisfying . . . fare." —*Sullivan County Democrat*

"Clever and sweetly dramatic." —*Booklist*

"Steel is a fluent storyteller renowned for taking . . . readers on both an emotional and geographic journey." —*RT Book Reviews*

"Steel's plots are first-rate." —*Newark Star-Ledger*

"Steel yourself." —*Library Journal*

"Ms. Steel excels at pacing her narrative, which races forward, mirroring the frenetic lives chronicled; men and women swept up in bewildering change, seeking solutions to problems never before faced." —*Nashville Banner*

"Steel has a knack for writing about real-life issues and invoking an emotional bond with her characters." —*My Reading Rainbow*

"Steel is a skilled storyteller." —*Booklist*

"One counts on Danielle Steel for a story that entertains and informs."
—*The Chattanooga Times*

"Steel writes convincingly about universal human emotions." —*Publishers Weekly*

"The plots of Danielle Steel's novels twist and weave as incredible stories unfold to the glee and delight of her enormous reading public." —United Press International

"Few modern writers convey the pathos of family and material life with such heartfelt empathy." —*The Philadelphia Inquirer*

"Ms. Steel can be counted on to please her faithful readers."
—*Richmond Times-Dispatch*

"FUN." —*People*

"Engrossing." —*San Antonio Express-News*

"She knows how to weave a story and that's no small achievement!" —*Bookviews*

"Humorous and clever." —*The Greenville Advocate* (Ill.)

"Spellbinding." —*The Dallas Post* (Pa.)

By Danielle Steel

THE WEDDING PLANNER • WORTHY OPPONENTS • WITHOUT A TRACE
THE WHITTIERS • THE HIGH NOTES • THE CHALLENGE • SUSPECTS • BEAUTIFUL
HIGH STAKES • INVISIBLE • FLYING ANGELS • THE BUTLER • COMPLICATIONS
NINE LIVES • FINDING ASHLEY • THE AFFAIR • NEIGHBORS • ALL THAT GLITTERS
ROYAL • DADDY'S GIRLS • THE WEDDING DRESS • THE NUMBERS GAME
MORAL COMPASS • SPY • CHILD'S PLAY • THE DARK SIDE • LOST AND FOUND
BLESSING IN DISGUISE • SILENT NIGHT • TURNING POINT • BEAUCHAMP HALL
IN HIS FATHER'S FOOTSTEPS • THE GOOD FIGHT • THE CAST
ACCIDENTAL HEROES • FALL FROM GRACE • PAST PERFECT • FAIRYTALE
THE RIGHT TIME • THE DUCHESS • AGAINST ALL ODDS • DANGEROUS GAMES
THE MISTRESS • THE AWARD • RUSHING WATERS • MAGIC • THE APARTMENT
PROPERTY OF A NOBLEWOMAN • BLUE • PRECIOUS GIFTS • UNDERCOVER
COUNTRY • PRODIGAL SON • PEGASUS • A PERFECT LIFE • POWER PLAY • WINNERS
FIRST SIGHT • UNTIL THE END OF TIME • THE SINS OF THE MOTHER
FRIENDS FOREVER • BETRAYAL • HOTEL VENDÔME • HAPPY BIRTHDAY
44 CHARLES STREET • LEGACY • FAMILY TIES • BIG GIRL • SOUTHERN LIGHTS
MATTERS OF THE HEART • ONE DAY AT A TIME • A GOOD WOMAN • ROGUE
HONOR THYSELF • AMAZING GRACE • BUNGALOW 2 • SISTERS • H.R.H.
COMING OUT • THE HOUSE • TOXIC BACHELORS • MIRACLE • IMPOSSIBLE
ECHOES • SECOND CHANCE • RANSOM • SAFE HARBOUR • JOHNNY ANGEL
DATING GAME • ANSWERED PRAYERS • SUNSET IN ST. TROPEZ
THE COTTAGE • THE KISS • LEAP OF FAITH • LONE EAGLE • JOURNEY
THE HOUSE ON HOPE STREET • THE WEDDING • IRRESISTIBLE FORCES
GRANNY DAN • BITTERSWEET • MIRROR IMAGE • THE KLONE AND I
THE LONG ROAD HOME • THE GHOST • SPECIAL DELIVERY • THE RANCH
SILENT HONOR • MALICE • FIVE DAYS IN PARIS • LIGHTNING • WINGS • THE GIFT
ACCIDENT • VANISHED • MIXED BLESSINGS • JEWELS • NO GREATER LOVE
HEARTBEAT • MESSAGE FROM NAM • DADDY • STAR • ZOYA • KALEIDOSCOPE
FINE THINGS • WANDERLUST • SECRETS • FAMILY ALBUM • FULL CIRCLE
CHANGES • THURSTON HOUSE • CROSSINGS • ONCE IN A LIFETIME
A PERFECT STRANGER • REMEMBRANCE • PALOMINO • LOVE: *POEMS* • THE RING
LOVING • TO LOVE AGAIN • SUMMER'S END • SEASON OF PASSION • THE PROMISE
NOW AND FOREVER • PASSION'S PROMISE • GOING HOME

Nonfiction

EXPECT A MIRACLE: *Quotations to Live and Love By*
PURE JOY: *The Dogs We Love*
A GIFT OF HOPE: *Helping the Homeless*
HIS BRIGHT LIGHT: *The Story of Nick Traina*

For Children

PRETTY MINNIE IN PARIS
PRETTY MINNIE IN HOLLYWOOD

Danielle Steel

The Challenge

A Novel

Dell | New York

The Challenge is a work of fiction. Names, characters, places, and incidents are the products of the author's imagination or are used fictitiously. Any resemblance to actual events, locales, or persons, living or dead, is entirely coincidental.

2023 Dell Trade Paperback Edition

Published in the United States by Dell, an imprint of Random House, a division of Penguin Random House LLC, New York.

Dell is a registered trademark and the D colophon is a trademark of Penguin Random House LLC.

Originally published in hardcover in the United States by Delacorte Press, an imprint of Random House, a division of Penguin Random House LLC, in 2022.

This book contains an excerpt from the forthcoming book *Palazzo* by Danielle Steel. This excerpt has been set for this edition only and may not reflect the final content of the forthcoming edition.

ISBN 978-0-593-60020-7

Ebook ISBN 978-1-984-82162-1

Printed in the United States of America on acid-free paper

randomhousebooks.com

2 4 6 8 9 7 5 3 1

Cover design: Derek Walls

Cover images: © Christoph Wagner/Getty Images (lake and mountain in foreground), © Ascent Xmedia/Getty Images (man and woman together), © Zing Images/Getty Images (man at far left), © Thomas Söllner/EyeEm/Getty Images (man second from right), © Lilkin/Getty Images (man at far right), © Peter Paterson/Arcangel (sky and mountains in background)

Book design by Sara Bereta

To my wonderful children,
Trevor, Todd, Beatrix, Nicky,
Victoria, Vanessa, Samantha,
Maxx, and Zara,

May you conquer all your challenges
and be forever safe.
You are my greatest blessings
every moment of every day.
I love you with all my heart,

Mom / ds

The Challenge

Chapter 1

The day after his fourteenth birthday in July, Peter Pollock still had to do all his usual morning chores on his parents' ranch in Fishtail, Montana. Fishtail was in Stillwater County, in the foothills of the Beartooth Mountains, an hour from Billings, Montana. The closest mountain to them was Granite Peak, with an elevation of 12,807 feet, the highest mountain in Montana and the most challenging to climb. The town itself was at 4,466 feet and had a population of 478 people. Peter had grown up in Fishtail and loved his life there, except for his morning chores.

He was a good-looking boy, tall for his age. He looked like his father, Pitt, with straight blond hair and sky-blue eyes. His mother, Anne, was blond too, petite and fine-featured, and a stunning rider. She had won blue ribbons at all the local horse shows and rodeos in her teens. She and Pitt had been high school sweethearts since freshman year, when they were Peter's age. They'd gone to the University of Montana together, and got married in June after they'd graduated.

Peter was born in July of the following year, when his parents were twenty-three years old. They were thirty-seven now, and had always said they wanted five or six children. Anne was an only child and had wanted a big family, but she had never gotten pregnant again. They'd gone to see a specialist in Billings, and another one in Denver. The doctors they saw marveled at the fact that they'd even managed to have Peter. A defect in Anne's fallopian tubes made it almost impossible to conceive, and she never had again, so they focused all their love and attention on Peter, and were grateful for the miracle of their only child.

Pitt's paternal grandfather had founded the Pollock ranch. They bred and sold the finest horses in the state, and it was the largest ranch in the area, well known and respected throughout the western states. People came from as far south as Texas to buy their horses, and as far east as Kentucky. The bloodlines of their horses were legendary. Pitt's father had run the ranch when his father died, and as an only child himself, Pitt had inherited it from his father when he died in an accident ten years before. Pitt Pollock was one of the youngest, most successful ranchers in Montana. Anne had never even thought about that when she fell in love with him at fourteen. Her father had been everyone's favorite local vet, and he had taken Anne with him many times when he tended to the horses on the ranch. It had never dawned on either father that their children would fall in love, and when they did, their parents figured it wouldn't last. They were just kids when it all started. Twenty-three years later, they were more in love than ever.

Anne worked side by side with Pitt in the office and was the chief financial officer. She had majored in business and economics, and had a great head for finance. Pitt knew everything there was to know about horses. He'd been taught by his father and grandfather, and had learned his lessons well. Peter knew that one day he would run the ranch. He was a serious, responsible boy and had never caused his parents any trouble. He got decent grades in school, but liked to have fun too. He planned to follow in his parents' footsteps and go to the University of Montana. His mother thought he should go to business school afterwards, to learn everything he could about running a venture as large as theirs. The world had changed since Pitt's grandfather's day. Now it was essential to know everything about the economics involved, not just about horses. It was a flourishing business. Peter was nowhere near thinking about graduate school yet, although his parents talked about it more than he wanted them to. He was starting high school at the end of August, which was as far as he wanted to look for now. He was excited about it.

He had grown up with a carefree life on the ranch, and rode some of the finest horses in the country whenever he wanted to. He had ridden in his first rodeo when he was five, his parents bursting with pride while they watched him. Their open adoration of him was embarrassing at times. For Peter, parents who were crazy about him, and madly in love with each other, was a given. All he wanted to do was ride, have fun, and spend as much time as he could with his three best friends.

The boys had grown up together, and they spent all the time they could with each other, riding their bikes to each other's homes and exploring. Anne and Pitt always made the boys feel welcome at the ranch. They had set up a bunk room where they could stay whenever they wanted. They didn't want Peter to suffer from not having siblings, and the four boys spent every possible moment together, although Pitt kept Peter busy doing chores on the ranch. He wanted his son to learn ranching from the bottom up, and didn't hesitate to assign him menial tasks, like the ones Pitt had done as a boy. Peter never thought about how successful they were, or what all this would mean to him one day. It was where they lived and what they did. His friends paid no attention to it either. They had no regard for the thousands of acres the Pollocks owned, or the volume of business they did, breeding and selling valuable horses. None of them understood how lucrative the ranch was, which Anne and Pitt thought was just as well.

Bill and Pattie Brown owned a smaller neighboring ranch. Bill's father had bought the land for it from Pitt's father when Bill was a boy. They had cattle as well as horses and sheep. They owned a successful dairy, and though their operation was smaller than the Pollocks', they did well. They were Anne and Pitt's closest friends. Pitt, Anne, and Pattie had gone to high school together. Bill and Pitt were best friends. And once the two couples were married, they were ecstatic when they got pregnant at the same time. Anne and Pattie talked about how their babies would become best friends one day, or marry. Their sons were born three weeks apart, with Matt Brown arriving before Peter. Anne and Pitt were Matt's godparents. And their wish had come true when the two boys were best friends by the time they went to nursery school together. Anne had been graciously happy for Bill and Pattie when they had a second child eight years later, although the Pollocks knew that a brother or sister for Peter was not in the cards for them. They had made their peace with it. The Browns' second child was another boy, Benjie. He was now six years old, and his older brother's adoring shadow, much to Matt's irritation most of the time. Matt grudgingly took Benjie with him whenever his parents insisted, but he loved escaping to the Pollocks' ranch to hang out with Peter and, whenever possible, he would leave Benjie at home.

Pattie had gone to nursing school while Anne and Pitt were in college. Bill was three years older and already working on the ranch. He and Pattie got married a year before Anne and Pitt. They had broken up for a while before that, and dated other people, but they married each other in the end. Pattie worked as a nurse for two years until Matt was born, and then became a stay-at-home mom after that. Her life with Bill was secure. Her family hadn't had the means that Bill's did, so she was grateful for the life he provided her and their two boys. She was the envy of her sisters, with a husband who owned a successful ranch, and she didn't have to work. Her sisters' husbands were ranch hands elsewhere in the state, as Pattie's father had been. Both Pattie's sisters had jobs, one as a teacher and the other as a secretary. Pattie was the success story in the family, married to a rancher.

Bill and Pattie's relationship was occasionally stormy, unlike Anne and Pitt's still-romantic relationship. Bill had a hot temper, and she had a fiery nature, but despite the occasional fights, Pattie and Bill considered themselves happily married. Pattie thought about having a third baby at times, and would have liked to have a girl, but the prospect of ending up with three boys made the idea less appealing. She had her hands full with the two she had. Matt had been much more mischievous and adventuresome than Peter when they were younger, and Pattie was constantly chasing after Benjie to make sure that he didn't get hurt in the cattle barn, or chasing after the sheep, or hanging around the bullpen. He wanted to do everything his older brother did, and she spent a good part of her day checking up on him, worried about what he was up to, and often scolding him when she found him.

The two families went on vacations together every year. One of their favorite pastimes was camping, and the boys loved it. They provided an extended family for each other. Peter and Matt were always at one home or the other, with a slight preference for the Pollocks' place, because Benjie wasn't there.

Matt's ambitions were very different from Peter Pollock's. Peter's future was set as the sole heir to the ranch. He would be the fourth generation to run it one day. He loved where they lived and the life of a rancher, and he watched his father carefully to learn from him.

Matt dreamed of city life. He was considered a computer wiz at school and wanted a job in the tech world one day. He knew who all the big players in tech were, and he was desperate to work for one of them when he graduated from college. He wanted to go to Stanford if he could keep his grades up, and then stay in California to work in Silicon Valley. It sounded abysmal to Peter, who loved the mountains and open spaces of Montana, and wanted to stay in the place where he was born. Matt couldn't wait for high school to be over so he could leave.

Benjie said he was going to be a rodeo clown and ride the broncos when he grew up. He'd had a narrow escape from one of the bullpens the last time they all went to the rodeo. At five, he had once followed a clown into the arena, with a bull pawing the ground twenty feet away from him, all in the two seconds his mother hadn't been watching him. She never let go of his hand at the rodeo after that. It was easy to believe he'd be a rodeo clown one day. That was not his parents' aspiration for him, but at six, it was all Benjie dreamed of.

Tim Taylor was the third musketeer in Peter and Matt's group of inseparable friends. He had faced greater challenges than Matt and Peter. His homelife had been less idyllic, and he was happiest when he was at either the Pollock ranch, or the Browns'. He was warmly welcomed at both. His parents were both natives of Montana from modest homes. His parents' fathers were both ranch hands too, like the men in Pattie's family.

His mother, June, had suffered a case of bacterial meningitis when she was pregnant with him, and survived it without losing the baby. But he was born partially deaf as a result of the high fever she'd had for several days. He wore two hearing aids, which helped. He had had extensive speech therapy, and although he still spoke with a marked speech defect, he managed well with the hearing aids, and lip-read and signed when necessary. After his mother's diligent work with him, and a good speech therapist, he was at the top of his class at school and nothing slowed him down. He read voraciously, and had a passion for horses, as well as great instincts about them. He wanted to go to veterinary school, then come back to Fishtail and work with horses.

He was extremely adept at rock climbing, like a mountain goat, his mother said about him. She was proud of the progress he'd made. He'd finished eighth grade at the top of his class as usual, and wanted to take advanced placement classes in high school, to get into a good college. His friends were indifferent to his hearing impairment. He managed so well in spite of it, and he had a great sense of humor.

After working closely with him on his speech therapy in his early years, June had gone back to school and become a licensed speech therapist. She worked in the nearby town of Red Lodge, and was recommended by several doctors in the area and Saint Vincent Healthcare hospital in Billings. She thoroughly enjoyed her practice.

Her marriage to Ted Taylor rapidly became a casualty of Tim's affliction. It had put a huge strain on their relationship, which had been on a bumpy road anyway. Ted was a proud man, who had grown up in intense poverty as a young man. His father had been an alcoholic ranch worker who'd died young, leaving Ted's mother to struggle to make ends meet.

Ted had been unable to accept the fact that his son was less than perfect. He had kept away from Tim at first, then had gone through a period of heavy drinking, which was how he handled most problems, like his father had. He had finally conquered his problem with alcohol through AA, but sought a "geographic" solution to their marital problems. He had left June and Tim, and taken a job in Oklahoma, working in the oil fields. He had done well, but came home seldom, unable to face the problems there. Then he took a job in Texas, which included working on oil rigs in the Gulf of Mexico, and later traveled in the Middle East. After four years of it, and his seeming inability to remember that he had a wife and son in Montana, June finally divorced Ted when Tim was five. He no longer remembered a time when his parents were together. He saw his father once or twice a year now. Ted sent him postcards from exotic places and called him once in a while, but rarely saw him. He still couldn't handle Tim's handicap, no matter how well Tim had mastered it with his mother's help. Ted never told people that he had a deaf son, except in AA meetings when he blamed his drinking on the divorce, rather than the reverse. He ignored the fact that he had run away from his wife and son to work halfway around the world, so he didn't have to face them. He could afford to send them enough child support so they could live comfortably in a house at the edge of town that June rented. He never stayed longer than a day when he came to visit, and he couldn't leave fast enough. He still couldn't face what he perceived to be Tim's imperfections. He felt guilty for having run out on them, but had never been able to turn it around. He never even tried. He had run away from his problems all his life, just like his father.

June tried not to be bitter about it, and refrained from making disparaging comments to Tim about his dad, but she felt cheated by Ted nonetheless. She'd had a few brief affairs in the nine years since her divorce from Ted, but her only real love was her son. Ted had turned out to be someone they couldn't count on, and Tim had in effect grown up without a father. The life Ted led sounded glamorous, working in foreign places, and Tim made him sound like a hero when he talked about him, but he and June knew he wasn't. Tim had had more fathering from Bill Brown and Pitt Pollock than he had ever had from his own father.

Matt and Peter were like his brothers. He and Peter were only children with devoted mothers. The main difference being that, other than in name and occasional brief annual visits, Tim had no father. Tim tried to impress his father with his grades and his athletic accomplishments, none of which seemed to interest Ted in his distant life on the oil rigs. June was well aware that if there were ever an emergency, she wouldn't even know where to reach Ted, but fortunately there had never been one. Tim was not a wild child, or prone to high-risk activities, other than his rock climbing, which he was responsible about, as he was in all things, unlike his father. The Browns and Pollocks often included him on their vacations, and they were well aware that he needed a stand-in father. They provided it as best they could, for which June was deeply grateful. Tim needed a man in his life, in lieu of the fantasy father he had, who was more of an illusion than a reality, and had disappointed Tim all his life. His mother was the person who never let him down. He wanted to be a speech therapist like her when he grew up, so he could help kids like him.

The fourth member of their gang lived at the edge of Fishtail too, near Tim's house. Noel Wylie had gone to school with the other three boys since kindergarten. His parents, Marlene and Bob, had moved to Montana from Denver right after Noel was born, and were Fishtail's two very respected attorneys. They opened a joint practice, and the Pollocks were clients. Living in Fishtail was a choice they had made, not an accident of birth, and they loved it. They had wanted to bring up their two sons in a healthy, wholesome, rural atmosphere, and to get away from cutthroat city lawyering. It had been the answer to their prayers. Fishtail had met all their expectations, and they had a busy, booming practice. They thought Fishtail was the most beautiful place on earth.

Their older son, Justin, was entering his senior year of high school at the end of August, and Noel would be starting as a freshman. Neither of the boys were enchanted with their parents' choice to live out of the mainstream, in Fishtail, and both wanted to return as soon as possible to the city life they no longer remembered but were sure they would prefer. They had both decided that growing up in a town with a population of four hundred was oppressive and a form of deprivation. Justin wanted to go to law school, and he dreamed of Chicago, New York, Denver, or L.A., wherever he got into college and eventually law school. His parents hoped he'd come back to Fishtail, to join them in their practice, but all he wanted was to get hired by a big city law firm, the bigger the better, and never live in Fishtail again once he left for college. He insisted that city life was in his DNA, and he didn't want to spend the rest of his life in Fishtail or the Beartooth Mountains. He was counting the days until he could leave.

Noel shared the same opinion. Their parents were highly intelligent, Ivy League–educated attorneys who had chosen the less traveled path, as the children of overachievers themselves. Justin and Noel wanted to try their hands at that kind of achievement in a more competitive, urban, challenging world.

Noel wanted to go to med school. The idea had come to him when he was diagnosed with juvenile diabetes at seven. He had faced the challenge well, and wore an insulin pump now, which spared him from having to administer insulin shots to himself. The pump monitored his sugar levels for him and gave him the insulin doses he needed. His three closest friends, some of his classmates, and all of his teachers were aware that he was diabetic. He had explained it in medical terms to his three closest friends in detail, showed them the pump on his side, and told them the implications of having juvenile diabetes. He wanted to treat juvenile diabetic patients one day, and, like Justin, he wanted to practice in a big city, at a teaching hospital in San Francisco or L.A. His parents had taken him to Children's Hospital Colorado, in Denver, and UCSF in San Francisco for diagnosis and treatment, and he loved the bustle and activity of the hospitals he'd seen. After a while, they no longer frightened him. He wanted to be a doctor like the ones on the teams that had treated him. He'd had some hard times with the disease at first, until they got it regulated. He'd handled it well, with the careful supervision of his mother. His brother Justin was knowledgeable about the disease as well, and knew everything he needed to in case Noel ever fainted, or had a reaction from high or low sugar or a problem with the insulin. Justin was as well versed as his parents about how to handle a diabetic crisis for Noel, but there had been none in many years. And Noel himself knew how to deal with it. His friends almost forgot that he was diabetic, and that their parents were well versed in it too, in case there was ever a problem while Noel visited them.

Justin and Noel were very different. Noel was down-to-earth, practical, and mature for his age. In some ways he was fearless. Because he'd been sick at an early age, and had to face the realities of his disease, he was undaunted by life, and didn't let anything stop him. He had an outgoing, more gregarious nature than his older brother. Justin was always more anxious, and more introverted. Because he knew that his brother faced risks with his disease, he felt protective and responsible for him.

His parents expected him to look out for his younger brother at home and at school, and whenever their parents were busy. Neither

Marlene nor Bob Wylie realized how burdened Justin felt by it, entrusted with the life of another human being. Justin even felt guilty sometimes that Noel suffered from an illness and he didn't. He was especially kind to Noel to make up for it.

In a way, Noel's illness had impacted Justin's childhood more than Noel's. Noel took it in his stride. Justin worried about everything, and never expressed it. Still waters ran deep, as his mother said about him. Justin had a much quieter nature than his exuberant younger brother.

Justin liked girls but hadn't had a girlfriend yet. Noel couldn't wait to get to high school and find one. He was a bright, handsome boy.

Their biggest medical problem at the moment was not Noel but Bob, their father. Bob had been diagnosed with pancreatic cancer the summer before, and had gone downhill slowly at first. But the disease gathered speed quickly, and by Christmas, he'd had to quit their legal practice, leaving it all on Marlene's shoulders. She had handled it heroically for the past seven months—Bob's care, their law practice, and mothering the two boys. There wasn't a spare moment in her day when she was not caring for someone: her husband, her two sons, or the clients in their practice. She was exhausted and hid it as best she could, trying to keep Bob's spirits up, not worrying her sons unduly while preparing them for what they all knew was coming. He had already outlived the prognosis by several months. She had tried to warn the boys as gently as she could, but she knew that neither of them fully understood how hopeless Bob's situation was. She couldn't even understand it herself. He had been so strong and capable, and suddenly so desperately sick.

Bob had stopped his chemo treatments in June. They were destroying what was left of the quality of his life and made him desperately ill. He wanted to enjoy the last months he would have with his wife and sons, although he was too weak to leave the house, and often his bed, now. The doctors had agreed that further chemo was useless.

Marlene had nurses come to help her regularly, when she had to work all day or travel elsewhere in the county and couldn't come home to check on him every few hours. Hospice workers had begun to visit them daily a few weeks before, and that made the process a little easier. But there was nothing easy about it. Marlene was losing the husband she loved and had been married to for twenty years. She was forty-five years old and could no longer avoid the fact that soon she would be a widow. Bob was facing it as gracefully and as lovingly as he had everything else in their life, but she couldn't hide from it anymore.

She couldn't imagine life without him. They had lived together, worked together, shared every task and burden. He had protected her and made all their important decisions. And now it was all going to be on her shoulders, and it had been for the last seven months, as he got weaker. Bob could hardly leave their bedroom now, and she could see that talking to him about their legal practice or any problem of the boys exhausted him. She tried to shield him from everything she could.

She had begun to have nightmares about Bob and both boys being in an accident, and all of them dying together, leaving her to face life alone. She was much more anxious about the boys now, and worried about them more, as though trying to protect them would help avert a tragedy, but she knew that Bob's death was heading toward them relentlessly, and wouldn't wait much longer. She had done what she could to prepare the boys, as gently as possible, and they were devastated. Justin was in denial and would talk about Bob being at his graduation from high school in a year. Noel, being more interested in medical issues, had read on the internet about his father's illness, and would go on walks alone sometimes, crying about what they all knew was coming. Marlene wished she could slow down the process, or cure him magically, but she couldn't. They would all have to face it, and every day she wondered how she would survive without him. She had always been able to rely on him. And without meaning to, she was relying on Justin more than before, since he was older than Noel. At seventeen, he was almost an adult and never balked at the responsibilities she put on him, like caring for Noel.

Their friends and neighbors had been wonderful, and did all they could to be supportive. They visited Bob when he was up to it, dropped off meals Marlene could just put in the microwave so she didn't have to cook, did errands for her, and offered to pick up Noel from his activities. Justin drove him most of the time, but it was a relief for him when others did it, so Marlene accepted their help gratefully, for her sake as well as Justin's.

The arrival in the past few weeks of hospice workers to care for Bob was an undeniable and ominous sign that they had entered a new phase, and worse times were coming. Marlene hadn't even planned a vacation with the boys that summer. She was afraid to leave Bob, even for a few days. She wanted to be there at the end, whenever it happened. They were living from day to day. She could see Bob fading before her eyes, and the strain was brutal for all of them.

All three boys, Matt, Tim, and Noel, were heading toward the Pollock ranch the day after Peter's birthday. They were going to swim in the shallow stream on their property, not far from the house, go riding into the hills if it wasn't too hot, and Peter's mother had promised to pay for dinner at the diner in town. As a special treat, the boys could dine there alone. They usually went with their parents for the variety of good homestyle food. Anne had told Peter that morning that she thought they were old enough at fourteen to go there on their own, eat dinner like adults, and behave themselves. She or Pitt would drop them off and pick them up, probably she would, since Pitt often finished at the ranch office late, after answering a last slew of emails from all over the country. Then he would come home for dinner with her and Peter.

She thought it would be a nice treat for Peter to go out with his friends. He grinned when she suggested it at breakfast. It was a first sign of what he could expect as he entered high school in another month, and it made him feel very grown up.

He was thinking about it as Matt arrived and dropped his bike on the ground outside the barn and went inside to find Peter. He was just putting away the heavy shovel he had used to clear away some hay, and Matt helped him spread out a fresh bale. Peter said he was finished with his chores, and then told Matt about dinner at the diner. Matt looked worried for a minute.

"I didn't bring any money." He never did. None of them ever had more than a few dollars on them. They didn't need it. There was nothing they needed to buy and nothing to pay for.

"My parents are treating," Peter reassured him, and Matt looked relieved. He spent the allowance he got on video games and candy every week. He tried to buy a girlie magazine once, with naked women in it, but the man who sold books and magazines in town knew him and wouldn't sell it to him, even though Matt had just turned fourteen, which seemed to him old enough to look at naked women. He would have shared it with Peter. He bought a video game instead.

"I hate living in a town where everyone knows my parents," Peter said when Matt had complained, but he was looking forward to dinner at the diner, just the four boys. They could talk about whatever they wanted, which was usually horses, or movies they wanted to see, or the next camping trip they were going on with their parents. Matt had had a brief flirtation with a girl in eighth grade that spring but it had evaporated quickly. Peter hadn't had any forays into romance yet, although he was always aware that his parents had fallen in love when they were his age, and been together ever since. He didn't want anything like that, but going to the movies with a girl, or watching a movie with one at home in their playroom sounded appealing. He just hadn't met the right girl yet. He'd rather hang out with his pals for the moment. He wasn't desperate for female company yet. Horses and video games still seemed like more fun and less mysterious.

Tim and Noel arrived a short time later, and they helped themselves to the sandwiches Peter's mother had left for them in the fridge, before heading to the stream in their bathing suits. They biked down a narrow dirt road to get there, left their bikes under a tree, and jumped into the stream, splashed each other, laughed as they teased each other for an hour in the water, and then lay on the grass to dry off. It was a perfect day, hot but not unbearably so. They rode back to the house around four o'clock, and agreed to go riding the next day. When they got back to the house, they headed downstairs to the spacious playroom Pitt had had built for them. He liked having Peter's friends around. He and Anne both did.

At six o'clock, Anne reminded the boys to put their jeans on and said she'd drive them to dinner at the Silver Spur Diner, as she put the money in Peter's pocket. It was going to be their first dinner out alone as independent young men, and a landmark moment for all four of them.

When she dropped them off, she watched them walk inside, sauntering like grown men, laughing and shoving each other. She drove away with a smile. Her baby was growing up. It was hard to believe he'd be starting high school in a month. It all went so fast. It seemed like only a few years ago that he'd been a baby. And now they were going out to dinner on their own.

Chapter 2

Juliet Marshall had been visiting her father, Tom, for nearly two weeks, and had another four weeks left in her six-week visit with him from mid-July until the end of August. Her parents had agreed to it, when her father moved from New York to Fishtail in January. Tom had discovered Fishtail when he came to the area on a fishing trip with a group of men from his office. He had fallen in love on the spot with the town and the Beartooth Mountains, and even the hundred-year-old historic General Store. The town had haunted him when he went back to New York. He had been longing for a change, and realized that Fishtail was it. He was tired of the rat race, the constant stress of his job, and living in New York. His marriage had been showing signs of stress for the last few years. They'd been fighting more than they ever had before.

He tried telling his wife, Beth, about Fishtail and the beauty of Montana when he got back. She looked at him like he was nuts. They were inveterate New Yorkers who had grown up there and lived there all their lives. She didn't want to live anywhere else. She was a freelance writer for magazines and highly respected in her field. She loved New York, and she had thought Tom's complaints about New York were just growing pains, and temporary, and had paid no attention to them.

Beth discounted what he'd said as some kind of midlife crisis, or burnout, which she thought was incredibly irresponsible and adolescent of him at forty-three years of age with a great job at a prestigious investment firm on Wall Street. He was highly paid and suddenly no longer cared. Money and success were the gods that he and Beth had worshipped. Now he wanted to walk out on all of it, and he expected Beth to do the same. He got six of his clients to commit their investment portfolios to him, and he was proposing to manage their money for them long-distance, from the wilds of Montana. He told Beth he couldn't live in New York anymore. The stress would kill him. He wanted a healthier, more wholesome life, which Beth considered a betrayal of everything they had built together. He thought all of it was meaningless, and they agreed to separate so he could pursue his new life.

She was furious with him. He had a great job, a wife, and a thirteen-year-old daughter, and he was giving it all up to live in Fishtail, Montana.

Juliet was heartbroken when they told her. They separated and he left his job, lined up his clients, and moved to Fishtail four months later. When Beth realized he was serious, she filed for divorce.

There had been no sign of what she called his "insanity" before. They'd had their squabbles like other couples, and minor disagreements, but there had been no hint that he would give up a career and a marriage and move to a town of four hundred people in Montana. The news had broadsided Beth, Juliet, and all of their close friends. There were other couples who appeared to have more severe problems, and no one would have been surprised by their divorces. In Tom and Beth's case, everyone was stunned. Overnight, they had nothing in common, except their daughter. He said he couldn't live in New York anymore, not even for Juliet. Tom simply said they had "run out of gas." He had felt pushed to the breaking point doing business in New York, the constant stress and pressure, the viciousness, the competition, never having time to smell the roses (which he was allergic to anyway, Beth pointed out), and the quality of life or lack of it, living in the city, pursuing goals that had become meaningless to him. He said it was a phony life that he no longer believed in. He didn't want to teach their daughter a value system in which the only thing that mattered was money and the pursuit of it, no matter what it cost the soul. He said that he felt as though he had wasted the first half of his life, and he didn't want to waste the rest of it. He wanted to live in natural surroundings, hike and fish and ride in his spare time, and not have to ride the subway to work every day. It was an argument Beth couldn't win. Their marriage had been shaky for the past few years, as they seemed to be going their separate ways and wanting different things more and more. Their relationship collapsed completely with the weight of the changes he wanted to make, and ultimately did make. He gave up everything Beth cared about in their marriage, all the superficial signs of status they had worked so hard for. Beth had no intention of giving up everything just because he had gone crazy. Tom had completely changed. Living in Montana was out of the question for her.

She had been working for a magazine when they'd met seventeen years before. She had felt much the same way about the magazine that he did about Wall Street now. She felt stifled so she had left to become a freelance writer, and had done very well in the years since. She contributed to their life and he envied the freedom she had working for herself. She no longer had to deal with office politics, which she had hated, and could work at her own pace. She worked harder as a freelancer than she had in her job, working for someone else. She thrived on the overachieving atmosphere of New York. He accused her of being a workaholic, which she conceded might be true. She loved all the cultural and status social events easily available in New York. Their parents had been high achievers too, and she and Tom had gone to the best schools. They had come from similar backgrounds, with the same values. She couldn't understand what had gone wrong. They had become strangers to each other. Beth wanted Juliet to go to the best private schools, as they had, then eventually to an Ivy League college and succeed at a career she loved, not live in the sticks in a hick town.

"Money, money, money, that's all you think about," Tom had accused her. She was a money machine. He didn't want to be one anymore.

"I want to provide the best for our daughter, and it takes money to do that," Beth insisted. "You went to Harvard, why shouldn't she one day?" Beth's father had run an ad agency and her mother was a successful publisher. Tom's father was the president of an investment banking firm. Success was important to Beth and Tom and always had been. Now he was opting to step out of the race. She was furious with him. "You want to waste everything we've accomplished and sit on a mountaintop in Montana? And what about Juliet? Where would she go to school?" That led to a ferocious argument about public schools, the advantages of rural living, the importance of nature, and the admission that he was sick and tired of competing with her and everyone else in Manhattan. He couldn't see the point of it anymore. He said he needed to breathe and wanted a "real" life, like a "normal person."

"For heaven's sake, Tom, grow up. You're not a Boy Scout anymore. You're forty-three years old with a great career, a wife, and a child. You can't just throw it all away and go hide in a cave somewhere."

"I don't want to hide. I want to breathe and live for a change. Living in New York isn't real and it costs a fortune. We could live in Montana for a fraction of what we spend here." He had a point, but Beth didn't want to hear it. She was profoundly committed to life in New York, and everything it represented. "I'm tired of trying to impress people I don't give a damn about." He had some valid points, all of which Beth refused to listen to.

"You're tired of being a responsible adult," she accused him, "and you want to return to the boyhood you never had." His parents had pushed him hard to achieve and so had she. "You want to be Tom Sawyer or Peter Pan. I don't want to be Heidi or Tinker Bell or play *Little House on the Prairie*. We're grown-ups for chrissake. We have a sophisticated, adult life I love, and Juliet has every advantage we can give her. I'm not going to take that away from her. All you think about is yourself. Try thinking about us for a change. You're being completely irresponsible, Tom. You can't just throw our whole life out the window because *you* need a change."

"You could work from anywhere," he reminded her, which was true. "You write freelance and you have a good agent."

"I write about politics, the economy, the world on a fast track, important current events, heads of state. What would I write about from there? The beauty of a tree? The sunset on a mountain? That's not what I do. Why can't you take a sabbatical if you need a break, or see a therapist or take medication?" He said she completely disregarded what he felt and needed, which was true. She couldn't understand what had happened to him, and she didn't want to. They had irreconcilable differences to an extreme degree.

"If I went on sabbatical," he said to her, "I'd be drowning again as soon as I came back. I hate my job and our life. I need to be true to myself. A therapist isn't going to change that." The sad fact was that, without noticing, they had drifted along the river of life going in opposite directions, and were shouting at each other from the distance. They could hear each other, but they were too far apart now to be able to reach each other, and neither of them wanted to change directions. She was thirty-eight years old and didn't want to turn forty living in Montana, having given up everything she had fought hard for in New York. She believed in what she was doing, and the life she lived, as much as he believed what he was discovering about himself. Neither of them were wrong, but they were wrong for each other. The battles got more bitter for the next three months. The tension Tom was feeling spilled over into his work and he got into an equally bitter battle with the senior partner of the firm. It was about one of his clients' investments, and how Tom was handling the account. Tom gave notice and left the firm two weeks later, which only made things worse between him and Beth. She accused him of creating the fight on purpose. A week later, they separated and he moved out, while Juliet watched in horror as their home life and her parents' marriage unraveled. Tom moved into a bleak furnished apartment while he made his plans. And he left for Montana after Christmas, in January, and advised Beth that he had found the home of his dreams in Fishtail, Montana. She gave up on the marriage and the hope of his returning to sanity. She filed for divorce when he left and came to a temporary agreement with him about visitation.

He flew to New York every six weeks for a weekend to see Juliet, which was the best he could do for now. Beth agreed to let her stay with him for six weeks in the summer, and they would have to figure out more permanent visitation after that, in the fall. The hardest part was that he hadn't moved to a city like Boston or Chicago, which was easy to get to. Juliet couldn't easily fly to see her father for a weekend in Fishtail, Montana, and from what Beth could learn, the area was snowed in for half the year.

Juliet was bitterly unhappy about the arrangements, and blamed her mother for filing the divorce and not giving Tom a chance to work things out. She blamed both of them for playing tug-of-war with her, and she argued with her mother constantly about everything. She was relieved to get away from her, but still upset at her father when she arrived in Fishtail in July, with no idea what it would be like. She was still crushed that her parents were going to be divorced. Many of her friends' parents were, but they lived across town from each other, not halfway across the country in a tiny town that was hard to get to.

Juliet was happy to see him when she arrived, and surprised to find that he had rented a pretty Victorian house and furnished most of it. He had become adept at ordering furniture and antiques from the internet, and had done a good job with the house, particularly with her big sunny bedroom, which had a four-poster bed he'd gotten on 1stDibs. He had wallpapered the room for her himself, and Beth had sent him a few of his things, and some paintings that he loved. She didn't argue with him over their belongings, but she still couldn't believe what he'd done. Their marriage had disintegrated in a matter of months.

Juliet could see that he was happy. The area was beautiful. He drove her up into the mountains, and they took hikes along the trails. Juliet was tall and athletic like her father. She enjoyed the outdoors more than her mother did. Although Beth had been a champion ski racer in college, and she had taught Juliet to ski when she was five. But everything Beth did was about competing and winning for money. Tom wanted more than that in his life. He wanted substance and real people and a job he enjoyed. Beth didn't, and she called him irresponsible and juvenile.

Tom took Juliet fishing at a peaceful lake. They made dinner together at night, and later tried the few local restaurants in Fishtail and neighboring towns. It wasn't New York, and she missed her friends, but it made her realize how much she missed living with her dad. She didn't think his ideas were crazy. They made sense to her, but not to her mother. Juliet didn't want to leave her friends in New York, but she didn't want to leave her father either.

She could see that he loved where he was living, the simplicity of it. He was happy there, and she realized that it might be the right choice for him. It was just terrible luck that Fishtail would have been all wrong for her mother. For Juliet, it now meant that growing up was accepting that she would have divorced parents, and a father who lived far away in a remote place with a completely different life. She could see that he was peaceful, less stressed, and he seemed content. He was much more patient now and had more time for her. There were things she liked about Fishtail too, but she couldn't imagine living there. It was too small and felt foreign to her. Like her mother, she liked her life in New York, and her friends, but she loved her father and was sad that he was now so different from her mother. She loved them both, even if she and her mother argued much of the time. She had always been so happy that her parents were together, and now she was going to start high school in the fall with divorced parents, like so many of her friends.

She wondered if her dad was dating but didn't want to ask. Her mother wasn't. She was still outraged by what Tom had done. She said he had betrayed her and completely abandoned their life and who he was. But Juliet was able to see that the changes in him weren't bad. He seemed younger and happier and free now in Montana. Her mother was more stressed and tense than she'd ever been before, with everything on her shoulders now and no husband to consult with or lean on. And she hated Tom for wanting a new and different life. Her fury at him was eating her alive, and she snapped at Juliet all the time. It was a relief to be away, and her father was nice to her.

Juliet and her father cleaned and cooked the fish they'd caught at the lake. The next day, Tom suggested they be lazy and have dinner at the diner. Juliet hadn't been there yet, and he said it would be fun. It was a funny little town, with antique shops and the General Store.

"They have a jukebox," he told her about the diner as they drove the few miles into town from his house. "Although the songs are pretty old." He jangled a pocketful of quarters he'd brought along so she could play it, and she smiled. "A lot of the local kids go there, mostly high school age." She hadn't seen anyone her own age yet, and her father hadn't made any friends in the few months he'd been there, so they were spending all their time together. It was why she had come, to spend time with him, and she'd enjoyed the time she'd been there, so far. There was none of the underlying tension she had with her mother. Her mother was planning to spend the time Juliet was away catching up on assignments and meeting deadlines on the weekends in a small house she had rented in the Hamptons. The rest of the time she was in the city. Juliet was going to spend a week in the Hamptons with her when she went back, before school started.

She was enrolled to begin high school in the fall at a very fancy, highly desirable and competitive private school. Getting into it had been a real victory, and her mother said it would assure Juliet a place in a good college if she kept her grades up. Beth put a lot of pressure on her and was very proud of her, but Tom was sorry to see Beth pushing Juliet to start the rat race of power, competition, and status so young. He didn't tell her, but he thought she should enjoy her childhood and adolescence. Juliet had no idea yet what career path she wanted to pursue after college. She was a little nervous about how hard her new school would be, and whether or not she'd like the other kids there. She didn't know anyone else who'd been accepted at that school. But her mother had wanted her to go there and made the decision. Juliet felt like she had no voice in her own life, and she wondered if her father had felt that way too.

Tom parked his new red truck outside the diner. It looked the same as it had in the 1950s, a relic of the past, which had a certain charm. There were a number of bicycles leaning against the wall outside and lying on the ground. Unlike New York, nothing was locked up here. Her father left his front door unlocked most of the time too, which had surprised her.

Juliet walked into the diner behind her father. She was wearing cutoff jean shorts, a T-shirt, high-top sneakers, and her long blond hair in a braid down her back. She looked more like seventeen than fourteen, even without makeup or fancy clothes. She had a mature look about her and seemed very poised. Tom had observed that the local kids seemed more relaxed, a little more boisterous, and dressed and acted more like kids than their counterparts in New York.

Juliet noticed a table of boys talking and laughing at the back of the diner, and she glanced around at the other diners. They all looked relaxed and were engrossed in conversations. Her father recommended the meatloaf or fried chicken when they sat down. She smiled because she couldn't remember his eating anything like it in New York. Her mother favored vegetable salads, kale, and healthy food, and no carbs. Juliet ordered a cheeseburger with everything on it, while he opted for the meatloaf, put a pile of quarters on the table, and pointed at the jukebox. "Have a ball. Let's have some music." He wasn't even sure if she'd recognize the songs—some of them were so old—but she took a handful of coins, slid out of the booth, and headed for the jukebox. She carefully read down the list, and only knew a few of the songs, but there were some she liked too, so she put a quarter in the machine and was pressing buttons, when one of the boys from the back table came up to her. He was tall and blond. She could sense that he was looking her over. She glanced up at him with a shy smile. Much to his horror, he blushed as soon as she did. He had his mother's fair skin, which betrayed him every time.

"My father says they haven't changed the records here since he was a kid. They're practically prehistoric," he said in a friendly tone. "Some of them are okay though, oldies but goodies." He felt awkward talking to her, but she was so pretty, he felt like he had to say something at least, standing next to her.

"They're from my dad's day too." She smiled at him. "Do you want a go?" She pointed at the machine, before she put another quarter in.

"Thanks," he said, put a quarter in, played three songs, and then let her drop another coin in as they stood smiling shyly at each other. "Where are you from?" he asked her. It was easy to see that she came from somewhere else. She didn't look local, and he would have known her from school if she was.

"New York. My dad moved here in January. I'm visiting him." She didn't add that her parents were getting a divorce. It was obvious anyway, if she was no longer living with him. "Are you from here?"

"Born and raised," he said, sounding like a cowboy for a minute. And then feeling very bold, and taken with her, he added, "Do you ride?" She nodded. "Do you want to come riding with me and my friends tomorrow? We're going to a lake to swim." She hesitated since she didn't know him, although the invitation was tempting, and he looked apologetic. "Sorry, that was rude. I'm Peter Pollock." He stuck out a hand to shake hers.

"Juliet Marshall." She smiled at him.

"We live a little way out of town on the main highway. I'll have my dad give you an easy horse to ride. The lake isn't far from our place." He gave her his cellphone number and she put it in her phone. "Just call if you want to come, or send a text. We're taking a picnic to the lake. My mom's always afraid we'll starve if we don't take food with us." He grinned and she laughed as her father waved to her. Her burger had arrived, and as she quickly said goodbye to Peter, she noticed that the portion of meatloaf on her father's plate was huge. She was still smiling as she slid back into the booth.

"I said to play a few songs, not a whole concert. Who were you talking to?" he asked, as she dropped the rest of the quarters back onto the table, and the first song started to play. It was an old song, but she liked it. The boy she'd been talking to was handsome and looked about her age. He had appeared almost as soon as she got to the jukebox. Tom realized that he was going to see a lot more of that in the coming years. Juliet was a beautiful girl. She stood out, even in cutoff shorts with no makeup and her hair in a braid. The blond boy was wearing jeans and a T-shirt, as she was, and the same high-top sneakers she had on. It was a universal uniform for kids their age, wherever they lived. But as a New Yorker, her hair was a little neater, her T-shirt was pressed, her sneakers clean, and her nails carefully done.

"His name is Peter Pollock. He invited me to ride to a lake with his friends tomorrow, for a picnic. Can I go?" she asked simply, and he thought about it. He didn't know the boy, but she'd be happier visiting him in the future if she made some friends in the area.

"Pollock," Tom said thoughtfully. "If it's the Pollock I think it is, they own one of the biggest ranches in the state. They raise horses."

"He offered to lend me one, to get to the lake. He gave me his number to call and let him know if I can come."

"Do you want to go?" her father asked her as they ate dinner. Juliet commented that the burger was pretty good, as she thought about Peter's invitation.

"Maybe. He seems nice. It might be good to know some kids here when I come to visit you." He agreed but hadn't made any friends yet himself.

"I should call his parents and see what the plan is. I don't want you riding off with some bunch of wild kids. Are there any girls going?" The presence of girls usually slowed down boys their age, in his opinion. Juliet knew that wasn't always true.

"He didn't say."

"I'll call his mom tonight," he said, and Juliet rolled her eyes.

"Do you have to, Dad? It makes me look like such a dork." He grinned at the look on her face.

"Your mother does that when you go to see people we don't know."

"Yeah, and everyone thinks she's neurotic. And I look like a dweeb with my mom calling. I'm fourteen!" she said, as though it were forty.

"I don't care if they think I'm neurotic. I don't know them, or their son, and I love my daughter."

"Why can't you trust me?"

"I do. It's everyone else in the world I don't trust. Not with my daughter anyway." He had always been that way.

"I swear, Mom's still going to be calling parents when I'm fifty."

He laughed at the thought, but knowing Beth, it was possible. She was an ultra, ultra cautious, suspicious mom who wanted to be sure that there would be parents present, and she could trust them to supervise properly. "I think she might let up by then. But probably not before," he teased Juliet. They had finished dinner and he ordered apple pie for dessert. She looked surprised.

"You're going to get fat here, Dad. You never ate like this in New York."

"Your mother wouldn't let me. And the air here makes me hungry." She grinned at his excuse. It was true. Her mother insisted that they eat healthy meals, with lots of vegetables and no desserts. Her father had gained weight since he'd moved to Montana, but he still looked good. He'd been a little too thin before, and stressed out.

He was finishing the slice of pie with vanilla ice cream when Peter and his friends walked past their table. Peter stopped to talk to Juliet again, and she introduced her father.

"Hi, I'm Peter. We're just going up to a lake not far from my house. I'll give her a really quiet horse." He turned to Juliet then, looking hopeful. "Can you come?"

Her father answered for her. "I'll give your mom a call tonight," he said pleasantly. "It's nice of you to invite her. It's been a little dull around here for Juliet with only me for entertainment."

"Do you play video games?" Peter asked her.

"Sometimes," she said cautiously. She wasn't crazy about them. That was a boy thing. She played chess masterfully though, and could beat her father now, even though he had taught her. They'd been playing every night since she arrived. She had missed doing things like that with him.

"See you tomorrow," he said, looking happy, and turned back to Tom. "Nice to meet you, sir," he said politely, and hurried off to join his friends, who were waiting for him in the doorway. Tom noticed a truck pick them up a few minutes later, with a woman driving. That reassured him too. Clearly, they kept a close eye on their son, as he did with his daughter. They all seemed young and innocent.

"They look like nice kids," Tom commented as they left the restaurant and got in his truck. He called Peter's mother when they got home. Anne answered the phone herself, and she sounded young and busy. All four boys were in her kitchen making s'mores and eating ice cream.

Tom explained why he was calling. "Your son very kindly invited my daughter to ride to a lake with him and some of his friends tomorrow, to have a picnic."

"That's true," she said cheerfully. "As far as I know, there are four of them going. I know all the boys well, they're like my own kids. They're always together and they're a pretty tame group. It's what Peter said, a picnic lunch and a swim at the lake. We don't let them ride any of our livelier horses, although they're all good riders. Your daughter can ride?"

"She can," he assured her. That had concerned her. She didn't want to take a risk with a girl who couldn't ride falling off one of their horses, getting hurt, and her parents suing them. She didn't know Juliet or her parents.

"Peter tells me you just moved here a few months ago. You'll have to come out and visit us sometime. Fishtail can be a little lonely before you meet some folks." She sounded friendly and warm.

"I've been enjoying just exploring and getting to know the place, and recovering from New York."

She laughed. "That's a big change for you! Well, I'll look forward to meeting Juliet tomorrow. I'll be here when they take off. They'll only be gone a few hours. She's welcome to hang around when they get back, if she isn't sick of the boys by then." She sounded easygoing and pleasant. He gave Juliet his seal of approval when he hung up, and she beat him at chess again that night. She looked happy to be joining the others for the ride to the lake and the picnic the next day. Tom was impressed that he would be meeting the Pollocks. He'd been hearing about them since he'd moved to Fishtail. They were practically considered royalty in the area, and thanks to Juliet, he would be meeting them now. Kids always had a way of meeting up, no matter who they were or where they were from. Juliet wasn't impressed. But her father was.

Chapter 3

Tom Marshall got directions at the local gas station about how to get to the Pollock ranch. It wasn't complicated. "Just stay on the highway out of town, look for the stone posts and the sign, take a right into their driveway and keep driving. You'll get there eventually," the attendant said. Tom had noticed the sign before, but hadn't paid much attention to it, since he had no reason to go there. You couldn't see the Pollocks' barns or pastures or the main house from the road.

The driveway seemed to go on for several miles and then he found himself in the middle of a compound with enormous immaculate barns around him, signs to the breeding barns, private roads going in several directions, and a large rambling stone house in a separate area with tall, old trees around it. As he approached, he saw a beautiful big pool behind the house, and several small outbuildings. It appeared to be a huge operation. There was an administration building where both Anne and Pitt had their offices.

Anne was standing on the front steps of the house herding the four boys when Tom pulled up, and he and Juliet got out of the truck.

"You're just in time," she said, smiling at Tom, as Peter introduced Juliet to his friends. They were all talking at once. Peter and Matt were carrying the saddlebags with the lunch Anne had packed for them. She was busy talking to Juliet's father, and reassuring him again.

"The boys know the area like their back pocket, and the lake isn't far. It's just a few miles up the mountain in the foothills, and it's an easy trail."

Tom and Anne followed the boys to the barn then so they could mount up, and as they got on their horses, Pitt came out of the barn and greeted Tom warmly.

"Happy to meet you. You'll have to come to a barbecue some Sunday night." He looked like he was in a hurry and left them a few minutes later, after asking Anne to come to his office once the kids left. Tom watched Juliet get up on a sleepy-looking horse who was as docile as Peter had promised.

"She's one of my old horses," Anne explained and patted the mare's neck. "She's very polite. She won't give Juliet any trouble," she assured him. "And by the way, I'm glad you called last night. I would have done the same with strangers who had invited my daughter somewhere, or even with Peter. You never know how responsible other parents are. It's always good to check. And it's good for Peter to see that other parents do it too, and that I'm not completely crazy when I call parents I don't know." He noticed how pretty Anne was. She was a little younger than Beth, but had a fresh, natural, wholesome look. Beth was chic, intense, harried, and a product of New York City living.

"Juliet hates it," he confided, "but her mother and I both do it. At least for now. When she's a little older, we won't be able to get away with it. But at fourteen, I want to know who she's with and where she's going."

"I completely agree." The five teenagers were mounted up by then, the lunch was stowed, and they were ready to leave. Juliet was wearing a cowboy hat her father had bought her for her stay there. Anne reminded them to have fun, and to bring their trash back from the lake, not just leave it there. Peter rolled his eyes, and they loped off, following each other on a back road of the property that would lead to the foot of the mountain, and the trail which would take them a short distance up to the lake.

Peter rode ahead of Juliet and led the way, and the others chatted easily on the ride up. Twenty minutes later, they left the trail they'd been on, went through a clearing in the trees and suddenly saw the lake. It wasn't vast, but it was picturesque with some lovely vistas and a narrow sandy beach. Peter and Matt got their supplies down, and they all helped each other spread blankets on the sand, unpacked the lunch and ate it quickly. It was delicious, with homemade chicken sandwiches, potato chips, cookies, and fresh lemonade Anne had made herself.

"Your mom makes the best picnic lunches," Tim said in his affected speech, which was noticeable, but they could all understand him clearly. "My mom is a terrible cook," he said and they all laughed. They knew it was true.

"My mom's not much of a cook either," Juliet added. She liked them. They were all nice boys, and she had enjoyed talking to Matt on the way there. She could tell he was crazy about computers. Matt said he was happy he didn't have to bring his pest of a little brother, Benjie, with him.

"They sent him to some kind of day camp this week. I think he's making mugs or decorating something. He always wants to come with me. He'd have wanted to come with us today." She was learning a little bit about each of them. Peter had whispered to her earlier that Noel's dad was really sick, which sounded very sad to her. She had noticed part of Noel's insulin pump clipped on his jeans and didn't comment on it. One of her girlfriends in New York had one too, so she knew what it was. She had heard about his older brother, Justin, who was helping his mom with his sick father, and took care of Noel a lot these days, since their mother had her hands full with their father, their office, and her two sons.

Juliet could tell that they had grown up together and were almost like brothers. She was disappointed to discover that none of them had sisters. There were four boys in their group and an older and a younger brother, but not a single girl. But they were good company anyway.

They wrapped up their garbage from lunch and put it back in the saddlebags to take home with them. Then they stripped down to their bathing suits and went swimming. They played water games for a while and dove under the water. Juliet kept up with them. She was strong and as tall as they were. She was taller than Noel, and they had fun with her. Peter stayed close and was attentive to her. After they swam, they lay on their towels on the sand and dried off in the sun. At four o'clock, they headed back and were at the Pollocks' barn shortly after. They walked their horses into the barn, took off their saddles and put them away, and filled the feedbags for them. It had been a really nice day, the best one Juliet had had since she'd gotten there.

Afterwards, they went into the house and played video games for a while. Juliet played with them. Anne had left snacks out for them. Juliet couldn't help thinking how lucky Peter was to have parents who were still together, and Matt too. Tim had mentioned that his parents were divorced, and his father worked on oil rigs all over the world, so he only saw his father between assignments for the company he worked for. Noel didn't say much about his father, and he looked preoccupied a lot of the time. He was about to leave on his bicycle to go home around the time Juliet's father came back in the truck, and he offered Noel a ride home. They put his bicycle in the back of the truck. Juliet thanked Peter, and said goodbye to Tim and Matt, and then they drove away. Noel told Tom where his house was. It was very close to the house Tom had rented. They stopped to let him out, and his brother Justin came out of the house to help him. Juliet's breath caught when she saw Noel's older brother. He was really handsome, and looked very grown up, with broad shoulders and long, powerful arms. He was striking looking with dark hair, and he paid no attention to Juliet whatsoever. He thanked her father for bringing Noel home, and then they headed into the house together as Tom and Juliet drove off. Juliet thought he looked very serious and acted like an adult, which wasn't surprising with their father so sick.

"They look like nice boys. They all do," Tom commented. Anne had told him in a quick aside about Noel's father, and how upset they all were. With hospice on the scene now, they knew he couldn't last much longer. She said that he and Marlene had had a nightmarish year, and they were all worried about how Noel and Justin would weather the last chapter.

Tom was quietly thinking about it as they drove away. It was a sad story, and they were clearly a group of very close-knit friends, who had some really lovely children. Bright, respectful, and well behaved.

They had all been kind to Juliet all day, and there was a nice spirit of camaraderie between them, even with a pretty girl in their midst. Peter seemed the most interested in her, but hadn't crossed any lines. Mostly, he had been a good host, and saw to it that she had a good time and everyone was nice to her. He even showed her his favorite video game, which was wasted on her. She had proven herself to be a good rider that day, as good as any of the girls they knew who had grown up on horses.

They had invited her to go fishing with them in the next few days, and she had invited them to go to the rodeo with her and her father, which was always good fun. Peter had added that his mother had been the rodeo queen two years in a row before she married his dad. Juliet liked her. She seemed like a warm, kind, loving woman, and it was obvious that she was crazy about her son and provided a warm welcome to his friends. Tim and Matt were spending the night with Peter that night, as they often did. Noel needed to be home with his dad, in case something happened. They were quietly waiting for the end to come now, which could be anytime. Marlene had encouraged both boys to go out and see their friends and not sit around the house, which was too depressing. Bob slept most of the time now, and was on heavy medications with a nurse to tend to him, while

Marlene went back and forth to the office, and nursed him herself when she was home. It was the hardest thing she'd ever been through, watching the man she loved slowly slip away, and there was nothing she could do to stop it. They had already lost the fight. It was just a matter of time now. How much time, no one knew.

On Saturday, after the picnic at the lake a few days before, Pitt Pollock and Bill Brown took the four boys fishing, as they had promised. Peter invited Juliet to join them, and her father let her go. They caught plenty of fish, and Pitt had invited Tom to join them for dinner that night. The Pollocks were going to cook the fish and plenty of other food. Juliet caught two fish, and was proud of them, and took the hooks off herself. The boys were filled with admiration. She wasn't like most of the girls they knew. She was braver and fun to have around. She didn't squeal and scream at the worms they used as bait, and did everything her father had taught her when she had gone fishing with him earlier. Peter was more and more impressed with her, and Anne smiled and chuckled about it at dinner that night. She sat next to Tom, while the boys and Juliet were playing kickball on the lawn, in the light from the patio. They had a beautifully built home and extensive grounds.

"I think my son is having his first serious crush," Anne whispered to Tom as Pitt walked over to join them. He had cooked a delicious dinner, and they had all enjoyed it.

"I think she's having fun too," Tom admitted. "She's never been too interested in boys before. She worked hard on her grades last year, so she could get into the very challenging high school she's going to in the fall. She'll have to work even harder this year. I'd like her to enjoy her childhood too, but her mother sets the bar pretty high for her." She had for him too, but he didn't say that. He had run away as a result. He wasn't proud of it, but he was happy to be out of the rat race he'd been a part of in New York.

"They're sweet together," Anne commented. "And it's harmless. None of them are ready for serious romance at this point." Pitt hooted at her when she said it.

"How quickly you forget," he teased her. "We were their age when I fell for you, hook, line, and sinker, and how many years ago was that? Twenty-three?" he reminded her. "Don't underestimate the power of the human heart, or of teenagers in love. We were both fourteen too."

She smiled at the memory. "The world was different then. Everything was more innocent. Kids are more sophisticated today. But I still don't think any of our kids are ready for all that. These kids would rather play video games and go fishing than get in too deep with romances." She sounded convinced of it.

"Give them a few months, or a year," Pitt commented. "It all changes when they start high school, and that's only a month away for them. That innocence will be gone pretty soon. If your father hadn't been breathing down my neck all through high school, I wouldn't have been nearly as well behaved with you. I was scared to death of him," he told Tom, and all three of them laughed. "I was sure he'd kill me if I did anything I shouldn't. That all changed when we went to college." He grinned at Anne and she leaned over and kissed him. They had their secrets too. "At least we held out 'til college. I'm not sure kids do that anymore."

"You're scaring Tom to death," she scolded her husband, and Tom laughed.

"I'm not worried about Juliet right now," he said. "And I can't imagine people falling in love as freshmen in high school today and still being together twenty-three years later, like you two."

"It doesn't happen often," Pitt admitted. "We were lucky." Tom could see that they had a strong marriage and a good relationship. He envied them what they so obviously shared, instead of the hostility he had with Beth now, and the arguments before that.

"It didn't happen for me that way in my marriage," Tom said. "It did for a while, and we were both on the same page when we started out seventeen years ago. And then it started to come off the rails about ten years into our marriage. She got more and more ambitious and caught up in her work. I got more and more disenchanted with what I saw going on around me on Wall Street. I saw the sacrifices you have to make to get ahead, and after a while it didn't seem worth it. I felt like I was being strangled by ambition and politics and lies. When I saw a chance to escape and start my own consulting business, I leapt at it. I didn't need to be in New York to do that, and all I wanted was to get the hell out of Dodge. My wife is the queen of Dodge. She couldn't live without it, and I couldn't live with it anymore. I wanted to get out before it ate me alive. So here I am," he said quietly. He sounded at peace but sad about it. He felt like he had lost a war, and a marriage, in order to save his soul.

"It must be confusing for Juliet to have you both leading such different lives, with such different goals and values," Anne said. She realized how lucky she and Pitt had been to stay on the same path after so long, and she was grateful for it.

"It is," Tom agreed, "but I don't know what to do about it. Her mother wants Juliet to have all the advantages she has in New York: good schools, Ivy League college, a race for success in a tough job. That whole world nearly destroyed me, and I don't want that for my daughter. But her mother wants to see that she gets on the fast track to success. I don't believe that's what success is anymore. I love my life here, and I want Juliet to see the value of it and make her own choice one day."

"We can't make those decisions for them," Pitt said. "We're lucky. Peter wants to stay here and run the ranch one day, after he gets an education. That's what I did, and what he thinks he wants at fourteen. Bill Brown's son, Matt, can't wait to get out of here. He wants to be in the tech world in Silicon Valley. I don't think they have a chance in hell of keeping him here. This is a special kind of life. It suits some people and feels like a death sentence to others. Some of our kids will stay, and some won't." Bill Brown came up and heard the tail end of the conversation and agreed with Pitt.

"Matt won't be able to get out of here fast enough. It breaks my heart not to have him take over the ranch one day, but it wouldn't be fair to stop him," Bill agreed. "My youngest, Benjie, who just turned six, swears he's going to live here forever. He says he's going to be a rodeo clown one day and ride the bulls. He just might. But probably neither of them will want to run the ranch when I'm too old to do it. If I'm lucky, one of them will come around. If not, neither of them will, and I'll have to sell when I get too old to run it. There aren't a lot of boys who spend their youth dreaming of being a sheep farmer, and running a dairy," he said, and the others laughed. "I never dreamed of it either, but it suits me to a T, and thank God Pattie loves it here too. But this is a very different life. It's not for everyone. I don't think any of us can predict what our kids are going to do. It depends on who they wind up with as partners too. That makes a big difference."

The conversation moved on to how Marlene Wylie was going to manage without Bob. They had been a perfect couple, and then he got sick. They were all dreading what would come next for her and their boys. Tom hadn't met the Wylies yet, but it sounded like a sad story to him, for their two sons as well, and they seemed like good boys.

The evening ended late, and Tom commented to Juliet on the way back to their house how much he liked their new friends, and what nice kids all the boys were. He told her how proud he was of her too. He was really pleased to have met the Pollocks and their friends, and despite Pitt Pollock's enormous success as a rancher, and all that he had inherited, he and his wife were simple, warm, unassuming people who had no interest in showing off. They had no need to, and had good, old-fashioned family values.

It was night and day compared to the people he had worked with in New York, and the coldhearted greed and arrogance he had had to fight through every day. He liked the clients he had now. He had handpicked them when he set up his consulting business. He couldn't understand how Beth could still want to live with that kind of shameless greed and inhumanity all around her in order to say that she was successful. To Tom, it was the epitome of failure as a human being—selling your soul to the devil for monetary success. He might not be setting the world on fire in Fishtail, but he was happier now than he had ever been, even though he didn't like being alone. But he had been alone with Beth anyway. They had become strangers to each other long before he left and enemies once he did. They weren't even friends anymore. Every contact he had with her was hostile and painful. The only bridge to each other they had now was Juliet, and it was a hard position for her to be in, as Anne had said that night. Juliet lived on the firing line between two parents who had come to hate each other, and had completely opposite views of life now. Beth wanted to keep her firmly in her camp, and Tom wanted to show her something different. As Anne had said, it had to be confusing for her, but so far she seemed to be weathering it. Tom felt guilty every time he thought about how hard it must be for Juliet to have parents who were so completely different and opposed to each other.

"Did you have fun tonight?" he asked her on the ride home, and she smiled and nodded.

"They're nice. I like Peter's mom a lot. Matt's mom, Pattie, seems a little more frantic, but Anne seems really happy." He knew now that Anne was happy because she and Pitt loved each other, genuinely and sincerely. It changed everything and blessed everyone around them. He thought it was what marriage should be but too often wasn't.

Juliet went up to bed a few minutes after they got back, and was already half asleep as she fell into bed. She liked Peter a lot and she thought he liked her too, but she didn't want to tell her father. For now, it was a secret. She wondered if he was going to kiss her before she left Fishtail, and she hoped he would. Then she drifted off to sleep, smiling. It was nice having a secret which no one knew.

Chapter 4

A few days after dinner at the Pollocks', Tom came downstairs in the morning and found Juliet making stacks of sandwiches, and putting them in plastic bags. She added some fruit and cookies and power bars. She looked like she was preparing food for an army.

"What's all that for?" he asked, pouring himself a cup of coffee.

"We're going swimming again today. I said I'd bring the lunch. It's the least I can do. They've all been so nice to me." She had emptied their fridge and cupboards to do it. She made chicken and peanut butter and jelly sandwiches. She'd asked and no one had a peanut allergy, and they said they liked it. Peter was going to bring some cake. Matt said he'd bring whatever he could. The boys had all been talking about a camping trip they always went on together at the end of the summer, and Juliet wished she could be with them. But she'd be back in New York by then, getting ready to start her new school.

She waited until her dad had eaten a piece of toast and finished his coffee, and then he drove her to the Pollocks'.

"I might stay there for dinner and play video games tonight," she told her father. "I'll call you when I'm ready to come home." He had nothing else to do and was happy to provide chauffeur service. He loved having her around. It gave his life meaning. The house was so empty without her, and so alive now that she was there.

"Be careful," he warned her, out of habit, when she got out of his truck and picked up the bags of sandwiches.

"We're just going for a swim, Dad." She smiled at him. "Like we did before." She'd been on the swim team at school, and she swam as well as the boys did. She was wearing a T-shirt, with a sweatshirt over her shoulders in case it got chilly that night before she came home. She had on a bathing suit and jeans since they'd be riding to a waterfall in the foothills of Granite Peak that the boys had told her about. They said it was a fantastic place to swim and she'd love it, and that it was an easy ride to get there, low on the mountain. The water came down from higher up. She could hardly wait.

Out of sympathy for what they were going through, Peter had told Noel to bring Justin if he wanted to come. They all loved going to the waterfall. The water was cold on a hot day. Justin accepted readily. He couldn't stand sitting in the house with the hospice nurses anymore. They were nice, but they were an outward sign that his father was going to die soon, and he was drained from waiting for it to happen. He didn't even realize it, but he needed some time off to just be a kid again.

Marlene had an important meeting at her office with a new client that day. Bob didn't want her to cancel it. She hated to leave Bob alone with the nurses, so Pattie Brown agreed to come over to sit with him while Marlene was out. He could talk if he wanted to, or just sleep. As a nurse, Pattie would know what to do if she needed to call 911 for him, or summon Marlene from the office. Bob had always loved Pattie and her sense of humor, so he was happy to have her come.

Pattie told Matt the bad news at breakfast. She was going to spend the day at the Wylies' with Justin and Noel's dad, Bob.

"I know you hate it, Matt, but I can't do anything about it. I don't know what you have planned today, but you have to take Benjie with you. I can't leave him alone, and I can't take him to the Wylies'. It's too sad over there now, and he'll get restless sitting around. You have to keep Benjie with you." Matt groaned.

"Why can't he stay with Dad? We're all going swimming again, and having a picnic."

"Your father's too busy to watch him, and swimming and a picnic will be perfect. He'll love it. Just keep an eye on him. Anne will take care of him when you go back to Peter's house. There's nothing else I can do about him today. I owe this to Marlene. She doesn't want Bob to be alone with just the hospice nurses. I promised her."

"Okay, okay," Matt said grudgingly, and he still looked upset about it when he got to Peter's, after Pattie dropped them off on her way to the Wylies'. "He always ruins everything," Matt said to Peter about Benjie. Peter thought about it and consoled his friend.

"No, he doesn't. He can swim. We'll take him to the waterfall with us. I'll put him on an easy horse on a lead line, and he'll be fine. We'll all help you watch him. We could go another day, but Juliet already made lunch for all of us," Peter said, smiling. Justin and Noel had just arrived, and there was a holiday feeling to the excursion. Peter was excited about showing Juliet the waterfall, since she'd never seen it.

Tim was the last to arrive on his bike. Justin and Noel had come by bike too, and were grateful for the outing, and the distraction. Juliet was playing guessing games with Benjie as they headed to the stables and saddled the horses. Pitt was at a horse auction, and had taken Anne with him right after breakfast. Everyone was busy. Peter put the lead line on Benjie's horse himself, and one of the stable hands handed it to him once he'd mounted his horse. He had chosen Black Diamond, a horse that was so slow and old but sure-footed that Peter liked to tease him and say he was dead. But he was exactly what Benjie needed so he couldn't get into any mischief while he was riding. Nothing was going to make Black Diamond move faster than the snail's pace that was his preferred speed, and he was never skittish around other horses. Peter knew Benjie was completely safe riding him, and for extra protection, he had put a strap around Benjie's waist and attached it to the saddle. He rode beside him as they left the main courtyard that led to the trail they would be taking to get to Granite Peak. They would be going higher than they had last time, up to where the waterfall was, which was at a higher elevation than the lake. But not so high as to be dangerous. The upper elevations of the mountain attracted the most serious and experienced mountain climbers, but they weren't going far and it was one of their favorite destinations for a hot day. They all loved the waterfall, and it was safe there.

As they left the yard between the barns, one of the stable hands waved to Peter as though he had something to tell him. Peter was leading the group, but he slowed to find out what the stable hand had to say.

"There are fire warnings on the other side of the mountains. The fire is still a long way away, but good to know." It had been a dry summer, and by the end of it, there were always fire warnings somewhere. Peter wasn't worried.

"Thanks, Joe." They started up again and headed for the trail at a slow trot. Peter didn't want to wear the horses out in the heat, and a short time later they were on one of the lower trails toward Granite Peak. Juliet was riding behind Peter's and Benjie's horses, and the other boys were strung out single file behind her. It took them an hour of steady climbing to get to where Peter wanted to go. The boys knew the trail, and here and there were beautiful vistas. They slowly gained altitude. Then they took another trail and could hear the waterfall before they saw it. It was spectacular. They reached the clearing where they all knew they could tether the horses and leave them in the shade. Peter was disappointed to see that the waterfall wasn't as full as it usually was because of the dry summer, but it was still beautiful, and the pool at the base of it would be even better for swimming.

Once the horses were tied up, they left their clothes in a heap near them, and raced each other to the base of the waterfall. They cavorted and played in the water for an hour, and Juliet kept an eye on Benjie so Matt could play with the others. They dove off the rocks into the deep pool. Justin stayed with Benjie then, and Juliet dove into the water with the others. They were all being careful and responsible with their young charge, and finally Matt took his brother in with him, and let Benjie ride on his back. Benjie squealed with delight and pretended to whip him like a horse until Matt threatened to take him out of the water. Then Benjie calmed down again. They had all cooled off and climbed out of the water, then lay on the rocks to dry off. Matt didn't let Benjie out of his sight, and Benjie sat near him begging to get back in the water again. They promised they'd go for another swim before they left, and then Peter suggested they hike upstream along the riverbanks that were around a bend. The water was deep there, they all knew, and Peter explained to Juliet that the water would be too turbulent for them to cross the river. They hadn't been to the river all summer, but they came to the waterfall every week.

They took out Juliet's sandwiches, spread out the blankets, and ate lunch. All the boys thanked her for having brought them, and as soon as they finished eating, they put everything away. Peter told her that up here at a higher elevation it was particularly important, so they didn't attract bears looking for something to eat. Juliet didn't find the warning reassuring, but Peter told her that they never saw bears. Then they took off on the familiar hiking trail to meet up with the river. They expected it to be roaring past them and were stunned when they rounded the bend to see a dry creek bed full of gigantic, jagged rocks. The river had gone dry, and there was barely a drop of water at the bottom of it. If they could find rocks that were smooth enough to walk across, they could easily get to the other side. They had never been able to do that before.

It looked like a landscape on the moon as they all stared at the dry riverbed, filled with boulders. After hiking a short distance up the trail, they found a place where they could cautiously let themselves down, lending each other a hand, and make their way across the riverbed to the other side. It was new terrain for them, but they made it with Benjie on Justin's back, and a short time later, they found a wider trail that headed up the mountain. Since they'd never been on that side of the river before, they were eager to explore. Even Justin looked excited and threw himself into the expedition wholeheartedly, and leading the way, with Peter and Matt right behind him, and the others following. Juliet was holding Benjie's hand. He skipped along and stumbled occasionally on a loose rock, and Juliet quickly pulled him up to keep him from falling and hurting himself.

They'd been walking for half an hour, when a bolt of lightning and a clap of thunder exploded over their heads. They all jumped. It looked as though the lightning might strike right next to them. There was no time span at all between the thunder and lightning, and a torrent of rain began to fall. They took refuge under some trees to wait for the rain to stop. They huddled together on some rocks. The clash of thunder and lightning was scary, and Benjie started to cry. Juliet held him tightly in her arms and told him that it was exciting, and there was nothing to be afraid of. He looked unconvinced, but his cries dwindled to a whimper as they watched the storm unleash on precisely the area where they had been minutes before. Beyond it, in the distance, they could see blue sky filled with smoke, and Peter realized it was from the fires the stable hand had warned them about. Below them, they could see that there were no rain clouds in the valley, they were only directly over the half of the mountain where they stood.

The downpour continued for an hour, and then they heard a roaring sound, like boulders rushing down the mountain. Within seconds, they saw that it was not boulders rushing toward them, it was water. Somewhere on the mountain, a flash flood had started and filled the riverbed that had been dry only an hour before. All the mysteries and calamities of nature were clashing at once: fire in the distance, a flash flood from an unknown source up the mountain, the sky seeming to fall, and a riverbed they could no longer cross, which had become a torrent between them and the other side. The boys looked at each other, trying to figure out what to do next. Juliet watched their eyes, trying to determine if she should be panicked, or if this was all an ordinary occurrence.

Peter looked confident when he spoke, which reassured her. "That water can't be coming from the peak. It's some kind of spring that surfaced. All we have to do is get above it, cross back over and come down the other side, and then get back to where we left the horses." It sounded sensible, and his theory presumed that the flood hadn't come from too far above them. Maybe some deep subterranean well had become unblocked. The water in the riverbed was getting rapidly deeper, and the rushing currents made the river too treacherous to cross.

They couldn't get across the riverbed where they were standing, and it was easy to guess that it would be even more dangerous as the water raced downhill, so the only choice they had was to continue up the mountain and get above the source of the flash flood which had filled the riverbed so quickly and turned it into a raging body of water.

They had their hiking boots on, and were dry from standing under the trees, and they continued to head up Granite Peak on the trail that began to narrow and get rougher as they got higher and it got harder to breathe. Noel was the first who said he needed to sit down for a minute, and his brother was quick to tell him to take it easy. There were more claps of thunder and more flashes of lightning, followed by another deluge, which drenched them as they continued up the steep trail.

They could no longer see the patch of blue sky in the distance, or the smoke hovering far away. The trees obscured their vision. The water fell periodically, and they saw fallen trees and debris rushing past them in the river. Peter thought of the horses and was relieved that they were tethered on high ground.

None of them were talking as they climbed. They needed the air for their lungs. It was getting chilly, their clothes were damp, and none of them wanted to admit that they were frightened. It seemed best to say nothing. None of them had the answers to their unspoken questions. They saw a dead deer float down the river. Justin thought it had been struck by lightning or perhaps by a fallen tree. They saw a mangy-looking wolf clinging to a log being swept downstream, and a family of otters clumped together. The logs disappeared quickly, and Peter doubted they would make it to safety if the logs were pulled under by the rapidly swirling currents. One thing was for sure: None of them could have made it across back where they had come from, near the waterfall. They had been hiking for nearly two hours by then, and had come a long way up the mountain. The flash flood continued on its path and the skies opened from time to time. The foliage got thicker around them. There was no sign of where the flash flood had come from, so they couldn't figure out how to get around it. They didn't say a word to each other as they climbed and kept their fears to themselves. They were wet, scared, and cold.

It was almost dark when they finally stopped walking. They sat down on a cluster of rocks to figure out a plan.

"It's going to be dark soon," Peter said in the calmest voice he could muster. "I'm not sure we should head up any farther. The flood must have started higher than we thought." The others nodded agreement, somewhat stunned by the situation. They hadn't meant to climb that high. "Maybe we should head back down the way we came," he suggested, but they had seen the river overflow the banks farther down and cover the trail, so they'd be trapped if they went that way.

"I don't want to scare my parents," Peter said, feeling both foolish and worried. It had been a rugged few hours on the trail, which ran parallel to the riverbank they'd been on earlier and could no longer reach. "But maybe we should call and let them know where we are." Justin thought it was the wisest course, before nightfall, and pulled out his cellphone, to find that the battery had gone dead. Noel had one too, and had carried it for years due to his diabetes, but he discovered he had no service. Juliet didn't have service either. When they checked, none of them did, and then Peter remembered hearing that there was no service on the mountain because of the altitude, so they were on their own. Suddenly, they realized that they had been cut off from the world, with no possible communication.

Benjie started to cry. "I'm hungry . . . and thirsty. . . ." He started to wail.

"Stop crying!" his brother said harshly because he wanted to cry himself and was afraid he would. Juliet put an arm around Benjie to calm him.

"I thought that might happen," Juliet said in a gentle voice about the lack of cellphone service. No one had paid attention to the fact that she had worn her backpack when they crossed the riverbed. She had brought some sandwiches for him in case he got tired. And some bottles of water. She passed around one of the bottles, and each of them took a small, conservative swallow, not wanting to be greedy or waste a drop, and then gave it back to her. She had suddenly become the keeper of their sustenance, like Wendy with the Lost Boys in *Peter Pan,* which was what they had become. She had a plastic knife in her backpack and cut a small wedge from a sandwich for Benjie and handed it to him, and then she wrapped the sandwich carefully again. She had brought four sandwiches, two apples, and two bananas in her bag, just in case. It would keep them going for a while, and surely they wouldn't be there long.

"Even if we can't call them," Peter said, "once they figure out that we haven't come back, they'll come looking for us," he reassured the others. They knew that what he said was true. Their parents would send out a search party. Peter just hoped that they'd come looking for them before dark. Matt nodded agreement, and Tim and Noel exchanged a look, with fathers who couldn't rescue them, with one in a foreign country and the other too ill.

Justin had another thought and looked at his younger brother with concern. "How are you with your pump? How much have you got left?" Justin knew from classes he had taken in order to help his brother that Noel's pump would last three days, and no more. After that he would slip into a coma. Without insulin in the pump, he would die.

"I'm okay," Noel said in a low voice, embarrassed to have his frailty revealed so openly. "I've got about two days left in it. We'll be home by then."

"You don't have a spare with you?" Justin asked, looking tense, and Noel shook his head. It added another element of drama to the situation. "You know you're always supposed to carry one. Why the hell didn't you?"

"I didn't think we'd be out overnight, or that we'd get stuck up here!" he shouted back at his brother. At worst, they'd be found by morning, and he had two days left. It was worrisome, but it wasn't a disaster . . . yet.

Unconsciously, Matt pulled Benjie close to him and put an arm around him, while Juliet moved nearer to Peter. Benjie suddenly seemed so little, like such a baby. He was only six, and had been a good sport all afternoon as they hiked up the mountain with the flood rushing past them, getting more and more lost. They should never have crossed the riverbed, even if it was dry. They all knew better. They lived in the mountains. They knew what one should and shouldn't do when hiking, and the risks of Granite Peak at the upper elevations with unexpected crevasses and sheer drops. They had forgotten all of it that afternoon, in a festive mood, sure that they were safe, and excited by the adventure. None of them had hesitated or sensed potential danger.

As night fell, they still hadn't decided if it was best to continue up the mountain or head down. Peter and Justin still thought they would get above the flood, but the others were afraid to go up any farther. And heading down, they would run into the overflowing riverbanks, which seemed even worse, especially at night. The rain had started again and was coming down heavily. Juliet found an empty cup in her backpack, which she had brought for Benjie, and she set it on a rock to gather rainwater. It started to fill quickly. They passed the water bottle around again, and each took a careful sip. Juliet cut several small pieces out of one of the sandwiches, and everyone took one, and she carefully rewrapped the rest. They needed to take care with the supplies they had, since they had no idea how long they'd be there. They were grateful she had thought to bring anything with her on the hike. Without that, they'd be starving, and very thirsty.

"What if we get attacked by *wolves*?" Benjie screamed as it got darker.

"We won't," Matt said, sounding nervous and trying not to, to reassure his brother. "They don't attack people." But they all knew wolves did, particularly if they were hungry or desperate themselves, which they would be after a dry summer. And it was cub season. Many of the animals on the mountain would be protecting their young from hunger and the flood.

"Or a *bear*!" Benjie offered as an alternative, and they all laughed nervously at the way he said it. But that was a distinct possibility if they stumbled on a bear who felt a threat to herself or her cubs.

"Or an elephant!" Justin added to lighten the moment, and even Benjie laughed.

"They don't have ephelants up here," Benjie said with a knowing look. "But tigers maybe." Or an elk or a moose, even an antelope. There were said to be bison on the mountain, but none of them had ever seen one. Getting charged by one didn't sound too appealing.

"What if we try to find a cave to sleep in tonight?" Tim suggested.

"Not if there's a bear in it," Peter answered. "I think all we can do is sit under the trees tonight, try and stay as dry as we can, and get moving again in the morning. If we stay on one of the trails, they'll find us tomorrow after first light." But which one? Up? Down? Or a trail they hadn't found yet?

"We should take turns keeping watch. One of us should be awake all night. Let's take it in turns for an hour each, just to make sure we're not all asleep if a bear wanders by." It was Peter's idea and they all agreed that he was right. Juliet had an alarm on her watch and set it for an hour later. Matt volunteered to take the first watch. They were hungry and tired, and they wanted more water but were afraid to drink too much. The rain had stopped by eight o'clock, and they huddled together like puppies to keep warm in the chill mountain air. It was going to be a long night, but they all agreed that by morning they would be found. It would be an adventure they would remember forever. The night they could have been eaten by a bear on Granite Peak.

"We could call this the Granite Peak Challenge!" Matt said, looking excited, and Peter laughed.

"Or the Challenge! We could make it an annual event."

"I'm not signing up for the next one," Noel said. It had seemed like such a good idea when they decided to have a picnic at the waterfall, and then cross the riverbed when they found it dry. Who knew there would be a flash flood, and they'd get stranded up here?

"They'll think we're heroes and call our names out at the rodeo," Benjie said and liked the idea as he cuddled up to his brother.

"I'd rather not be a hero and be home in bed," Tim said, wondering if his father would be impressed the next time he called and Tim told him about spending a night on the mountain. His father always liked demonstrations of manhood.

Juliet was hoping her father wasn't worried. She closed her eyes and thought about it, and felt Peter's hand gently take hers, then he whispered in her ear so the others wouldn't hear. "Don't be scared," he said ever so softly. She nodded, smiled at him, and held his hand tight until she fell asleep. She had her shift to keep watch later. For now, all she wanted to do was sleep, and forget how thirsty she was.

Chapter 5

Pitt and Anne were working on their accounts that night and stayed late at the office. They had been at an auction, sold three breeding mares and bought two very expensive stallions. They were still talking about them, and Pitt's plans for them, when they got home and found the house dark, which Anne thought was strange.

"They must have gone to the diner for dinner. They probably came home wet and tired and hungry from the flash storms today," Pitt said. Anne always worried more than he did, and he put an arm around her and kissed her. "Maybe they went out for a pizza." He always thought of the simple solutions first.

"Peter would have texted if they went out for dinner," she said, visibly worried.

"Maybe they went to Bill and Pattie's, with no food service here." He smiled at her. "You feed them too well. They eat here more often than I do. They'll be back soon. I'm sure they didn't stick around the waterfall for long once it started raining." It was nine o'clock at night by then. They hadn't had dinner themselves and went to make sandwiches in the kitchen while they waited for the boys. Pitt had calmed her fears.

At ten o'clock, Pattie Brown called.

"What time do you want me to pick up my monsters? You must be sick to death of my family by now. But I appreciate it. I stayed at the Wylies' with Marlene 'til eight o'clock and made dinner for her. Bob is quietly slipping away. I don't think it will go on much longer."

"I thought the boys were with you," Anne said, frowning. "We got home an hour ago, and they weren't here. Pitt thought they were at your place or that they went to town for dinner." She hadn't thought to look for their bikes at the barn, since she assumed they'd taken their bikes with them.

"He's probably right," Pattie said calmly. "Benjie is going to be hell on wheels tomorrow if they have him up this late. I hope he's asleep in a booth at the diner, or somewhere. If he's still awake, he'll be a mess tomorrow. They'll probably be home in a few minutes. I'll let you know if they show up here first. They can camp out here if they want to."

Anne was about to text Peter and Pitt told her to relax. Tom Marshall called a few minutes later and apologized to Pitt for the late hour when he answered. "I'm sorry, my daughter seems to have joined the group of musketeers. She was going to call me but I guess she's having too much fun at your place. When do you want me to come and get her? I can be there in a few minutes if she's ready." She couldn't sleep over with a bunch of boys, so she'd have to come home. The boys could stay at the Pollocks'.

"We think they're out to dinner. They'll probably be home any minute," Pitt said. He hated to treat them like babies and wanted to give them time to show up.

"She's not with you?" Tom sounded surprised, then worried.

"Actually, no. We just got home a little while ago ourselves. We were at an auction all day, buying breeding stock. I'll call around and see where they are. I'll call you back in a few minutes." Pitt looked at Anne when he hung up. "Where the hell are they? They're not at the Browns', or here, and Tom wants to know when to pick Juliet up."

"They're not at the Wylies'. Pattie was there with Bob, and they wouldn't go there now with Bob so sick. And I'm sure they're not at Tim's. They never go there. Tim comes to us. June works late and they all hate her cooking." She looked embarrassed when she said it, and Pitt laughed.

"I'll call the guys in the barn and see what time they brought the horses in. They're too young to go to a bar," he said with a grin, "so they have to be at someone's house."

The head stable hand answered the phone in the barn, and Pitt was startled by his response.

"The horses never came back tonight. I figured they took them over to the Browns', and were staying there, and would bring them back in the morning. The trails have been pretty slippery tonight. I thought maybe they were afraid to lame one of the horses. And their bikes are still here."

"Thanks, Jack," Pitt said, then hung up on him and turned to look at Anne. "The horses never came back in. Maybe one of them slipped and got lamed in the storm, or one of the kids fell and got injured.

Their bikes are at the stables." He went to put on his rough work boots and a heavy rubber raincoat he wore when he rode in bad weather.

"Where are you going?" Anne asked with a look of panic.

"I'll take some of the guys with me and have a look at the trails and see what we find. They're out there somewhere, and something must have happened, or the horses would be back in the barn, since they're not at Pattie and Bill's." He called the Browns and asked Bill if he wanted to come with him.

"Give me five minutes. I'll meet you on the trail. I'll bring a couple of my guys too." Pitt called the barn again then to ask Jack to bring one of the other stable hands, and Pitt told him which of his workhorses he wanted saddled. He took a solid horse he knew he could rely on. He debated about calling Tom Marshall, but he didn't want to frighten him and tell him that the kids were missing and so were the horses. The trails were bordered by steep ravines, and even some of the most experienced riders had fatal accidents on Granite Peak every year. He wanted to have a look around first before he called him.

"Should I call Harvey?" Anne asked him as he hurried through the front door and put his hat on. He thought about it for a minute and shook his head.

"Not yet. Let me take a look first. Bill and I know those trails as well as Harvey does. And we can't have lost seven of them. They're out there somewhere, probably cold, wet, and scared to death. Maybe one of them is hurt. Or some of the horses."

Harvey Mack was the chief ranger for the area. He and Pitt were old friends and had known each other for years, since Pitt was a boy. Pitt didn't want to call Harvey this late unless there was a problem. He didn't want to drag him out for nothing. And if there were fires starting on the other side of the mountain, Harvey would have his hands full trying to get that under control. He didn't need to have seven kids lost in a rainstorm to worry about too. Pitt was sure that he and Bill could handle it, and if not, they'd call Harvey when they got back. The kids were probably under a tree somewhere waiting to be found.

He ran to the stables. It was raining hard again. The stable hands had his horse ready, and gave him a leg up. He and two ranch hands left at a fast trot, careful not to give the horses their heads, with the ground slippery. Bill and three of his men were waiting at the entrance to the main trail to Granite Peak, and all seven men took off on the trail to the waterfall. It took them twice as long as usual to get there. And the river was a rushing torrent overflowing its banks when they did.

"I was up here a few days ago," one of Bill's men shouted in the wind. "The bed was dry. There was a flash flood today."

"I'll bet the damn fool kids crossed over when it was dry, the flood came, and they couldn't get back," Pitt guessed and Bill nodded. They had both done things like that when they were kids, but they had never gotten lost on Granite Peak and spent the night.

Pitt's stable hands had brought high beam searchlights with them. They shone them on the water and the opposite bank, into the trees. Bill had a bullhorn, and he shouted the boys' names and Juliet's, then listened for a response. There was none.

"They either walked up or down the trail, if they did cross over. They wouldn't have just sat there waiting for us to show up. They're on foot now, so God knows which direction they went." They found all seven horses tethered to the trees where they'd been left. The stable hands tied three of them together to lead them back, and Bill's men took the four others. They'd have to be careful that they didn't slip and fall into a ravine, just as the kids might have, especially now if they were on foot.

Pitt took the searchlight himself and shone it slowly on the opposite shore, and then he stopped and gave a shout for Bill. There was a small scrap of red fabric flapping in the breeze on a bush at the water's edge. He squinted as he looked at it. It was a bright red plaid. "Peter has a shirt like that. I'm right. They crossed over and couldn't get back. God knows which direction they went. Hopefully, they didn't try to swim back." He said it in a hoarse voice with tears stinging his eyes in the rain. If they had tried to swim across, they would never have survived. That would have been the surest course to disaster, but they knew better. "Harvey has to get his boys out here at first light. The terrain is too rough and the brush too thick to find them now in the dark. It's a hell of a lesson for them." He didn't add, "if they survive."

Pitt and Bill rode back in silence as quickly as they could, with their stable hands leading the horses, careful to avoid the slippery places. Twice they nearly slid over the edge into a ravine, but stopped in time. It took them an hour and a half to get back, even longer than it took to get there. Bill went home with Pitt. It was one in the morning by then. As soon as Anne saw their faces, she assumed the worst, but Pitt was quick to reassure her, as best he could.

"We don't know where they are, but I think they crossed the river and couldn't get back. We found the horses. The kids are probably huddled under a tree somewhere along the trail, miserable and scared."

"Or fighting off a bear," Anne said, clutching Pitt. "Oh my God, Pitt, what if something happens to them?"

"We'll find them tomorrow. I'm going to call Harvey right now. You call Marlene and June. I'll call Tom Marshall as soon as I get hold of Harvey." Pitt had the chief ranger's private cell number, and he answered immediately in a deep gruff voice, but he didn't sound as though he'd been asleep. He told Harvey what had happened, as much as he knew, and what he could guess.

"We had a bad flash flood up there today," Harvey told him. "And it's raining at the midline tonight. But on the backside of the mountain, they didn't get a drop of rain, and we've got a hell of a fire growing and coming around to the south side. I want to meet with all the parents at your place at six o'clock in the morning. We can't do anything until then. I'll get my boys out in the choppers after that. And Pitt, I'm sorry. We'll bring them home. Don't worry. That mountain is nothing to mess with. I imagine they've figured that out by now." And they knew it from the stories they'd heard all their lives about climbers who'd run into trouble and gotten lost. Granite Peak could be merciless.

"We've got some extenuating circumstances on our hands too.

Noel Wylie is a fourteen-year-old diabetic. He's Bob Wylie's boy. Bill Brown's six-year-old son is with them. And we have a fourteen-year-old female in the group."

"Oh God, what else? Thanks for the heads-up about the Wylie boy. I'll get the medevac team alerted. How is Bob doing, by the way?"

"He's not. He's in the homestretch," Pitt said. "Hospice is with him. This is all Marlene needs on top of everything else."

"She's a wonderful woman. She doesn't deserve this." They both agreed. "We'll get the kids home tomorrow. I want to get them off that mountain, before the fires move any closer. This is a worry none of us needs. See you tomorrow morning," he confirmed. Pitt called Tom Marshall as soon as he hung up from Harvey. Harvey always had a way of making you feel as though everything would be all right, even if you didn't see how it could be. He found a way, and pulled a rabbit out of the hat more often than Pitt would ever have thought possible. Pitt was counting on him to do it again this time. He took a sharp breath when Tom answered immediately. This was one call he didn't want to have to make, to tell him that his fourteen-year-old daughter was MIA somewhere on Granite Peak. But no human bodies had been found as the river rushed downstream, Harvey had assured Pitt of that. The kids were up there somewhere, the question was where and how soon they could find them. Pitt was hoping the helicopter pilots could do their job and get all seven kids off the mountain safely. They had done some remarkable rescue missions before, in worse weather. He just hoped that none of the kids were at the bottom of a ravine, or severely injured. He was praying that his son was alive, that they all were.

"Tom?" Pitt said when Tom answered. "We have some mixed news here. The kids are still on the mountain somewhere. They didn't come home. We think they may have crossed a dry riverbed before there was a flash flood, and then they couldn't get back. We found the horses, but not the kids, so we know where they were, and they couldn't get too far on foot, especially with a six-year-old with them. The chief ranger wants us all at my place at six in the morning for a meeting, after that they're sending out the rescue helicopters and a medevac team to look for them. If you know what Juliet was wearing, it will help a little."

"Oh my God, how did that happen?" Tom was shocked. He hadn't expected to hear that they hadn't come back.

"I don't know. Seven kids exploring on a mountain, with no concept of how dangerous that can be, is how it happened. We can give them hell when they get home, but let's get them off the damn mountain first. I'm sorry this happened. I'm going to ground my son until his thirtieth birthday." Pitt sounded serious.

"I'm sure with seven of them, they all contributed some foolhardy ideas," Tom commented. "I'd better call Juliet's mother. She'll give me hell for not calling her sooner, and not keeping an eye on Juliet well enough before this. I was hoping you'd call me to tell me they turned up at your place."

"I wish I had. The chief ranger is a good man. He'll find them. I just hope none of them are hurt." Tom fell silent as he thought about it and felt sick, and a moment later they hung up. Pitt met Anne in the kitchen. She had just hung up with Marlene.

"I don't know how much more that poor woman can take. Her husband is dying, and now her two sons are missing on Granite Peak. If she loses them, I don't think she'll survive it."

"Neither will we if something happens to Peter," he said with tears in his eyes as he held his wife, and they clung to each other. Neither of them could imagine sleeping that night. The morning couldn't come soon enough. They wanted the helicopters out there to find the children.

Marlene sat watching Bob breathe heavily in a deeply drugged sleep, as she prayed for him and her children. Almost as though he could hear her thoughts, he opened his eyes and looked at her, suddenly awake.

"Are the boys okay?" He looked agitated.

"They're fine. They're at the Pollocks'," she lied to him. He nodded as though he believed her and looked at her again.

"You wouldn't lie to me if something was wrong, would you?"

"Of course not," she said, trying to make him believe her.

He closed his eyes, and drifted back to sleep, as she sat next to him, praying he wouldn't die, and her boys would come home safe. She kept trying to calculate how much insulin Noel had in his pump, and hoping he had brought a spare with him. Sometimes he did. If he didn't, they were racing against the clock for Noel's life. Justin knew it too, as he sat next to his sleeping brother under a tree on Granite Peak. His father was dying, and his little brother might die too. It was more than he could bear, and he was sorry he hadn't stopped them from coming up here. He should have, and he blamed himself, but it was too late now for that. All he knew was that if Noel died, he would never forgive himself, and he was sure his parents wouldn't either.

* * *

Tom waited until it was five A.M. in Montana to call Beth. It was seven A.M. in New York, a respectable enough hour to call her, without terrifying her more than he had to. He told her as quickly and as simply as he could.

"Juliet went up a mountain with a bunch of local kids here yesterday," since it was the next day for her in New York. "They're all good, wholesome kids. They rode up to a waterfall where they went swimming, and they didn't come back last night. They found the horses tied to some trees, and we think the kids went hiking, and got stuck somehow. There is no evidence that they got hurt. They're sending out rescue helicopters to search for them in a few hours, and a medevac team. That's all I know, Beth, and I'm so sorry to have to tell you this. I think she's going to be okay." He had no grounds for saying that, but it was all he had hoped for since Pitt called him. Beth said everything he thought she would.

"Are you insane? You let her go up a mountain with a bunch of kids? What were you thinking? How irresponsible are you in that dream world you live in? Are you ever going to grow up? I can't trust you with her for five minutes. You're never taking her back there again, if you can't keep her safe."

"I shouldn't have let her go," he admitted. "Most of them are her age. They're all good kids. All boys, except Juliet. I thought they'd take care of her, but something must have happened. I just hope they're okay. I think they got turned around and lost somehow. I'm sorry I didn't call you sooner, but I just heard a few hours ago, and I didn't want to wake you with this kind of news."

"I'm coming out there," she said with both vengeance and terror in her voice. "If something happens to Juliet, Tom, I'll never forgive you," she said angrily.

"I won't forgive myself either. Life can't be that cruel." But they both knew it could be. Other people had lost children in circumstances like this. Accidents, illnesses, plane crashes, motorcycle and car accidents. No one was exempt from the whims of fate. He couldn't bear the thought that their beautiful, innocent daughter might be injured or dead or afraid. It ripped his heart out when he thought of it.

"How do I get there?" his ex-wife asked him in a shaking voice. He told her what airline to take, the connection she'd have to make, and what airport she'd arrive at. Fishtail was situated between two fairly major airports, each an hour away, and flights from JFK landed there.

"I'll meet you if you want me to. We have a meeting with the chief ranger at six A.M., an hour from now. Some of the most important ranchers' kids are in the group, they'll push everyone to organize the search parties quickly and keep looking 'til they find them. No one wants these kids to be lost, no matter who their parents are."

"I'll see you soon," she said. "I'll text you what flight I'm on." It was only after she hung up that she started to sob and couldn't stop as she threw some clothes into a carry-on bag, dressed rapidly, rushed downstairs, locked the apartment, and took a cab to the airport. The last thing she wanted was to go to Fishtail, Montana. All she wanted was to bring her daughter home, alive and whole. And then she never wanted to see Tom Marshall ever again. If his carelessness and irresponsibility were the cause of Juliet's death, she would never forgive him. Tom knew it too.

Chapter 6

When Chief Ranger Harvey Mack walked into the Pollocks' living room at six in the morning, he filled it with his presence and the aura around him. The word Anne always used to describe him was "huge." It referred to his size, the power of his presence and personality, and the way people responded to him. He was six feet five with the widest shoulders Tom had ever seen. He had a stern expression, which broke into a smile at regular intervals, long arms, big hands, long legs. He had a deep voice, which seemed appropriate, a mane of dark hair with gray at the temples, and piercing dark eyes. He was someone whose authority was unquestionable.

He could be tough when he needed to be, and gentle as a child when a situation warranted it. He was a born leader. He had played college football at the University of Michigan, been a Navy SEAL for ten years after that, and had been decorated several times. He had been a forest ranger for more than twenty years now. He had frequent dealings with the military, when they needed to call in the National Guard for emergencies, and was one of the highest-ranking forest rangers in the state.

He came to the meeting in his ranger's uniform, and still had his military bearing. His size made him seem ominous until he spoke, and his face creased into a warm smile when he saw Anne and Pitt. He hugged Anne and told them both how sorry he was that their son was momentarily out of sight, but he assured them convincingly that they would find him soon and have him back home. Harvey was someone you immediately believed in and knew you could count on. He spent most of his time on horseback, but had flown a reconnaissance and rescue plane early in his career as a ranger, and had come up through the ranks quickly and steadily over the past two decades. He lived nearby in Big Sky. Fishtail and the Beartooth Mountains and Granite Peak were all part of his territory. He knew the area, and particularly the mountains, like his own backyard.

When he walked into the Pollocks' living room, the parents gathered there stopped talking and stood up to greet him. Anne had put a basket of muffins and pastries on the table, and had handed each of them a cup of coffee when they came in. Most of them had been awake all night worrying about their children. Harvey knew all of the local residents, and made it his business to know the people in his district. Pitt introduced him to Tom, whom Harvey had spotted immediately, and explained that he was Juliet's father. Pitt had given him all seven names of the missing children the night before. Harvey knew each of the children too, except for Juliet. He appeared frequently at community events, and spoke at the local schools about responsible use of the national and state parks, how not to cause forest fires by careless camping procedures, and the potentially dangerous animals that lived in the mountains. They had several injured tourists every year who fed the bears or did other foolish things. The locals knew better, but kids sometimes tried to show off their bravery or taunted the animals with disastrous results.

He stopped to speak to Marlene for a minute and asked about Bob. She had left him sleeping with a hospice nurse watching him so she could come to the meeting about her sons. She told him briefly about Noel's insulin. He already knew about it since Pitt had mentioned it to him the night before. Harvey was acutely aware of the dangers the seven kids were facing, and he had a medevac team in place, ready to take off in a helicopter within the hour. He explained to them that they would have two rescue helicopters in the air all day, combing the area. They knew the point the kids had started from, where the horses had been tethered. They had a map of all the trails and had calculated how far the children could have gotten on foot within twenty-four hours. There were a number of trails they could have taken. Some were blocked by the flash flood now. There were also red zones, which presented the greatest risks to the kids because of the sharp drops, dangerous ledges, and ravines and crevasses. One or several of them could have fallen, and might be trapped now, while the others tried to extricate them. This could be why they hadn't come home.

"Are they likely to have any tools with them, or camping equipment? Could they have been planning to spend the night and just didn't tell you? Kids don't always share their plans with us," Harvey said with a smile, and they all shook their heads.

"I think they would have told us," Anne volunteered.

He asked what kind of food and water supplies they had, and who had been responsible for it. Tom answered that Juliet had been making a stack of sandwiches that she took with her. And Anne guessed that they probably had about six large bottles of water, and maybe some canteens.

"So they would have been all right for food and water last night," Harvey estimated. Marlene guessed that Noel would have about two days of insulin left in his pump, or maybe less, and she didn't believe he had a spare on him, although he should have. She said that Justin was well versed in emergency procedures for problems with Noel's diabetes. Most of them knew what their children had been wearing. Pitt told Harvey about the little scrap of red plaid fabric he'd seen snagged on a branch, and Anne confirmed it was the shirt their son was wearing. He asked Tom some details about Juliet, what she was wearing, her height and weight, how strong and athletic she was, and if she'd done any rock or mountain climbing previously. Harvey jotted down a few notes, but committed most of it to memory. All seven of them were his highest priority at the moment, and he knew everything he needed to know about them. All of the parents were adamant that neither drugs nor alcohol would have been a part of their plan.

"We think they just started hiking up a trail to check things out, went farther than they meant to, and got stuck somewhere," Pitt said simply.

"One of them could be injured, and the others are trying to help, which would slow them all down," Harvey explained to them. "And if they crossed the riverbed, which the fragment of plaid fabric suggests, then their return by the same route would have been impossible after the flash flood when the riverbed filled. We've got fires burning on the other side of Granite Peak, but they couldn't have gone far enough for that to be a problem. The fires are moving slowly and are contained at the moment. Unfortunately, the rainfall didn't happen on that side of the mountain, so it didn't help us with the fires, but I don't think that's our prime risk at the moment. I'm more concerned about the ravines, or something untoward, like their disturbing a mother bear and a cub in a cave. We're going to be looking very closely with our recon planes. I think it's very unlikely we won't have them home by tonight, with a whole new respect for wandering around the mountains without adult supervision, adequate supplies, and a plan." He smiled at them.

"We'll be going up the mountain on horseback too. I'll be with them, and we'll all be connected by radios, so we'll be in constant contact with you. I'm going to leave a radio with each of you today, set to our frequency. You'll hear the folks in the recon planes too, so you'll know as much as we do at all times."

"Could Bill and I ride up with you?" Pitt asked, and Harvey hesitated. He knew what excellent riders they were, but it could be emotional for them if any or all of the seven were severely injured or worse. He couldn't rule that out.

"I think you'd be better off here," he said, "but I won't stop you if that's what you want to do." Pitt nodded and looked at Bill, who nodded too. They wanted to be on the ground, helping with the search. Maybe they would recognize some scrap of something that one of the rangers and rescuers might miss.

The chief ranger spent three quarters of an hour with them, and then he glanced at his watch and stood up. "We want to get on the road as soon as we can, and in the air. We're set to start in half an hour." He signaled to his driver from the kitchen door, and he came in with a box of radios, one for each of them, and showed them how to operate them. They were already on the frequency, listening to communications about preparations. They were taking several additional horses with them, in case some of the young people would need to ride to an area where the helicopters could pick them up. They had a dozen paramedics in the medevac plane, and Saint Vincent Healthcare hospital in Billings had been notified and were ready for them. They had a very efficient trauma unit. Most of their rescue missions happened in winter during snowstorms, with hypothermia and icy conditions involved. Summer rescues were rare and they hadn't had one in several years.

They all followed Harvey to the door and thanked him. Marlene was rushing back to Bob, to relieve the hospice nurse. Bill and Pitt agreed to a meeting place where they would join up with Harvey and the rangers on horseback. June had patients to see in her office and was going to keep the radio on. And Anne invited Tom to spend the day with her and Pattie, while they waited for progress reports from the search in the air and on the ground. Then Harvey stopped on his way out as he thought of something else.

"I almost forgot. Press. If we don't find them pretty fast, this is going to turn into the hottest story of the hour. It could go national, which means we'll have news trucks, reporters, and cameras all over town, and in your faces. Brace yourself for that. It's always best not to get tangled up with them, and best not to comment. They'll put words in your mouth whenever they can, and once they get caught up in the technical aspects of a rescue, they cause a lot of confusion and slow us down. You're free to talk to them if you want to, of course, but I always prefer to keep it to a minimum. As far as I'm concerned, nothing good ever comes from too much contact with the press." Harvey knew too, the press's involvement would also depend on whether there were fatalities or not. If there were, it would be an even bigger story, and it would make headlines everywhere.

"God, that's all we need," Pitt said with a glance at Anne. He could just imagine what that would be like, particularly if any of the kids were hurt or, God forbid, dead. He hoped not.

"If we don't solve this very soon, it is going to be very big news. Brace yourselves. The press makes it all a lot harder. They want anything sensational, and they love rescue stories. We'll be hearing from them soon. They'll want an update on our progress every hour. Press conferences are not my favorite in situations like this, a lot of misinformation gets passed around, so you won't be seeing a lot of me on TV. We have a press aide for that."

Harvey took off a minute later, talking into his radio, as his assistant ranger drove the car. They were sending forty rangers on horseback into the mountains, and the planes were taking off twenty minutes after he left.

Anne offered them all another cup of coffee before they took off. Bill and Pitt had already gone to the barn to saddle up. They didn't want to waste any time.

Marlene was right behind Harvey in her car, on her way back to

Bob. She was normally a pretty blonde, and he thought she had aged ten years in the past few months. He knew what those days were like.

The kids woke up having slept fitfully through the night. They had spelled each other off hour by hour so that one of them was always awake in case of an animal attack, or any other untoward experience. They had heard coyotes the night before, howling and obviously in a pack. An owl had hooted at them from above. Only Benjie had slept well because he didn't have to do a shift. Juliet had a spare sweater in her backpack, so it was dry and she put it on him. He'd been shivering. And Matt took him to attend to his needs in the bushes, as they all did.

They started the day with a small square of the remaining peanut butter and jelly sandwiches, and a good swallow of water for each of them.

"I never knew water could taste so good," Peter said with a sigh. "I could drink a gallon of it." They had gathered two full cups of water from the rain the night before to add to their supply, and Juliet put the cups back in her backpack after they poured the rainwater carefully into the two big bottles.

They heard the helicopters in the distance a short time later, but they were still far in the distance, flying a set path. The children could hear them, but barely see them. Peter frowned.

"Why don't they bring them closer? They'll never find us from there," he said, worried, as Justin watched the sky too.

The helicopters headed in the wrong direction then, farther up the mountain and farther away from where they were.

"Shit, they have no idea where we are," Matt said, looking disheartened. "I hope we don't have another night out here." He had worried about the bears all night, but there had been no sign of any. They had kept out of caves though.

"Or a lot of nights," Justin added. They all looked tired. It had been a long night, and they were hungry and uncomfortable, and chilled from the night air on the mountain. Their damp clothes had dried by morning.

Tim suggested they pick berries then, which cheered everyone up. He knew which berries to pick, from a Boy Scout camping course he had taken. They didn't have any receptacles, so they used their hands and their T-shirts to hold them. They were less hungry after that. Then they conferred about which way to go. In daylight, a small narrow trail was visible past some trees they were sitting near. It went neither up nor down, but appeared to go around the mountain, and they decided to try that for a while. There were plenty of berries on the new trail as well, so they ate those too, until Benjie said he had a stomachache.

"Are you sure you know which kind we can eat?" Justin asked Tim, who assured them he did. Otherwise, Justin was quiet and pensive, trying to think of creative ways to get down the mountain, and worried about his brother. As the oldest member of the group, he felt responsible for all of them, and even more so for his brother. He should never have let him come, or at least he should have thought to ask Noel if he had a spare pump with him. But they'd been planning to ride back after lunch, and had gotten carried away. There was no reason to think he'd need another pump.

Justin was thinking about his father too, and wondering how he was doing. He felt terrible about the worry they were causing their father, who was in no condition to weather more stress, if he even knew what was happening. Justin wondered if their mother would tell him. He somehow had a feeling she wouldn't. She always protected Bob so carefully, and he got more upset now than he used to, and cried over things he never would have before. Justin hated worrying his mother too, when she had so much on her plate. He felt like he had failed them both, letting Noel get into a situation where he was now at risk. He told himself he should have stopped him before they crossed the riverbed.

They'd been walking for almost two hours when they came back into a small clearing that looked familiar, and they realized that it was where they had spent the night. They had been going in a circle for the last two hours.

"I vote that we head down," Matt said. "That makes the most sense." But every path they tried to take was blocked, and the trees and bushes got thicker and thicker. No recon plane or helicopter would be able to see them in the thick brush. They headed up the mountain then. It was the only path open to them at the moment, and they all gave a start as they walked along a narrow ledge and looked straight down into a ravine. One misplaced step and they would have fallen. They passed it without mishap but were all very quiet. In the dark, they would have fallen to their deaths for sure. Nothing about this adventure was fun anymore.

Juliet doled out another tiny ration of their sandwiches, with a sip of water, and a few slices of the banana she had in her bag. They divided up two power bars, and all felt better after they ate, even though the quantities were small.

"It doesn't make sense to me to head up the mountain," Peter complained. So far they had all agreed on the best route to take.

"We could still get above the flash flood so we can cross over," Justin reminded him. They watched the recon helicopters in the distance all day, but they never came close enough to where they were, so the children could wave or give any kind of signal. The pilots were far from where they were climbing, which was discouraging to watch.

The rangers on horseback had come up with nothing either. Not even a shred of clothing stuck on a branch, or any clue that the seven kids had passed by there.

In the trailer Harvey was using as an office, he scowled at the computerized maps they were using.

"I have the feeling that the trail is getting colder and they're headed in a different direction," he said to two of his assistants. One of them pointed to a paper map on the desk, and Harvey nodded and instructed one of the pilots to fly through that zone, and see if they saw anything. Harvey felt like he was throwing mud balls at a barn and nothing would stick. They had come up dry at every turn so far.

"Dammit, they're out there somewhere. I wish they'd give us some kind of sign, or we'd catch a glimpse of just one of them, which would lead us to the others."

"Do you think they split up?" the younger ranger asked him, but Harvey shook his head, and studied the maps again.

"No, I don't. They know better. They're safer as a group. Six of those kids are local, they know something about the mountain. And they're probably too scared to try to get out alone, or even in pairs." The younger ranger nodded. He agreed.

In the Pollock kitchen, Anne had been making stew all day. Pattie had gone home for a while, and Tom and Anne sat at her kitchen table. When she turned off the stove, she ladled a good amount of the stew into a Tupperware box and pressed the lid on it.

"What's that for?" Tom asked, curious.

"I thought I'd drop it off for Marlene. She'll need something to feed the boys when they get home." Her eyes filled with tears as she said it. They all would, if they were lucky. She couldn't even let herself think of what her life and Pitt's would be like if they lost Peter. There would be no meaning to their life anymore without him. She couldn't even put her fears into words, but Tom could see it in her eyes, and hugged her. They'd heard Pitt on the radio a little earlier. The rangers and other men on horseback had come up with nothing. There had been no trace of the kids anywhere so far, on the ground or from the air.

"I can drop the stew off at Marlene's place if you want," Tom offered. He needed to stretch his legs and get some air, and to do something useful. Anne had called her earlier, and mercifully Bob had slept all day, while Marlene sat and listened to the radio for news of the boys. "I have to pick Beth up at the airport in a couple of hours. I can stop at Marlene's on the way. Will you be okay here by yourself?"

She smiled sadly at him. "It's not my place to say, and I don't know what went wrong in your marriage, but you're a good man, Tom Marshall. She was a fool to let you get away."

"I'm not sure I know what happened either," he said seriously. He'd been thinking about it a lot lately, more than he had in the beginning, when he first left New York. The anger had gone out of it for him. "We grew so far apart. We both changed. We had all the same goals when we got married, and then suddenly we didn't. I think we were focused on all the wrong things. Or the wrong things for me. She thinks I let her down. I guess I did. I got to hate New York, and everything about our life. I just couldn't do it anymore. I couldn't see myself living there for the rest of my life.

"It was an epiphany for me, and a death sentence for our marriage. My job was soul-crushing. I tried to explain it to Beth, and she thought I'd lost my mind. Maybe I did.

"I came out here for a weekend with a bunch of guys, and all of a sudden everything came into focus. I knew I was leading the wrong life, and I had to get out. I wanted her to come with me, and when she wouldn't, I ran. So maybe I'm not such a nice guy after all. I let her down. But I love my life here. It's what I needed, but it wouldn't have been right for her. She would hate it here. It's not New York. I love everything about it, or I did until Juliet got stuck somewhere on a mountain. God, Anne, if something happens to her, it'll kill me."

"It'll kill us all," Anne said grimly. She had been thinking about it all day. They all were. "Pitt and I are lucky. We've always loved what we do. We love it here. And we really are partners. I couldn't live in New York either, and neither could Pitt. We love our work, which makes it fun, and we'll hand it off to Peter one day, and hope he loves it too." As she said it, she shuddered and could feel a chill down her spine. If Peter wasn't there to step into their shoes, it would lose all meaning for them too.

"I want Juliet to have a meaningful life, doing something she loves, not just chasing all the big prizes of success like her mother. You have a better shot at a real life here than I did in New York. I guess I wasn't cut out for that life after all. And the only one who didn't know that was me. In the Bible, it says "know thyself," and I didn't. I didn't meet myself until last year, at forty-three. It's a little late, but I figured I'd make a run for it before it was too late. It killed my marriage, but if I hadn't done it, it would have killed me."

"You're a brave man, Tom. It takes a lot of guts to walk out on a life like that." She could guess that he'd been successful there, and his ex-wife still was.

"I hurt Beth," he confessed to Anne. "I hurt Juliet too when I left. I hate that part. Fishtail is a long way from New York. We have to work out a better visitation schedule. I need to see more of Juliet than a weekend every six weeks, with me staying at a hotel in New York. I'd like to have her spend time with me here, but she's going to be busy in high school, starting in the fall, and it'll be hard. Her mother wants her in New York. She wants her to go to a 'killer school,' so she gets a great job, and has a big career one day. I want more than just that for her. Maybe she can have both worlds, with me here," he said quietly.

"She'll figure it out for herself. They all do. I see that with kids here all the time. Some stay and love it, others can't wait to get the hell out and head for a big job in the big city. And others fall in love with all this later in life, and they find their way here from a very different place, like you. I think we all end up in the right place in the end."

"I hope you're right," he said with a sigh. They were all exhausted waiting for good news that hadn't come yet. He picked up the stew for Marlene. "I'll drop this off on the way to the airport. It's going to be tough. Beth is even more pissed at me now. She thinks I'm a total loser because I gave up on New York. And now I let Juliet slip through my fingers. She thinks I'm completely irresponsible. Maybe she's right."

"They all slipped through our fingers," Anne reminded him. "And we keep a close eye on Peter. I think they just got distracted and were having too much fun. The mountains here are beautiful, but they can be treacherous. We can't forget that, and I think they did. Who knows? Maybe they thought it was some kind of challenge, to see how far they could go. Boys are like that. They love a challenge just for the sake of it."

He smiled. "That's what happened to me in New York. I got so caught up in the challenge that I never noticed that the prize wasn't worth a damn. Now I know."

"So will they, when they come home," she said quietly, and he kissed her cheek. He knew that in this ridiculously small town of four hundred people, he had found real friends. They were going through hell together, but at least they weren't alone.

"Pitt is a lucky man," he said to her, and he knew that Pitt was well aware of it. She was lucky too. "I hope I find a woman like you when I grow up. If I ever do."

"You are grown up, Tom. You just need a woman who wants the

same things you do, now that you know what you want. And good luck with your ex-wife." She smiled at him and he nodded.

"She's going to beat me to death when I pick her up at the airport." He was expecting it. "And maybe she's right. I hope we get good news by tonight."

"So do I. Give my love to Marlene." He took the stew and waved as he went out the door, and put the ranger radio in his pocket, so he could keep listening.

"See you later."

Pattie was just arriving at the Pollocks' as he left, and they waved at each other. It was comforting sharing the experience with friends. They all had so much at stake, but at least he knew for sure now that Fishtail was home.

Marlene was grateful for the stew when he dropped it off. There was a sign on the door not to ring the doorbell, so he knocked gently and she came to the door and smiled when she saw him.

"Thanks," she whispered and beckoned him in. "I didn't want to wake Bob," she explained.

"I figured. Anne said to give you her love."

"No news so far," she echoed what he already knew.

"They're tucked in somewhere. They'll find them sooner or later," he tried to reassure her, but they were all afraid that it might be too late when they did. The mountain could be cruel.

"After tonight, Noel will have about another twenty-four hours left in his pump, and I don't know what kind of food they have with them. That makes a difference for him too. Thank God Justin is with him. He knows what to do, if they can't get help." She had even more to worry about than the rest of them, with Noel's diabetes putting him at greater risk.

"How's Bob?" he whispered.

"The same." They had been through hell for the last year, and now her sons were lost on a mountain. It was one of those times when you just had to keep going, there was no other choice.

"Do you need anything?" he asked her, and she shook her head. "Why don't you try to get a little rest, while he is. When was the last time you got some sleep?" He was genuinely concerned.

"Last year?" she said with a grin.

"At least lie down until he wakes up. I'm heading to the airport to pick up my ex-wife. She's ready to kill me. She blames me for letting Juliet go up the mountain with the boys."

"You let them go to the waterfall. None of us knew they'd head up the mountain. They've been to the waterfall a million times before. You can only control so much with kids. In the end, they do what they want. And most of the time they survive it." She'd been telling herself that all day.

"I hope you're right." He gave her a hug and told her he'd be back in town in a couple of hours, and if she needed anything she should just call.

Then he hurried down the steps and headed to the airport to pick up Beth.

Chapter 7

Tom picked Beth up at Bozeman Yellowstone International Airport, which was less than two hours from Fishtail. It was the only flight she could get. Beth had had to change planes in Chicago, and had a long layover. She looked exhausted when she got there, with her dark hair pulled back tightly in a ponytail, in jeans and a safari jacket, and Chanel loafers. Beth always looked stylish whatever the occasion.

"Any news?" she asked Tom as soon as she saw him, before she'd even said hello. He didn't blame her. She had been on planes all day. He had kept her informed by text, but she had been in the air most of the time. It had taken her nine hours to get there in all.

"Not yet."

"For chrissake, what are they doing?"

"They've got forty rangers on the ground on horseback, covering all the trails, and two recon helicopters in the air. The area is heavily wooded. It's not easy to see them if they're there, and it's a big mountain." He didn't say that they could be at the bottom of a ravine, but that was a possibility too. "I've been listening to the radio all day, between the rescue teams. They're covering as much ground as they can." He led her to the garage to get his truck while they talked.

"I still don't understand how you could have let her go." Her face was taut as she said it, with barely concealed fury.

"They went to a waterfall, pretty low on the mountain. The boys have been there a million times before. No one thought they'd head up the mountain, if that's what they did. Apparently there was a dry riverbed, and everyone seems to think they crossed it, and a flash flood blocked them from coming back."

"You couldn't keep her with you? What were you doing?" The reproach in her voice was glaring, like the look in her eyes.

"I can't keep her locked in the house, Beth. She met some nice kids her age. They invited her on a picnic."

"All boys?" She sounded skeptical. He was on the carpet, and he had expected it.

"All boys. Good kids from nice families. You'll meet the parents. Oddly enough, none of them have daughters. There's a six-year-old with them, and one boy's older brother. He's seventeen. That may be a good thing. One of the boys Juliet's age is diabetic, which is a serious problem." She calmed down a little when she heard a six-year-old had been allowed to go, although it didn't change anything. "I'm hoping to hear good news any minute."

"I was hoping it would be all over by the time I landed in this godforsaken place. It takes less time to get to Europe. It's pretty country, but I still don't understand what you're doing here. I never will." He suspected that was true. "You were born in New York. Your father was successful in investments. Your mother was from a fancy family, and you want to be a hick, and live like a mountain man when you grow up. I guess that's the whole point. You haven't grown up yet." He expected her to bash him, and she did, but given the fact that their daughter was missing on his watch, he let it go.

They got in his truck then and headed for Fishtail. He had reserved a room for her at a small guest lodge near the famous General Store. She wasn't going to love the hotel, but there was nothing in town up to her standards. They had both gotten spoiled over the years. Comfort no longer mattered to him, and in the circumstances, he was sure she wouldn't care about that either. All she cared about was Juliet. They both did.

"When can I talk to the head ranger?" she asked him.

"He's probably still on the mountain with the others. You can reach him when he comes down. They can't search after dark." It was still light, but wouldn't be for long. He handed her the radio then. "You can listen to the radio. The pilots in the rescue and recon helicopters are on the same frequency too." She listened for a long time as they drove to Fishtail. There was nothing new in the exchanges, just a lot of reports about their position, and that they hadn't seen anything. It had been the same all day.

It took them almost two hours to get to the hotel he'd booked for her. She didn't comment but she didn't look happy when she saw it.

"It's not the Ritz in Paris or the Carlyle in New York," he conceded, "but it's about the best you can do here. There are some Airbnbs and a couple of guest ranches. I didn't think you'd want to stay with me."

"You're right, I don't." She sounded hard with him, but he could see how terrified she was. She had cried most of the way on the plane, and her eyes were puffy. They were all facing the horrifying possibility that their children might not be alive. It was hard to consider, and she loved Juliet as much as he did, even if they expressed it differently, and wanted different things for her. They both loved her. "What happens if they don't find them today?" she asked him before she got out.

"They keep looking," he said quietly. "There's a diner up the street if you get hungry. They have pretty decent food."

"I'm not hungry." She never ate when she was upset. She was always on a diet, and she had a slim figure. At thirty-nine, she had changed very little physically since they'd met in graduate school. She was studying journalism, and he was in business school at Columbia. They were native New Yorkers and were going to set the world on fire one day. They had, and it still mattered to her, but it had turned out to be meaningless to him. It was just fireworks with nothing behind it. Her beliefs and her goals hadn't changed. He wondered how much money and how much success would have satisfied her. Maybe if he'd become the head of a company, or a startup, and she won a Pulitzer. It all sounded empty to him, which was why he was here.

"Can I get you anything?" he asked before he left her, and she shook her head. He could see that she was on the verge of tears. He pulled her into his arms and she didn't resist. They needed each other now, even if she hated him and he had disappointed her. They no longer loved each other, of that he was sure. But they loved their daughter. It was the only bond they still had, and a strong one. He stroked Beth's hair as he held her, and wished he could promise her it would be okay. He hoped it would be. "We just have to get through this," he said softly, and she nodded. She wiped her tears when she pulled away. "The waiting is killing us all. I hope they find them soon. Call me if you need anything at all. If Chief Mack wants to meet with us, I'll call you and pick you up." She nodded again and looked less aggressive than she had when she got off the plane. She was a mother who was worried sick about her daughter, not an angry ex-wife, for now. She suddenly seemed smaller and more human, and he felt sorry for her. He had friends here, she didn't. All she had was him, all the recent bad history between them, and a pending divorce. It would be final soon. They were both eager to have it behind them, and if they lost Juliet, it would be like erasing the best part of the history they'd shared. It would make it all seem pointless. June Taylor felt that way too.

Losing the child of a divorced marriage made the marriage seem irrelevant. There would be nothing left to show for it.

He drove back to his house after he dropped Beth off, and sat on the couch, staring into space, waiting for news, and trying not to think of what he and Beth had once shared. The blackboard of their life together had been erased.

The kids walked all day, and had no idea where they were by the end of it. They were higher up the mountain, the trees were thicker and hard to navigate around, and the foliage made it even harder for them to be seen on the ground. They had seen helicopters in the distance, but they were too far for the band of seven to catch their attention. They could see smoke in the sky now, coming from the other side of the mountain, and there was a thin film of ash falling around them like early snow. They tripped over tree roots frequently. Benjie had fallen several times and hurt his knees and his hands, and cried when he did. Matt carried him for a while, and Justin took a turn since he was bigger and stronger. Noel was looking pale, and all of them were hungry and tired by the end of their second day on the mountain. All sense of adventure had gone out of it, if there had ever been any. This was no longer a challenge. It was only about survival.

Their food had almost run out. Juliet had no power bars left and only a few mouthfuls of the sandwiches. And they could only take small sips of the water from what was left. They still found berries along the way, but if they ate too many it gave them a stomachache. They looked exhausted, but they had agreed to keep moving all day, hoping that rescuers would see them, but none of the helicopters even came close. They had somehow guessed the young people's position to be entirely different from what it was, and the kids had no way of getting to the area the rescue planes kept flying over. Two deep ravines separated them from the low-flying zones of the planes. The ravines were entirely unnavigable without risking serious injury or death. So they just kept walking up the mountain, around to the side, and as close as they could get to the helicopters that were much too far away to even catch a glimpse of them between the trees. It seemed too late to head down the mountain now.

"Maybe we should try that tomorrow," Peter suggested to Justin when they stopped for the day. They had thought that the trees would thin out if they went up the mountain, but the foliage had gotten thicker, and it was getting harder to breathe, especially for Noel, who was slowing down noticeably. He was well aware, as was Justin, that he had another twenty-four hours of insulin left in his pump, and after that he would slip into a coma. He bitterly regretted not having brought a spare pump, and swore he would from now on. But this time he hadn't, and it might cost him his life.

They were sitting, catching their breath and taking small sips of water, discouraged by how far the helicopters had been from them all day. They had all disappeared from the sky just after seven, with the day still bright. The sun would set soon. The kids were talking about their plan for the next day, sitting in front of a small cave, when suddenly a giant brown ball emerged from the cave, and stood on its haunches. It was a bear with a cub right behind her, and all seven of them shrank in terror as the mother bear showed her teeth, and almost danced in front of them. The very small cub ran into a clearing and looked confused. Its mother stayed standing to protect it, as they all watched in terrified silence.

"Don't touch the baby!" Juliet shouted at all of them. It looked adorable, and very scared. The mother seemed to be deciding between whether to attack them or remove her cub from the scene she obviously considered dangerous.

"Holy shit!" Justin said out loud, as the bear gave a roar, and they tried to figure out what to do. There was nowhere for her to run to.

"What do we do? Do we throw rocks at it?" Peter asked in a terrified voice, as Justin spotted a boulder and leapt onto it, which made him considerably taller than the bear. He made no sound but towered over her, as he had read to do if one encountered a bear. The bear dropped to all fours, nudged the cub with her muzzle to push it forward. They disappeared into the forest a minute later. Justin tried to jump from the rock on shaking legs and fell backwards. He narrowly missed hitting his head, and the others rushed toward him.

"You saved us!" Juliet said as he tried to stand up and winced.

"I read somewhere that if you try to make bear sounds, they attack but if you look taller and stay quiet, they take off. I've never tested the theory though." Peter gave him a hand to get up from where he lay, and Justin grimaced in pain. "I think I sprained my ankle," he said. He couldn't walk when he stood up. "So much for walking down the mountain tomorrow." He appeared to be in serious pain as they moved around, glancing between the trees as they did, to make sure the bear didn't come back. They guessed that she would be looking for another lair to hide her cub, but they kept a close eye on the area around them. They were amazed that Justin's ruse had worked, except that now he was incapacitated.

"Lie down," Juliet suggested. He did, looking miserable. Peter brought a log over so Justin could rest and elevate his foot on it, but within minutes his foot had tripled in size and looked like a football. Juliet could see Justin was fighting back tears from the pain and the shock of scaring off the bear.

"Maybe it's broken," Peter whispered to her, when they walked away for a minute, before Juliet returned to give Justin a sip of their precious water.

"I hope not," she said, worried. Things seemed to be deteriorating. They had been on the mountain for two days and no one had found them. They were beginning to think that no one would, despite Justin's promises that they'd be home soon, to keep their spirits up.

"Matt, Pete, and I can carry Justin tomorrow. We'll take turns," Tim said gamely. All three boys were strong, although Justin was taller and heavier. They had been good sports so far.

They all calmed down after the bear incident, but Benjie clung to his brother and Juliet once it was dark, terrified that the bear would come back. Noel was quiet and getting weaker without food. Juliet had reserved all the juice she had for him. They still had some left, and she gave it to him. Justin was quiet but groaned whenever he moved. They were all resigned to going without food that night.

"I think we definitely win the challenge," Peter said when they settled down for the night. "The bear wins it. Justin wins first prize." He grinned and they all took turns again, watching for predators at night. But the bear didn't return. She was protecting her cub somewhere, hopefully far away.

Chief Ranger Harvey Mack called the Pollocks at eight o'clock that night and asked them to round up the parents so he could explain the next day's strategy. He was discouraged at the lack of results that day, but by no means felt defeated. He didn't intend to lose the seven children.

Tom called Beth on her cellphone and told her he'd pick her up in a few minutes. She was dressed and waiting for him when he drove by her hotel, and she jumped into his truck.

"What did he say?" she asked nervously about Chief Mack. Tom noticed she had her fighting face on, which wasn't a good sign.

"He's just bringing us up-to-date on the plan for tomorrow. You wanted to meet him, so now you will."

"I don't understand what's taking them so long. For God's sake, there are seven of them on a mountain. How hard can it be to find them?" Tom didn't like the sound of her tone, but he knew better than to lock horns with her, and he reminded himself that he wasn't responsible for her behavior. She was no longer his wife, and he knew what a bitch she could be if she was angry. He had experienced it often enough in the last year.

They were the last to arrive at the Pollocks'. All the others were there. Tom introduced Beth to them, and they all told her how sorry they were that they were in this boat together. Beth was polite to them, but not warm, as though she blamed them for the situation, along with Tom. He could tell she was gunning for Chief Mack too, when he arrived. He looked calm, but Tom could see a muscle tighten in his jaw. He'd obviously had a hard day, and made it clear that he wasn't happy with the results so far either.

"Neither are we," Beth said harshly, and spoke for them all. The other parents looked startled when she spoke up. Harvey Mack looked exceptionally calm.

"This is where we are now," the chief ranger said, ignoring her for a moment and pointing to a map. Tom was embarrassed by her outburst and was trying not to be. "We're moving to a different area tomorrow. It would have made sense to find them where we've been looking all day. But on the chance that they've gone seriously off course and don't know where they are, we're going to try another sector tomorrow."

"Are your pilots competent?" Beth asked loudly, and Tom winced, with an apologetic look at the chief ranger, who looked unimpressed.

"Extremely, Mrs. Marshall." She was no longer using Tom's name, and had reverted to her maiden name, Turner, but she didn't correct him. "And they'll be well accompanied tomorrow. The fires on the back side of the mountain are creeping up on us and coming around the sides of Granite Peak. The National Guard is sending us planes and rescue pilots for tomorrow. They're arriving at midnight. We'll have six recon planes in the air tomorrow, and a hundred people on the ground. It's the largest rescue operation we've had in the area, ever. I want to get your kids home, or at least locate them, tomorrow if we can. We can drop them supplies, if we can't get them out when we first spot them. And we'll have a pump for Noel in those supplies," he said pointedly to Marlene, and tears filled her eyes as she nodded gratefully. "We'll parachute some men and paramedics in to wait with them if we can clear the trees, depending on where they are. We start at dawn tomorrow," he told them. There were subdued nods and tears of gratitude among the parents. The tension was wearing on them all.

"And what if you don't find them?" Beth said in a sharp voice, and Tom wanted to strangle her to shut her up. They were doing everything they could with the National Guard and a hundred men on the ground and six planes in the air. They couldn't do more.

"If they're on that mountain, we'll find them, if I have to go up there myself every day until we do," Harvey answered her. He had spent twelve hours on horseback that day on the mountain with his team, directing all aspects of the rescue mission. He fixed Beth with a look that surprised her. It wasn't anger, it was pity, and she suddenly realized that she had met her match. He wasn't cowed by her. He felt sorry for her. "I realize that you're frightened, Mrs. Marshall. We all are. So am I. I don't want to lose a single one of your children. This is taking too long, but it's hard terrain to negotiate. I'm going to ask you to trust me. I am going to do everything in my power to bring those kids home. Do whatever you can to stay calm. You don't need anger to convince me. I have the kids' best interests at heart, and I want to see Juliet in your arms this time tomorrow." He had totally disarmed her, and she was crying when he finished. He walked over to speak to her after he spoke to the other parents. She had melted like so much ice cream and could no longer conceal her terror.

Harvey gently touched her arm when he spoke to her. "I'm sorry if I was hard on you. I know how frightening this is. We know it too. I'm not going to let you down, or the kids. They're coming home," he promised, and she believed him.

"Thank you," she said in a shaken voice. "I'm sorry if I was rude."

"Anger is just a cover for fear," he said kindly.

"I'm so afraid she'll die up there, or is already dead," she said in a whisper, and he gave her a hug. He was like a mountain himself, and it was comforting being in his arms.

"I don't think she is," he said. "If they were, I think we'd already have found them. I think they're a bunch of bright kids who got themselves in a mess, and they're trying to figure it out the way we are, so they're moving around, which makes them harder to locate. I'm just guessing, but I think they're a moving target. If they just sit still for a minute, we'll find them. They'll wear out before we do, and they'll slow down. I'm counting on that tomorrow. The mountain will be swarming with troops too. We need to outsmart them and outrun them to catch them. They're younger than we are so they can keep moving, but we outnumber them, and we're smarter." He smiled at her, and she smiled back. "I'll see you tomorrow, Mrs. Marshall. Try to get some rest." Tom marveled at the way he handled her. It was exactly what Beth had needed to calm down. A strong man to take charge. Tom knew that he hadn't been strong enough for her. Maybe that was what had gone wrong. The chief ranger saw right through her and didn't let her attack him. Beth was as docile as a lamb when he left.

They were all encouraged by what he had said. Tom couldn't sleep when he got home, thinking about the operation that would begin at dawn to save his daughter. It was like a war, perfectly planned with precision, and a hundred rescuers to find seven children and bring them home.

June Taylor was thinking about it too when she made herself a cup of warm milk and her phone rang. She didn't even recognize his voice at first. It was Ted, her ex-husband, calling from somewhere in the Middle East.

"I've just gotten back to my apartment. I've been away. You left me about ten messages. What's up?" He sounded annoyed. He had never completely forgiven her for divorcing him, nor she for abandoning them and rejecting their son all his life because he was deaf. It wasn't Tim's fault. He was such a great boy. He didn't deserve a father like the one he had, who thought postcards from foreign places and child support were all he needed to contribute to his son's life.

She told him what had happened. He sounded shocked.

"How long has he been up there? Do you think they're still alive?" They'd been on the mountain for two days in warm weather, which was a plus, but they were probably without food or water, and might be injured, which wasn't good.

"I hope so," she said with tears in her eyes again. What Harvey

Mack had said that night had made her cry too. They were all worn out from the strain and lack of sleep. "If they aren't, you missed your son's whole life, Ted, just because he has a hearing impairment from a fever I had when I was pregnant. You've punished him for it all his life." She had wanted to say it to him for fourteen years and finally had. It was long overdue. He didn't respond at first, and when he did, she could hear that he was crying too.

"I'm sorry, June. I hope to God he's okay up there."

"So do I," she said, sounding choked.

They talked for a few minutes and she promised to keep him posted. She told him about the rescue plans for the next day, with the National Guard. He said he was too far away and couldn't come home, which didn't surprise her. But it was the most civil conversation she'd had with him in ten years. She just hoped that Tim didn't have to die for his father to wake up. He deserved a real father, and not a handful of postcards every year.

She sat at the window that night. The moon was bright and she thought about her son, and prayed he was still alive.

Beth was doing the same thing, thinking about her daughter. They all were. There was no way any of them could sleep that night, waiting for the rescue operations to begin again at dawn.

Chapter 8

Tom only dozed for an hour or so before the increased rescue operation began. He lay awake thinking about Juliet, praying for her safety, and worried about the day ahead. He finally got up to make himself a cup of coffee, and was startled when he looked out the window. There were four TV news vans outside and a sea of reporters. Harvey had predicted it in the beginning, and it had taken the press two days to catch on. Calling in the National Guard had obviously done it, although it was surprising they hadn't picked up the story before, with ordinary rescue procedures in place. But now, as Harvey said, it had become the biggest rescue operation in the history of the area, even in snow season, which was theoretically more dangerous. But there were plenty of potential dangers now too, everything from bears and all the other wildlife on the mountain, ravines and gullies, the fires burning an ever-larger area on the back of the mountain, possible injuries, to Noel's health issues. There was plenty to worry about. Tom had no desire to talk to the press. He just wanted to get the kids home.

He waited until eight in the morning, and then called Pitt and Anne. They had been up since five and already seen news trucks and reporters at their house too.

"I don't see what it adds to the story," Tom said, annoyed, "to stalk us, when we're already so worried."

"It's the nature of media," Anne said. Pitt was upset about them too. And they felt sorry for Marlene, who had enough happening with Bob, and now worrying about both her sons. They wondered if the press knew Noel was diabetic and would use that to add more color to their story. "We're staying out of sight today. Apparently, they've already been over to the stables. The stable hands told them it was private property and chased them off. They were taking videos of everything in sight, and tried to get into the barns to photograph the horses."

"They're so intrusive," Tom complained. "They should leave us all alone, and the kids, when they get home."

He called Beth shortly after and warned her. She peeked out her window, and saw two TV trucks parked outside, and half a dozen reporters. It was apparently a national story. They were swarming all over the Pollock and Brown ranches, which made for better visuals, and trying to interview whoever they could for their reactions. He told Beth to stay inside and avoid them.

He called Marlene to make sure she was okay, just to be friendly, and she said reporters were grilling the hospice nurses when they arrived, about Bob's condition, and had asked how much longer they thought he would live. Tom thought that was disgusting and Marlene agreed.

"Do you want me to come over and run interference for you?" he asked, and she hesitated.

"You have your own problems. You have your ex-wife to deal with. She seems like a handful," she said with a smile.

"That would be correct. I was mortified when she went after Harvey last night."

"He's a big boy. He can take care of himself. He defanged her right away. I heard her apologize to him later."

"He handled her masterfully. I never did. I had to run all the way to Montana to get her teeth out of my neck," he said, and she laughed. It was a relief talking to him. He had a light touch, and she thought he was a good father. She couldn't imagine him married to a woman like Beth, who seemed very hard.

"Keep your doors locked," he advised her, "and warn the hospice people not to give them information." It was so wrong of them to stalk the home of a dying man.

"I already locked them," she said. He forgot sometimes that she was a capable woman, an attorney, who ran her own business. She seemed so vulnerable as the wife of a man so desperately ill, and now with two missing boys on top of it. It was a lot for anyone to handle. She seemed fragile to him.

He went out to pick up Beth later, so she wouldn't have to stay trapped at the hotel. As soon as he left his house, a young woman wearing too much makeup with a mass of blond hair, an impressive bust, and a low-cut sweater made a beeline for him. She trapped him just as he was getting into his truck.

"Tom Marshall?" she asked, but he could tell that she knew who he was.

"No," he denied it, but she pressed herself between him and the truck door so he couldn't get in.

"How do you feel about how the rescue mission for your daughter is being handled?" she asked him, looking for dirt or criticism of the rescue operation.

"It's been beautifully handled," he said, outraged on behalf of Harvey.

"Then why do you think the children haven't been recovered yet?" she pressed him, and he wanted to shove her away to get into his truck, but he knew better and wouldn't have dared. "They've been up there for three days now, this is the third day. Don't you think that's a long time to leave seven young people up on the mountain? Do you think they were slow getting started?"

"No, I don't. I think it must be damn hard to find anyone up there. They've been doing everything they can, right from the beginning."

"Do you think there were drugs or alcohol involved on the kids' part?" she asked, her face almost pressed against his. He thought the question outrageous. They might even be dead, but she was trying to make the kids and everyone involved look bad.

"I do not," he said, incensed. "Except maybe the six-year-old. Maybe you should do a story on six-year-olds on drugs." She was unfazed by his response, and was obviously used to being given inappropriate responses, given the nature of her questions, and her aggressive style.

"Are you concerned that the fires are starting to burn out of control on Granite Peak? What if they can't get to your daughter in time?" He couldn't believe what she was asking.

He looked horrified. "Are you seriously asking me how I'll feel if my daughter is burned alive on the mountain before they rescue her? Are you insane? What kind of morality do you have to ask a question like that? How do you live with yourself, exploiting people who are potentially facing tragedy and worried sick about their kids?"

"Do you think any of them will die?" she asked in a morbid voice, and the muscle went taut in Tom's jaw.

"Get away from my truck or I'm calling the police," he said in a low growl, but she heard him.

"How do you feel about the amount of tax dollars being spent on this rescue, with the military called in, what it must be costing, many millions of dollars, and the poverty programs that could have been funded with that money?"

"You mean just let the kids die? Is that what you would suggest?"

"I just wonder if you feel a social responsibility for the way that money is being spent."

"I'm grateful that the authorities are spending what they need to, to save my daughter and the six other children lost on the mountain with her. Now if you don't move your ass away from my truck door, I am calling the cops. And by the way, what's your name?"

"Selma Thornton," she said proudly.

"If you come near me again, or camp outside my house, I'm suing the station for stalking me, and then demanding your job. Are we clear?" Tom was livid.

"Crystal," she said with a broad smile, completely indifferent to what he had said. "Thanks for a great interview." He was on the verge of telling her what she could do to herself, but he refrained. But a later report said that he had threatened the reporter, and they implied that he was crazed with grief.

Marlene Wylie didn't leave her house all day. Pitt and Anne got in their car from the garage. The Browns stayed home and pulled down the shades. Beth snuck out of her hotel and said no one had recognized her. She had gone to the General Store. They got June on camera running to her car. The press was a menace, and all the parents thought they were disgusting. Ideally, the media would have liked photos of all of them crying.

But the most important thing was that the rescue operation was going well. A hundred men on the ground was a huge number. And the six planes were covering areas they hadn't before. They were systematically exploring areas where the young people could have gone or taken refuge, and eliminating them one by one.

The third day for the kids was the hardest. Noel wasn't feeling well. The food had run out, except for berries they couldn't eat anymore. They had tiny, little sips of water left in the bottle, and they cut two apples in quarters and each of them got a quarter of an apple and that was it for the day. They saved the last of the orange juice and the one extra quarter of the apple for Noel. The others had agreed not to eat.

They walked downhill instead of uphill this time, looking for new trails. But the ones they found all stopped at dead ends. They were stumbling and falling, from weakness and rough ground, as they wended their way downhill. Justin couldn't walk at all, and Matt, Tim, and Peter took turns walking in pairs, and making a seat with their hands to carry Justin downhill. It was slow going, since he was heavy for them. They were visible for a minute or two between the trees occasionally. The helicopters sounded closer, but they couldn't see them, with the heavy foliage of the trees, which obscured both the kids and the helicopters from sight. But the kids at least had a sense that there were people nearby, and realized that the rangers were still looking for them. They had no idea that the military was involved, and the National Guard had been brought in, since they couldn't see the men or the helicopters.

It was almost six o'clock, and the rescuers were about to end for the day, when Peter looked straight up between the tall trees and saw a helicopter just above them. He could see the pilot's face and then the chopper flew away, as all seven kids screamed, but no one could hear them in the noise from the motor. The pilot flew in a circle and his copilot looked at him and asked what he was doing, as he dropped as low as he could over the tall trees.

"I swear, I thought I just saw a boy looking up at me, in a red plaid shirt. Maybe I'm hallucinating and it's what I wanted to see. I'm trying to get another look." He was staring down intensely.

"You can't see shit with all this foliage," the copilot commented.

But Peter had seen him and so had Justin and Juliet, and Justin had an idea.

"Quick! Everyone! Take off your clothes. Now!"

"Now? Why?" Tim asked. He hadn't seen it.

"Just give me your shirt . . . shirts! Everybody!" Juliet pulled hers off without hesitating, and so did the others, and she and Justin tied them together, as long as they could, tying the sleeves to each other until they had a long rope of shirts and sweatshirts in a makeshift flag of sorts, in bright colors. "Go to that rock over there and wave it!" he shouted to Peter, who dragged the rope of shirts onto a high rock and started waving it like a lasso over his head. It snaked up between the trees, just as the helicopter flew overhead. The pilot and copilot saw it flying up through the trees and gave a shout. They could see Peter standing on the rock, using all his strength to wave it aloft. They radioed the other five helicopters, who flew into the area and they circled again and again, and caught glimpses of an arm or a face, and there were shouts going back and forth over the radio to the base.

"Bonanza! We got 'em!" They gave the exact location, and then flew a wider circle for several miles, but they could find nowhere to land. Harvey came onto the radio himself minutes later, with deep emotion in his voice.

"Is there anywhere you can land near them?"

"Not close enough, sir. We've got twenty miles of trees here, maybe twenty-five." And it was almost dark.

"Can you drop some guys in?"

"Negative. They'll get stuck in the trees. No way in or out from here. We'll either have to walk in to get them, or they'll have to walk out to us. It'll be a long walk for them." It was getting late. They didn't know what kind of shape the kids were in. But they had been healthy enough to make a flag and wave it.

"Did you get a head count?"

"No, sir. Just glimpses, faces, arms. They made some kind of flag. They're in there, and they're alive. But I can't give you an accurate count. There are definitely several of them. Maybe all seven, we couldn't tell." They were a long way from where the reconnaissance had started. They had traveled many miles, halfway around the mountain, which had brought them closer to the fires. Ash was still falling like snow where they were.

"If you can't get them out tonight, you need to drop in supplies. They may not have eaten for three days, or had water. And one of them is diabetic. We have a Medipak for him. He needs it now. He's got an insulin pump, which will give out by tomorrow morning." Harvey gave orders after that for ground troops and first responders to start walking toward their location, even if it took all night. He wanted them out by morning. He ordered the helicopter pilots to do a drop of supplies. His voice was so powerful, everyone responded to his orders immediately. The parents had heard him and were crying.

"The supplies are liable to get caught in the trees, they're pretty close together up here," the pilot told him. It was why they couldn't drop any men in. They would have either gotten injured or trapped in the branches, and even packages of supplies might not get through.

"Drop as many as you have to. The boy needs the pump, and they all need water and food." The ground troops and paramedics on each of the helicopters started bundling up the packages to drop out of the helicopters. At least one was bound to land in their hands, or close enough. They were dropping rescue rations of high sustenance food, bottles of water and juice, bandages, splints if they were injured, some Mylar thermal blankets, and an insulin pump for Noel in each package, so he'd get at least one he could use. Ten minutes later, the packages were ready to drop. Each of the helicopters circled the trees as narrowly as they could, and dropped their load, as the supplies rained down on the waiting group below. There were at least a dozen bundles, and then the helicopters flew off. They would be back in the morning. They had put a note in some of the packages explaining the plan, that ground troops were walking in to meet them, and carry them out of the forest if necessary. They only had one last night to wait, and then they were going home. But they hadn't seen the notes yet. Every single one of the packages that had been dropped sat in the tree branches like Christmas ornaments above their heads. They could easily guess that there was food and water in them, and possibly other things they needed, but they had no way to reach them. They hung in the trees, trapped in the branches. Not a single one of them had reached the ground.

There was pandemonium on the radios, as the helicopters flew back to the base. They had finally located the children. They didn't know how many had survived—hopefully all. The parents had another night to get through before they would know if their children were safe, and the nightmare was truly over. There was guarded celebration in each of their homes, and only hours left before it would end. They already knew that the ground troops were heading toward the kids up the mountain and would reach them by morning. Then they would know the rest of the story, and who had survived, maybe all of them. They had been located at last, miles from where they started, in an unexpected direction no one had guessed.

The fires were still raging near them, but Harvey was sure they would have them out in a matter of hours, before the flames that were spreading rapidly engulfed the mountain. They couldn't lose them now, and he didn't intend to. He dropped in at the Pollocks' that night and said that they had battled water, fire, and the mountain itself to get to them. It had been the most complicated search and rescue mission they'd ever undertaken. His guess had been right. The kids had moved at surprising speed, and had kept on the move, changing directions and trying different trails, which made it even harder to find them. It was like chasing a target that moved with no particular plan or direction. They had energy, youth, and ingenuity on their side, to their own detriment. It was like chasing a flea, as Harvey put it. It was almost over now. He just needed the winds to slow down enough that night so the fire didn't get to them before the rescuers did.

All seven of them stood looking up at the trees in dismay, at the silver packages resting on the branches, after the helicopters left. The pilots didn't know if any of the packages had reached the ground. They needed Noel's pump, and they were desperate for food and water.

"Someone has to climb the trees, and knock the packages off the branches," Justin said, counting how many there were: a full dozen. It looked like treasure to them.

Matt had always been the champion tree climber when they were younger, but he was too heavy now, with broad shoulders and strong legs and arms. And the branches were brittle and dry. If he climbed the trees, a branch could break and fall to the ground and kill him. Peter was even taller, and not as heavy, but he had a man's body. Justin was taller and heavier and he was in no condition to climb a tree. He still couldn't stand. His ankle was painful, and probably broken, after his encounter with the mother bear. They estimated that Tim was too heavy, too. Benjie wanted to try and they unanimously said it was too dangerous for him, and Noel was dizzy and weak without food and his blood sugar issues.

"I'll do it," Juliet volunteered, looking up at the dozen packages that hung there. "I used to climb trees all the time when I was a kid." They looked skeptical. She was tall but very thin, and she had a much lighter frame than the boys. She weighed much less than they did, and there was a chance she'd get away with it. But if a branch broke and she fell, she could break her neck. The question was, how hungry and thirsty were they? But it wasn't about food or water, it was about getting a fresh pump for Noel if there was one, before he went into a coma, maybe as soon as the next morning, or even that night. As far as Juliet was concerned, there was no choice.

"Are you sure?" Peter asked her before she started. He was worried.

"Yes," she said without hesitating, and he bent over, so she could stand on his back. She jumped lightly up on him, and then shimmied up the tree at a surprising speed. She slowed as she got to the upper branches. Some of them were creaking and she heard one give a loud crack as she went past it. A few smaller, very dry branches fell, but she wasn't on them. She tried to keep her arms wrapped around the trunk, but she needed the branches for support too. The tree scraped her bare arms as she went. Finally she reached the first three packages. She tapped them lightly and they fell neatly into Peter's hands, and then Matt's. Tim caught the next one. Noel caught the fourth. She had to switch trees then, and she felt like Tarzan as she did. There were three packages she couldn't get to, but she got nine to the ground in all, and then cautiously made her way down. She got splinters in her arms and through her jeans as she descended, but paid no attention to them.

It was like Christmas when they opened the packages. They had nine pumps for Noel in all. Water, juice, dried meat, fruit, all different kinds of food, chocolate, thermal blankets, inflatable splints, one which fit Justin perfectly. They had everything they needed, including matches, eating utensils, and several flashlights. They all drank many bottles of water. Justin helped Noel change his pump, and within a few hours he felt better. His had been almost out and wouldn't have lasted through the night.

They lay at the base of the trees, having eaten enough for the first time in three days. They had drunk all they wanted, and were warm under the blankets. They saw the night sky glow red from the fires through the branches. Later that night, as Peter and Juliet lay talking side by side, they saw two wolves rush past them. The animals paid no notice to the humans on the ground. They were fleeing the fires, and they saw several deer run past them too. There was a herd of bison grazing near them when they woke in the morning. They took off quickly.

The children had found the diagram of where they were supposed to go to meet their rescuers, and they headed straight downhill, through the thick trees. Peter and Matt supported Justin. The inflatable splint eased the pain enough for them to move him more easily. They had eaten more of the food before they started, and an hour later, they ran straight into their rescuers heading toward them. They walked for another hour to a clearing, with one of the paramedics carrying Justin on his back. There were two paramedics to make sure that Noel was fit to be moved. Two helicopters landed in the clearing, and all seven of them climbed aboard. Benjie sat with the pilot, and they flew off to Saint Vincent Healthcare hospital in Billings, where they would be examined.

Harvey was first to get the message, which he relayed immediately to the parents. He had cut the frequency to their radios until he was sure they were all alive, and now he was. He hadn't wanted them to hear bad news over the air.

He reactivated their radios, and announced in his deep voice, "Seven Little Indians are on their way home!" All had survived.

They wheeled Justin into the hospital in a wheelchair, and the others walked in under their own steam. Benjie was jumping up and down, and Peter had an arm around Juliet. They were all beaming. And they were startled when they saw all the photographers and TV cameras in the hospital parking lot. They were taken in quickly. Sitting at his desk, Harvey was smiling, and wiped the tears off his cheeks.

Chapter 9

Tom was alone in his house when he heard Harvey's announcement on the radio. He burst into tears, and sat there sobbing in relief. He called Beth immediately, to make sure she'd heard it, and she was crying too. She had stayed in her hotel room to avoid the press, but she wasn't dressed yet anyway.

"They all made it. They all survived," Tom sobbed. It was a miracle, and had been an enormous effort on the part of the Park Service and the National Guard. "I'll drive you to the hospital if you want," he offered. It felt like the war was over between them too. They were no longer together, but they weren't enemies anymore. There was nothing left to fight about. Their daughter had survived, which was all that mattered.

"Where's the hospital?" she asked him.

"In Billings. About an hour from here."

"Okay."

"I'll pick you up in ten minutes."

When he left his house, the same blond reporter headed for him with about thirty others, snapping his picture, and she put the mic in his face first. "How do you feel?"

"Elated, thrilled, grateful. So happy and relieved that they all made it." She was smiling at him, and when she turned off her microphone, she looked at him, embarrassed. "I'm sorry I pushed so hard the other day. Sometimes you lose perspective in this business. I listened to the recording of our interview after, and I felt like an idiot. I'm so happy it all worked out, for all of them. And fuck what it cost the taxpayers." She smiled at him. "That's what we pay taxes for. Better that than nuclear arms. What else matters except kids' lives?"

He was smiling at her and leaned over and kissed her cheek.

"Thank you. It's a reminder to us all about what does matter. I've got to go pick my daughter up now." She nodded and waved as he walked away and got in his truck, and she went back to the van from her TV station. She still had some wrap-up interviews to get, but he could tell she wouldn't be harassing him again with dumb, offensive questions.

Beth was waiting for him outside her hotel, and there were no TV vans there. "You took twenty minutes, not ten," she said tartly, and he smiled. Same old Beth.

"I got waylaid by a reporter whom I insulted the other day. She apologized."

"*You* insulted *her,* and *she* apologized?" Beth laughed.

"Something like that," he said, looking amused.

"She must want to sleep with you," Beth said.

While they drove to Billings, Harvey was giving a press conference in his office about the recovery of the seven young people who had been recovered from the mountain that morning, after having been lost for three days. In winter, they would never have survived it, and in summer they might not have either, for a number of reasons: the treacherous mountain, the ravines, hostile wildlife, their health. But all had ended well. He wrapped up with the press, consulted a bulletin about the progress of the fire, and headed to Billings himself. All the parents were on their way there to be reunited with their children.

Benjie was jumping up and down on his hospital bed when Bill and Pattie walked into the room.

"Justin scared away a big bear!" he screamed, and then gave a terrifying rendition of it. Matt confirmed that it was true and hugged his parents. Bill and Pattie hugged them until the boys could hardly breathe. And they were all crying.

Justin had broken his ankle when he fell off the rock, and was already in surgery to put pins in it when his mother got there. Marlene looked worn to a nub, and the doctors were keeping Noel at Saint Vincent's for a few days to make sure that his blood sugar levels had stabilized. He hadn't eaten properly in days.

"How's Dad?" was the first thing Noel asked his mother, and Justin when he returned in a cast.

"About the same," she said quietly to both of them. She didn't tell them that he had had a sixth sense that something was wrong with them.

The Pollocks had their arms around Peter, and he told them about Juliet climbing the tree to get the supplies, and the flag they had made. They had reclaimed their shirts that morning. Peter was wearing the plaid shirt his father had remembered, with a piece torn out of the elbow. Tom and Beth were alternately hugging Juliet. A nurse had been working on removing her splinters from when she had climbed the trees. She had dozens of them in her arms and legs. None of the kids looked as bad as their parents thought they would. The food they'd eaten the night before had helped.

Harvey Mack appeared a little while later and toured all their rooms. He talked with each of the children and their parents. The police had cordoned off the end of the hallway for them, so they'd have privacy. The parking lot was full of photographers and journalists.

Harvey stopped to talk to Beth for a few minutes, while Tom talked to Pitt, with ecstatic grins on their faces.

"I told you we'd get her back," Harvey said to her in a low voice so no one would hear him. "You didn't believe me."

"You were right. I was scared. She's my everything." Especially now with Tom out of her life.

"You should spend some time here and relax," he suggested. "It's a good place to think, and to write." She nodded but didn't know what to say to him. He was an overwhelming presence, and not just because of his size. She had the feeling that he could see right into her soul and know what she was thinking. It made her feel safe just standing near him. He patted her shoulder and then moved on to the other parents. He was sure she'd be leaving soon. He couldn't imagine her spending time in Fishtail, Montana. She looked so typically New York. The thought of it amused him, as she watched him move on to another room.

He and Marlene were old friends and he wanted to ask her how Bob was. He hated the fact that he was dying and she had so much on her shoulders now. But, thank God, at least she hadn't lost the boys.

The return of all seven children was a miracle and a blessing for them all.

Tom and Beth waited while they examined Juliet at Saint Vincent's, and said that she could go home. Tom drove them back from Billings, and Juliet was excited to be back at her father's house, take a shower, wash her hair, and see her room.

"I thought I'd never see this place again," she said with a look of wonder, when she first walked in. "I thought I'd never see any place again. The nights were terrifying, wondering if we'd be attacked by something. I thought we were dead when the bear came out of the cave and stood there roaring at us to protect her cub. And the days were exhausting. We just kept walking with no idea where we were going, and then we'd look over the edge of a trail and see a ravine we could have fallen into. I thought we were going to starve to death at the end. Luckily, I'd brought some sandwiches with me in my backpack when we went for a walk after the waterfall. We lived on them for three days." Listening to her made Beth shudder, and Tom feel grateful all over again.

"Do you want to stay for dinner?" Tom asked Beth. He hadn't asked her when she was going back to New York. He didn't want her to feel he was pressing her. He was afraid that after her whole misadventure, she'd want to take Juliet with her, since she had called him irresponsible. Beth had calmed down markedly just in the few hours since Juliet had returned.

"I'd like to stay for dinner, if that's okay." They both wanted to be with Juliet, just to revel in the joy and relief of having her back with them. The whole experience seemed surreal now. Beth had been so terrified that Juliet was dead. Now it all seemed almost normal again. She wanted to touch her daughter and hug her and hold her to make sure it was real and she wasn't dreaming.

Tom was making pasta and a salad while Beth poured two glasses of wine and handed one to him. Juliet was upstairs taking a shower. "I'm sorry I called you irresponsible," she said, looking humbled. "It was an incredibly stupid and dangerous thing for the kids to do. Luckily, they all seem to have handled it as intelligently as they could in the circumstances, but it wasn't your fault. You were right. They really are good kids, and their parents are all nice people. I guess kids just do incredibly dumb things sometimes."

"I don't think any of them will ever do anything like that again," he said, and took a sip of his wine. It was nice being able to talk to her when she wasn't furious or half crazed or all wound up. They hadn't had a decent conversation in a year.

"You're not irresponsible, Tom. I was just so mad at you when you wanted to turn your whole life around and leave New York. I can almost see why you love it here. Not quite," she said, and smiled at him, "but almost."

"I couldn't fight the wars in New York anymore. The prize at the end of it wasn't big enough, or worth it to me. Something changed for me. I felt like I was living someone else's life. And we became strangers to each other, heading in opposite directions."

"I don't think I understood that until now. You're different here. You seem happier," she said quietly.

"I am. Everything got downsized to something I can live with. The only thing I don't like is being so far from Juliet. I guess I'll have to come and see her more often. Every six weeks isn't enough. But if I were to move back to New York, it would eat me alive again. It's just not worth it to me anymore."

"Somehow I can't see you as a cowboy either. Are you sure Montana is the right place for you?"

"It seems to be. I like the people I've met here. They lead wholesome lives and spend a lot of time with their kids. I'm kind of the odd man out, with Juliet in New York and my being single, but they've been very good to me. My clients don't seem to care where I am. I can do pretty much everything I need to from here. I guess I'm a little old to be finding myself, but I like who I am here. I felt like a robot in New York, and I was coming apart."

"You don't miss it?" she asked him with a wistful look, and he shook his head.

"No, I don't."

"How did we end up so different?" she asked, looking mystified. "We didn't used to be."

"I don't know. We lost each other somehow. I'm sad we did. You're still happy with your life in New York." He looked hard at her.

"I still want to win at the end of the day, but you were right, sometimes I think I pay too high a price for it. If we had lost Juliet on that mountain, my life and everything I've built would have meant nothing to me." He nodded. He had felt the same way. But he realized now that Beth had always been more ambitious than he was. It just got more obvious as they got older. Her career meant more to her than his meant to him.

"I'm sorry everything got so screwed up for the last year. It was a hard transition to make, and I didn't handle it gracefully. I panicked and left," he said seriously.

"I felt like you had betrayed me, just because you didn't want to do things my way anymore," she confessed. She had gotten away with that for a long time. They both knew it now. He had cashed in his chips and refused to play the game after a while.

"I think you need a tougher guy than I am," he said. "Or someone who wants to play the same game."

"Maybe so." It was a huge admission coming from her. She didn't hate him anymore. She wasn't even angry at him. The man who lived in Montana wasn't one she'd have chosen now. She had no idea what kind of man would suit her, but she could see now that it wasn't Tom. They both loved their daughter, but it was the only bond they had left.

Juliet appeared in the kitchen a few minutes later in a fluffy pink bathrobe, with freshly washed hair. She had charged her cellphone and it rang as soon as she walked into the room, and she disappeared for a few minutes. They guessed that it was Peter, asking how she was. Beth and Tom exchanged a look.

"Do I smell romance in the air?" Beth whispered.

"You might. I suspect it's Peter Pollock. He's a sweet kid." Juliet breezed back into the room a minute later, with a mysterious smile at her parents.

"Peter says hi."

"Your point," Beth said to Tom under her breath, and he laughed.

They had a nice dinner together, savoring the joy of having Juliet back. It had been the worst three days of their lives.

"Can Peter come over tomorrow?" Juliet asked her father, and Beth raised an eyebrow again.

"Sure. For dinner?" he answered, and she shook her head.

"No, just to hang out." Her parents exchanged a look.

"You're not tired of seeing him after three days on the mountain together?"

"No," Juliet said primly. Then out of nowhere, she said, "His mom and dad were together from the time they were fourteen." And her mother nearly choked.

"What about boarding school?" she teased her. "Doesn't that sound like a good idea?" All three of them laughed. "You'll be back in New York soon anyway, so I guess it doesn't matter." Juliet didn't say anything, and she went back to her room a short time later.

"Should I be panicking?" Beth asked Tom, once Juliet had gone upstairs.

"I don't think so. It looks pretty tame, and they keep a close eye on him."

"Yeah, a great eye as of a few days ago," she said, and Tom grinned at her. "I get the feeling I'm not going to love these teenage years. It's so easy when they're babies. I'm not sure I'm up to the next chapters."

"We'll figure it out," Tom reassured her. He was happy that the war was over, or it appeared to be for now. What he had said to her earlier was true. She needed a tougher man than he was, or wanted to be. She had always been in competition with him, and he didn't want to live that way. He wanted a woman he could be equals with, and share things with, not one who wanted to compete with him and be the winner every time. Beth couldn't help herself, it was who she was.

Bob was sleeping, as he did almost all the time now, when Marlene brought Justin home. Justin's ankle was hurting him less now that it was in a cast, and the stress of the last three days was over. As the oldest in the group, he had felt responsible for all of them, and was so relieved that they were home and everyone had survived.

He limped in to see if his father was awake, and Bob opened his eyes and smiled at his oldest son. Justin had been so afraid that his father would die before he got home, but he hadn't. Justin knew that Noel had been worried about it too.

"You okay?" he asked in a whisper.

"I'm fine, Dad. What about you?"

"I'm okay. You weren't fine for a while. I could feel it. You and Noel. Your mom said you were, but I knew it wasn't true." It was eerie listening to him. As sick as he was, his father had sensed that something was wrong while they were lost on the mountain. Justin would have told him about the bear, but he knew that it would worry him now. His father was just a shadow of his former self. He was barely recognizable, with no hair, and he had lost so much weight. "Is Noel okay?"

"He's fine, Dad. They're just checking his sugar levels. We're both fine. Except for this." He held up his cast so they'd have something to talk about. It was hard finding subjects now that seemed safe and wouldn't upset him.

"How'd you do that?" Bob frowned when he saw it.

"I fell off a rock." Bob grinned. It was the kind of thing boys did. Justin didn't tell him that he had fallen off a rock scaring away a bear.

"No broncos at the rodeo for you," Bob teased him. And then he looked at his son seriously. "Take care of your mom for me." It brought tears to Justin's eyes.

"I will, Dad," he promised. He didn't want to talk about that now. But he could see that the end was coming soon. No matter how much they didn't want to face it, it was happening, and Bob knew it. His eyes drifted slowly closed then, and he went back to sleep. Even a few minutes of conversation wore him out, but he had been happy to see Justin. And Justin was glad he was still alive when he got back. He left the room, with tears streaming down his cheeks.

The press continued to hound them even once the kids were back. They wanted follow-up pictures, and lay in wait outside their homes. They tried to get brief interviews with the boys and Juliet, asking them what it was like, what they had been afraid of, how they felt about each other after being stranded together for three days. They wanted to know how Justin had hurt his ankle, why Noel was still in the hospital, if Benjie had been traumatized after being lost in the mountains for three days, and if their parents had punished them for getting lost. They all sounded like stupid questions to the kids, who didn't sense the malice behind them. Eventually, the reporters started to lose interest in the story and drift away. They had milked it for all it was worth, and the Fishtail kids were old news now.

The fires on the mountain were the biggest news of the hour. The winds had come up and shifted after the kids were rescued, and within days the front of the mountain was in flames. The mountain looked like a volcano, glowing red at night.

Harvey had his hands full. He was sleeping in his office, coordinating firefighters from other counties and states. He gave a daily press conference at the local TV station, and journalists from all over the state were camping out with camera crews to take dramatic photos of the fires. There had been no loss of human life yet, but it was a challenging time for him.

Anne had sent a basket of food to his office, grateful to him for bringing Peter and the others home.

Beth was watching him on the news one night, a few days after Juliet got back, grateful that the fire hadn't been raging to that degree while the kids were trapped on the mountain. She sat listening to his deep voice, and was impressed by how efficiently and graciously he handled the press. There was something about his voice that was reassuring. She smiled at the idea of being attracted to a forest ranger. She could see herself with the head of a corporation, a famous writer, a publisher, a venture capitalist, but there was something about Harvey that intrigued her. His imposing height, his wise eyes, his deep voice, his grace under fire. He looked like a man you could trust. She realized that she'd probably never see him again. But he had saved her daughter, and she owed him a huge debt. She decided to send him an email before she left, thanking him again. She didn't expect a response, particularly given what he was dealing with: the fires burning out of control on the mountain. She was surprised when he called her at her hotel.

"You haven't gone back to New York yet?" he asked her, surprised.

"I'm enjoying a few days with my daughter. I'm leaving soon," she said vaguely, as his voice resonated. He filled the room with his presence, even on the phone. He was a charismatic man with a powerful personality, a figure of authority, a person who was used to commanding.

"I hope you come back and see us again," he said warmly. "Maybe I can show you around next time. I've got my hands full right now."

"That's an understatement." They were the worst fires in the state in a century, and he had the press breathing down his neck all the time about how it was being handled. "How are you holding up?" she asked him.

"It's part of the job. I've been doing this for a long time. We'll get the fires under control eventually, just like we brought the kids back." He was a man who got things done. She couldn't imagine him running away from anything. She wondered if he'd ever been married. He didn't seem to be now. She didn't have that impression. She didn't even know if he had children. She didn't know anything about him, except that he was an interesting man, and he had saved Juliet's life.

"Maybe I should write a profile of you," she suggested.

"I'm not someone who likes to be in the spotlight," he told her. "It gets in my way. I get more done when I'm behind the scenes than when I'm center stage."

"That's a fabulous opening quote," she said, smiling as she thought about it. "I've written about presidents, foreign heads of state, royalty, movie stars."

"When I star in a movie, I'll let you know," he said, and she laughed. "Take care of yourself, Beth. That's all I wanted to tell you.

Watch out for New York. Make sure it doesn't eat you alive." She thrived on it, which was the main difference between her and Tom. He had run away. Beth had never run away from anything in her life. She realized now that when Tom had left it had been a blow to her ego, more than to her heart. Neither of them had noticed, but somewhere along the way, she and Tom had fallen out of love. She knew that now without a doubt.

"You take care of yourself too, when the fire gets too hot." She meant it in all senses of the phrase.

"I'm not afraid of the heat, Beth. I work better when I'm under fire."

"So do I," she said softly, thinking about him and listening to his voice. He remembered the way she had confronted him, the night he met her. She wasn't afraid of anything, and it was easy to see why she and Tom weren't a match. Tom was a gentle man and Harvey guessed that she must have eaten him alive. There were so many facets to her, all of which intrigued him.

"I hope you come back," he said in his deep, powerful voice.

"Maybe I will," she said, sounding mysterious for a minute. As soon as she said it, they both knew she would. A minute later, they hung up. They had both said enough for now.

Chapter 10

Juliet threw her mother a curve the day before she left. She had liked having her mother there, especially since her parents seemed to be getting along for the first time in a year. Their shared concern for their daughter had brought them closer together, as friends. It was a new chapter in their lives, that they were both enjoying, especially since Juliet's adventure in the mountains had had a happy ending. If it hadn't, things between them would have been very different.

Juliet and Beth walked around town together. Peter had dropped by several times, almost every day, and the Pollocks had Juliet to dinner. They included her in their open-door policy, where all kids were welcome. She was the first girl to be included in Peter's group of friends. The only thing his parents didn't do was invite her to spend the night. But she could stay as late as she wanted with the boys, and then her father would come to pick her up.

Juliet and her mother went to the Tippet Rise Art Center, and they had lunch in town. There wasn't a lot to do, but there was enough to keep Beth busy for a short visit. She bought cowboy boots for herself and a matching pair for Juliet before she went back to New York. She enjoyed her mother's company. It was different staying with her father. They did things like riding, bowling, and fishing. She had always enjoyed girl time with her mother too, and her mother had mellowed after nearly losing Juliet.

They stopped for lemonade after they bought the cowboy boots, and Juliet looked at her.

She was nervous, but dove in. "I want to ask you something." Beth was suddenly panicked that it might be about birth control. She didn't want her getting serious about a boy at her age. A crush was fine, but more than that wasn't, at fourteen. "I want to stay and go to school here," she blurted out. Beth was stunned and stared at her.

"Is this about Peter?" she asked, looking at Juliet intensely. Juliet shook her head.

"No, it's more about school, and Dad. I like it here. I don't like the school we picked in New York." It was one of the best schools in the city, and very demanding academically. Juliet had always been a good student, but the school Beth had pushed for was extreme, to get their students into the best colleges. But it had been her mother's choice, not Juliet's.

"You haven't even tried it yet."

"I like the kids here, Mom. And the way people hang around home, and spend time with their families. I can see why Dad likes it." She sounded like him when she said it.

"So can I," Beth admitted. But Juliet had taken her breath away. She couldn't imagine her own life if Juliet lived in Montana with her father. Their apartment in New York, and Beth's life, would be empty without her daughter.

"Would you ever consider spending time here? You could work from here too," she pointed out to her mother. It sounded like her arguments with Tom a year before.

"Did your father put you up to this?"

Juliet shook her head again. "I didn't tell him I was going to ask you. I have friends here now." She felt a special kinship with the boys she had survived the mountain with, but Beth knew that might dissipate in time. It had just happened.

"You might not get into the same kind of college if you go to school here."

"I will if I take AP classes and get good grades. I'd just like to try it. I like the way people live here. New York is so tough sometimes. That school felt more like college than high school when we visited it. I want to have some fun too."

"I don't know." Beth was too shocked to make a decision. "I have to think about it. And I have to talk to your dad. It would be a big decision to let you stay here." For all three of them. Suddenly Beth was about to lose a husband and a daughter all in the same year, and she wasn't ready for that. She realized now that the divorce had been the right move, but letting Juliet stay in Montana would be a huge change for her too. "We have to decide soon. You start school in four weeks."

"Thank you for thinking about it. I could come to New York to see you every month."

"You won't want to," her mother said. "You'll get busy with your friends once you start school. And you'll be snowed in here all winter. Think about that too."

"Best of all would be if you'd spend time here too," Juliet said with a pleading look, which reminded Beth of Tom again. She was her father's daughter. Beth was quiet when they walked back to the hotel. After Juliet left, Beth called Tom and told him. He was as shocked as she was.

"She hasn't said anything to me. I don't know if that would be the right decision for her. Do you think it's about Peter?" He sounded more worried than pleased.

"No. She likes it here. He's probably part of it, but not the whole thing. I think getting stuck on the mountain and surviving it with her friends affected her. They feel related to each other now."

"I don't know, Beth. I'm not sure it's such a great idea. It's one thing for me to decide to get off the merry-go-round. She hasn't even gotten on it yet. It's a little soon for her to be giving up New York."

"A year ago you wanted all of us to move here," she reminded him.

"I know, but that was crazy. I realize that now. I can't see you living here, and I don't want to take her away from you. That was never what I had in mind."

"Me neither. Well, let's both think about it and talk in a few days."

"Maybe she'll change her mind," he suggested, but Beth doubted that she would.

"That's not how she operates. Once she gets an idea, she hangs on to it."

"I wonder who she gets that from," he teased her.

"Both of us," Beth said, and he laughed.

"That could be true. I have to admit, I'm stunned. She hasn't said a word to me about it."

"I think it's a new idea. All those boys she's hanging out with are starting high school in a few weeks. She wants to go with them. It would be fun for her, but I don't know if it would be the right thing academically, or in any other way. She has a lot of opportunities in New York she wouldn't have here." It was part of the reason Beth had fought so hard against their moving there.

"Let's see how it develops," he said. Beth could tell he wasn't sold on the idea. And she wasn't ready to let her daughter go at fourteen. It had never occurred to her that Juliet might want to stay.

She and Juliet said a tearful goodbye the next day, and Beth left for the airport. She had time to kill once she got there so she called Anne and asked her what she thought, and if the local high school was any good. She liked Anne and respected her as a mother.

"It's as good as the effort the kids put into it. If she's a good student, she'll be fine. If she's lazy, she'll get lost. That's true at any school."

"She's always been a good student."

"It would be fun for her, and we'd love to have her, but she's young to leave you, Beth. It won't be the same living with her dad. Girls need their mothers, even if they hate them for a while." They both laughed but it was true. "Wow. I don't know what I'd do in your shoes. I think I'd want her in New York with me. You don't want to miss out on these years with her. It's too soon to let her go."

"That's how I feel about boarding school at her age," Beth said. "I'd never consider it. I don't want some twenty-five-year-old teacher telling her about his values, instead of ours."

"I agree. I want to keep a tight grip on Peter until college. After that, there's not much you can do." They called Beth's flight then, and she had to go. "Let me know what you decide, and if there's anything I can do. It's a good school. I just don't know if it's for her."

"Tom and I are going to talk in a few days. He doesn't seem too keen on it either. Having her with him full-time would be a big commitment for him. That's a lot different from a weekend once a month and six weeks in the summer."

Beth thought about it on the two long flights back to New York, and for several days after. It was a harder decision than when Tom told her he wanted to move to Montana. Given the state of their marriage, she had been willing to lose him, but not her daughter. Juliet didn't press her for an answer, but they had to decide soon. They were down to the wire. Beth was glad she had taken out tuition insurance, though it seemed redundant when she did it. Now it suddenly seemed like a good idea.

She made the decision while she was alone in the apartment over the weekend. The decision she made was a sacrifice she had been unwilling to make for Tom, but she was willing to make for her daughter. She couldn't see it any other way. It would have to be an experiment for a year, and then they'd see if it was working.

She called Tom a week later and asked him to put Juliet on the phone with them. It had to be a joint decision between the three of them.

"I'd be willing to let you go to school in Montana under one condition," Beth said. "I don't want to be away from you most of the time. It wasn't what I had planned for myself, and I have no idea how it would work. But I could do it for a year, if I rent a small place in Fishtail myself—like two bedrooms, so you have a room there too, and you could go back and forth between me and Dad. I would work there some of the time. I need to be in New York too, but I can do some of my writing in Fishtail and keep an apartment in both places, for when I need to work there. How does that sound to both of you?"

"You weren't willing to do that a year ago," he reminded her. "You said you'd rather die than live in Montana."

"That's true," she admitted. "But I would definitely rather die than not live close to my daughter for the next four years. You'll have to kick me out of your life when you go to college, but I'm not willing to let go when you're fourteen," she said to Juliet. "How would both of you feel about my living in Fishtail part-time? It's a small town and, Tom, I don't want you to feel that I'm encroaching on your turf."

"To tell you the truth, I'd love it. And I think it would be great for Juliet," he said. "She'd have both of us, at least part of the time. Do you think you'd be happy here?"

She had thought about it and asked herself the same question. "I'd be a lot happier than I would be alone in New York without my daughter. There are sacrifices you just don't want to make for a man, but you will for a child. What about you, Jules? What do you think?"

"I think I'd love it, Mom. I didn't want to leave you either. It's the best of everything if I have you and Dad, even if you're not together. And when you're in New York, I could stay with him."

"And we wouldn't need formal visitation rights," Tom said, warming to the idea. "Juliet could go back and forth between us, and stay where she wants. In some ways, it might really work, if you don't hate living here."

"If I do, I'll move back to New York full-time in a year. But something tells me this might work for all three of us, especially if I have the flexibility to be in New York when I want to. Or need a fix at Bergdorf's." They all laughed at that. "So, shall we do it?"

"Yes!" Juliet sounded ecstatic.

"You have my vote," Tom added.

"I'm in too," Beth said. "Tom, please go to the school tomorrow and get that all worked out, before I cancel the tuition here. We don't want her to end up with no school at all."

"That would be cool too," Juliet said, giddy with the decision. They talked for a few more minutes, and Beth said she'd come out in a few weeks and find a place to rent, but she had work to do in New York first.

"Well, it took a year, but you got me out there after all," Beth said to Tom, but they both knew she wasn't doing it for him, and she wouldn't have. She was doing it for Juliet. It seemed like a compromise that might work for all. And Beth wouldn't be trapped there. She would still have one foot firmly planted in New York.

The next morning, Tom called Absarokee High School, and made an appointment to enroll Juliet for freshman year. When Juliet told Peter, he couldn't believe it. The weird thing was that she and her mother hadn't gotten along for the past year, but ever since Juliet had gotten lost on the mountain, everything had changed. She and her mother were enjoying spending time with each other again. Beth had changed after those three fateful days and almost losing her.

They appreciated each other more than they had before, and Tom and Beth had made peace at last.

Beth still couldn't believe she was moving to Montana part-time a week later when she told her agent, but she wasn't sorry.

"You're moving to a place called Fishtail?" he said, sounding horrified. "How does that compute?"

"It computes just fine because I love my daughter." So she was moving to a tiny town called Fishtail, Montana. It made perfect sense to her, and with any luck, she'd have the best of both worlds: the excitement she thrived on in New York, and time with Juliet in Montana before she grew up and flew away. It was worth a try, and she was hopeful it would work. It was a bold move for Beth.

Before she left New York, Beth had lunch with a friend she'd known since her magazine days, before she'd married Tom, and told her that she was moving to Montana part-time. Her friend, Natalie Wyndham, looked at her like she was crazy.

"You? Montana? Have you lost your mind, or are you having an affair with a handsome cowboy who ties you to the bed?" Natalie asked her. She ran a small publishing house now, and she knew Beth well, although they didn't see each other often. They were both busy, and Beth hadn't seen many people during the year her marriage unraveled. She was too upset when Tom threw their whole life out the window to move to Montana.

"The cowboy idea sounds interesting, but actually, no, I'm not. I'm trying to be grown up and open-minded, and a good mother."

"That sounds awful." Natalie winced at the thought. She didn't have children. She had lived with the same man for thirteen years and was happy with their life that way, committed but unmarried. She said it gave her the illusion of being free and independent. And the idea of children had always terrified her, after an unhappy childhood herself. "Why Montana?"

"Tom had some sort of personal crisis last year. He quit his job, went 'back to nature,' decided he hated everything we had worked our asses off for and that our life stood for."

"Fell in love with your best friend's brother and discovered he'd been born to be a woman?" Natalie asked as they ate their salads, and Beth laughed.

"No, not that. But our marriage had died while we weren't looking. Or maybe we knew and just didn't have the guts to say it. It was actually the right move for him, and maybe for me too. We filed for divorce, and he moved to a town the size of a doorknob in Montana. He loves it. Now my daughter does too. So I can either drag her back to New York and force her to live here and go to a school she doesn't like, while she hates me for it, or let her live there with her father, and never see her, and I don't want to miss the few years I have left with her before she leaves for college. Or, I can try to do a juggling act and go back and forth myself and see how that works. I can work from there, as long as I maintain all my contacts in New York, and I'll be able to spend some time here every month. If I'm going crazy there, I can come back whenever I want for a quick fix. I know this sounds weird, but I was out there this summer, and I actually like it. Tom wasn't entirely wrong to want to live there. It's perfect for him. Living here was killing him, and it killed our marriage. So, there you are. Fishtail, Montana, here I come." She smiled and Natalie shook her head in dismay.

"You obviously drank the Kool-Aid. Now you know why I never wanted kids. They make you crazy and force you to give up everything you love, like New York City. I'd rather commit suicide than live in the suburbs for a kid, let alone move to Montana. You should get Mother of the Year for that," she said somewhat in awe, and Beth laughed.

"I didn't do it for Tom when he wanted me to live there full-time. I'm not sure I could have done that. Maybe for the right guy, but not for him. But I'm doing it for her. I never thought about it that way before, but motherhood is about making sacrifices you thought you'd never make, and suddenly you're doing something you swore you'd never do, for them. I thought I'd lost her this summer. She got lost in the mountains with some other kids for three days. I'd die if something happened to her," Beth said. "They were the worst three days of my life, so spending time in Montana to be with her doesn't sound so bad to me. Maybe sacrifice is the nature of loving someone. I didn't love Tom enough to move out there. I'm happy to do it to be with Juliet. And I like the people I met there this summer."

"Now you need to find that cowboy I mentioned, to spice things up for you. I have to say, I admire you, Beth. I'm sorry to hear about you and Tom." They were having lunch at a restaurant that was fashionable with the literary set, and Beth realized she was going to miss it. The Cowboy Bar and the diner in Fishtail were not quite the same.

"Yeah, me too," she said. "I think we were bored with each other. All the fun had gone out of our marriage. I didn't realize it until he forced a showdown about moving to Montana. But maybe it will work like this, not for him and me, but for Juliet."

"Commuting to Fishtail, Montana," Natalie said, "sounds very jet set." Beth laughed.

"It could happen to you. Wait 'til Charlie decides to retire and wants you to move to a retirement community in Florida, or a dude ranch in Wyoming."

"I'll pick dude ranch, go by myself, and float Charlie on an iceberg down the East River," she said as they finished lunch. She brought Beth up-to-date on the latest publishing gossip, who was sleeping with whom, who was going to get fired, and what big author had a new contract. It was always fun having lunch with Natalie.

"Well, good luck, cowgirl," she said when they left each other outside the restaurant after lunch. "Send me a postcard, and call me when you're in New York. Just don't forget to come home now and then. I can't wait to hear about the cowboy you find out there."

"Me too." Beth laughed and waved as she got into a cab to go home to finish an article she was doing for *The New Yorker*. It was definitely going to be an interesting experience commuting between Fishtail and New York. But New York would always be there, and Juliet would be off to her own life in a few years.

When she finished the article for *The New Yorker,* she'd start packing. She still had to find a place to live in Fishtail.

Chapter 11

By the second week in August, the worst of the fires on Granite Peak were eighty percent under control. There were a thousand firefighters from seven states on the mountain, and Harvey was no longer giving daily press conferences. Three of the firefighters had lost their lives, and the summer was coming to an end.

Juliet was spending most of her time at the Pollocks', with a dozen other kids in their swimming pool. Fishtail felt more like home to her now, knowing that she would be going to school with them. Her friends were excited about it. The boys she had been lost on the mountain with were protective of her, and talked about how brave she had been, and how she had climbed the tree to get the supplies the night before they were rescued. She had met a few of the girls she'd be going to Absarokee High School with, but she wasn't close to any of them yet. She was closer to the boys she had been spending time with, and when she wasn't at the Pollocks', Peter was at her house with her dad. He had taught her to play video games. She was getting good at it, and beat him some of the time, enough to satisfy her ego and not bruise his unduly. They saw the others from their mountain adventure nearly every day. Justin's ankle was still in a cast and would be for another month. Noel was feeling fine, and their father was still alive. He slept almost all the time now, heavily medicated to ease the pain.

Pattie had called Anne to see how Peter was sleeping, and she said he was fine. Pattie was worried because Benjie was having night terrors and recurring nightmares about the bear that had nearly attacked them. He was sure he could hear it outside their house at night, and he was afraid the bear would show up on the ranch and find him. Anne suggested Pattie take him to a therapist and told her to call June and ask her for a recommendation since she was dating a pediatrician from Saint Vincent's and knew a lot of doctors in Billings. It sounded like a good idea, although she said Bill didn't like shrinks and didn't think Benjie needed one.

"The poor kid hasn't had a decent night's sleep since they got back, and neither have we," Pattie said, worried. She thought the therapist was a good idea, and had thought of it too. She called June, who gave her the names of two child psychiatrists she had worked with who had needed speech therapy for their patients. When Pattie called, the first one offered her an appointment in September, and she took it.

The Pollocks gave their annual end-of-summer barbecue, and Anne could see that Pattie was worried. Benjie was quieter than usual, and less exuberant. She noticed that Justin seemed withdrawn too, but he and Noel were going through a hard time as their father slipped away by inches. Marlene was rail thin and had dark circles under her eyes. Bob was hanging on to life by a thread, he was like a candle that was flickering before it went out. The Pollocks felt sorry for them, and had the kids over all the time, but there wasn't much anyone could do.

Tom Marshall made a point of checking in with Marlene whenever he could, and offered to do chores and errands for her. He often had the boys over to dinner. Justin seemed to have become a man over the summer, between their three days in the mountains, and his experience with his father. He had told Tom, too, that he had felt responsible for the others when they were lost, because he was older. The incident with the mother bear had marked him too. He seemed very withdrawn these days, and he had to apply to college in the fall.

But the Pollocks' barbecue was particularly jovial this year. They had a lot to celebrate with Peter and the other kids having come home safely. The whole group was excited to be starting high school in two weeks.

The Pollocks had invited Harvey Mack as they always did, but they felt especially close to him this year, because of all he'd done for them. He made a point of speaking to each of the seven kids. He was pleased to see that they all appeared to have recovered and had bounced back from the traumatic days they had experienced. He had a long talk with Benjie, who told him all about the bear again. It had gotten bigger and taller in the telling, but Justin's quick thinking and heroism were unquestionable, and had won him two pins and a steel plate in his ankle. He wouldn't be playing football again, or not for a long time. He had been the star running back for his high school team. But the damage could have been worse. The bear could easily have killed him, or several of them.

All the parents made a point of talking to Harvey at the barbecue and thanking him again. It had been the biggest event of the year in Fishtail, and Harvey was the hero of the hour for marshaling the troops and bringing in the National Guard. He had handled the Granite Peak fires well too. He was good at his job.

Tom enjoyed talking to Harvey. He was an erudite, interesting man, and his stories about his years in the Navy SEALs were exciting. Harvey told Juliet to say hello to her mother for him, and she said she would. Then she ran off with Peter to play Marco Polo in the pool with the others. Justin couldn't play with his cast, and sat apart, watching the others and looking sad. It was no mystery to anyone why the Wylie boys were quieter than usual. Noel had perked up by the end of the evening, but Justin was taking his father's imminent death very hard. It was a brutal rite of passage for him, and a huge loss.

Marlene said something to Tom about it, when they sat together eating dinner by the pool. Tom enjoyed her company, and liked the boys. He felt terrible about what they were going through and volunteered every day to help.

"I've been relying on Justin too much," Marlene confessed to Tom as they ate Pitt's excellent barbecued ribs. He was the master chef of barbecue in the area, and everyone loved the food. "I don't mean to put a burden on him. He's the man of the house now, and he wants to help. With his ankle in a cast, he can't do much with his friends. He's really going to miss football, and he probably can't ski this year either." But at least he was alive and had come back from Granite Peak. "Pattie says Benjie is having nightmares. I think my boys are too, but they're even more upset about their dad."

"Don't hesitate to call on me," Tom reiterated, and she had, more often than she thought she should. She didn't want to take advantage of him, but he was very kind. Noel and Justin and Juliet were good friends. They treated her like a sister, and Justin was the big brother she always wished she'd had.

"We're all so happy that Juliet is staying for the school year," Marlene said to Tom, and it was easy to see that she was a very attractive woman, despite the tired eyes and the dark circles. She was under a tremendous strain, and more than the other parents even, it had been a nightmarish summer for her.

The barbecue went late, as it always did. Everyone was having fun, and relieved that the summer had turned out as well as it had. Peter and Juliet disappeared for a little while. They went to sit on a bench behind a shed and kissed, as they had been doing ever since they'd been rescued. It had been an exciting summer for Juliet. She and Peter were crazy about each other, but they didn't let their youthful passion get out of hand. They hadn't done anything they'd be sorry for yet, but the temptation was great. Peter had a very adult body, and Juliet had womanly curves. They both looked older than their years and were mature for their age. Even more so as only children.

Juliet went back to the party first when things started getting too heated between them. They didn't want their parents to see them come back together, although nobody was fooled. Tom and the Pollocks were keeping an eye on them whenever they were together. They knew that young bodies had minds of their own that defied reason, and they hoped that Peter and Juliet wouldn't do anything foolish. Anne and Pitt were on the same page with Tom on that. They were also aware that the intensity of what they'd been through together had deepened their feelings for each other. They had survived a life-and-death experience, which made them feel like adults overnight.

Juliet was on her way back from the bench behind the shed when she saw Justin coming out of some bushes, looking disheveled with an open bottle of wine in his hand. He looked startled when they nearly ran into each other. She noticed the bottle of wine immediately, and his eyes looked glazed.

"What are you doing here?" he said to her in a harsh tone, and they both felt awkward being there.

"I went for a walk," she answered, but didn't ask him the same question. She could see what he was doing. He'd obviously been drinking, but she didn't blame him, knowing what he was going through with his dad.

"You shouldn't be out walking alone," he scolded her. She didn't want to tell him she'd been with Peter. She didn't tell him that he shouldn't be drinking either. He dropped the bottle behind him in the bushes and staggered once as he walked her back to the party. She could see that he was drunk, and she wondered if anyone else would notice. His mom had been so distracted these days that he could have passed out cold in front of her, and Juliet wasn't sure she'd see it. But she didn't want anyone to think she was drinking with him.

She left him as soon as they got to the pool, and he slid into a chair. Tom had seen them return and questioned her when she walked by him.

"You were out walking around with Justin?" He seemed surprised, and wondered if she was interested in him too, maybe because he was older.

"I just ran into him on my way back from the bathroom," she said casually, and noticed Peter's return out of the corner of her eye. He came up to them two minutes later with a Coke for her and one for himself.

"Hi, Mr. Marshall. Have you had fun?" Peter asked, the perfect host. He had lovely manners and was always polite to Tom and all adults.

"Your parents give a great party." Tom smiled at him. He liked Peter. He just didn't want them to do anything foolish and get in over their heads. But he was equally aware that sooner or later, if they were determined enough, their parents wouldn't be able to stop them. Young love, and young bodies, usually won out. He just hoped they would wait a few years, until they were mature enough to deal with an adult situation. It was like holding back a tidal wave. "Your father makes the best barbecue in Montana," Tom said, and Peter grinned. "I want to take lessons."

They'd all been talking about their annual camping trip to Yellowstone on the last weekend before school started. The parents of the Lost 7, as some people called them, were less enthusiastic than usual. They were afraid that it might bring up bad memories for their children, but the kids seemed game to go anyway. Tom had suggested a weekend in Las Vegas, where there would be plenty for the kids to do, but it was more complicated to organize, and some families thought it was too expensive. No final decision had been made yet.

Peter sat with Juliet and her father for a while, then left to say goodbye to some of the guests with his parents, and Tom suggested they call it a night. It was one in the morning, and they'd been there since six o'clock. Juliet noticed Justin leaving with his mother and Noel. She hoped Justin wasn't driving, and saw his mother get behind the wheel. She saw him stumble once on the way to the car, but no one seemed to notice.

Tom and Juliet left a few minutes later and thanked the Pollocks warmly for a terrific evening. "I want barbecue lessons!" Tom told Pitt, who laughed.

"Family recipe!" he said. "But for a couple of bottles of wine, or a hot stock market tip, I'll share." The two men liked each other. Tom noticed Bill then, leaving with his boys.

"Where's Pattie?" he asked casually. He had seen her earlier.

"She wasn't feeling well," Anne explained. "She gets migraines. I think she had one."

"Too much barbecue," Pitt said, laughing. A few of the guests had had too much beer or wine, but not many. It was easy to get carried away on a fun evening where everyone was relaxed.

"Are you on for the camping trip?" Pitt asked him.

"Is it still on?" Tom was surprised when Pitt said it was, and he looked at Juliet. "I was hoping for Vegas myself, but it's up to Juliet. I didn't know how she'd feel about camping after Granite Peak." Pattie had already said she didn't think Benjie should go, with his bear terrors.

"I want to go, Dad," Juliet said in a firm voice, and Tom suspected that a weekend in tents with Peter had something to do with it. He'd have to be vigilant, and so would the Pollocks.

"We can't lose our traditions," Pitt said. "There are usually forty or fifty of us, and we still have the campsite reserved in Yellowstone. It's a fun event, and very civilized, no big challenges or uncharted territory."

"I'm game if Juliet wants to go." Tom smiled at his daughter, and she looked relieved. She and Peter had been talking about it for weeks, and now that she would be going to school in Fishtail, she'd be there. If she weren't, she'd have been back in New York by then with her mother. Beth wasn't coming back until after school started, and Juliet was nervous about that. But Peter said he'd take care of her on the first day of school. They were hoping they'd be in the same classes. "I guess we're in," Tom said to Pitt about the camping trip, and Pitt looked pleased. So did Peter and Juliet.

They left a few minutes later, and Juliet yawned on the way home.

"Did you have fun?" her father asked her. He'd had a good time, enjoyed everyone he talked to, and had been happy to see Marlene out for an evening. They had talked for quite a while by the pool, and sat together for dinner when he brought a plate back to her so she didn't have to move. She was grateful for his thoughtfulness.

"I did," Juliet said with a sleepy smile.

"How did you think Justin was?" her father asked her, and she only hesitated for a fraction of a second. She had already decided that she wasn't going to tell anyone about seeing him with the wine bottle, not even Peter, and she hadn't.

"I think he's fine," she said innocently. "Why?"

"His mom thinks he's having nightmares, and he's very upset about his dad, understandably. It's hard for all of them, watching him die slowly every day. It's gone on for a long time."

"I know." Juliet looked serious when she nodded. "They were afraid he'd die while we were lost. It's so sad." Everyone felt sorry for them, and Tom did especially for Marlene. He could see how painful it was for her, and her boys.

"Marlene's worried that he's depressed, and maybe suffering some kind of trauma from your adventures." Justin was the only one who had gotten physically injured, which was hard too. Eventually, he'd have to have surgery to take the pins out.

"He seemed okay to me," Juliet said, looking out the window. She hated lying to her father, but she didn't want Justin to get in trouble. He was like her big brother now.

"It's a wonder you all came out of it as well as you did." Then he looked at her. "Have you had nightmares about it?"

She shook her head. "I dreamed about it a couple of times, but not like real nightmares. The bear was really scary. She stood up on her back legs and roared at Justin. I thought she was going to kill him, but he scared her off, by getting up taller than she was and not acting scared. We were all shaking when she left."

"Brown bears are nothing to mess with. We forget that these are dangerous animals and this is still wild country in places. Pitt says the camping trip in Yellowstone is pretty tame."

"It sounds like fun, Dad," she said, smiling, and he laughed.

"You and Peter better behave, or I'll chain you to the steering wheel of my truck and take you home."

"I know, Dad," she said and rolled her eyes.

"I mean it," he said more sternly, but they were both in a good mood and had had fun at the barbecue. He was relieved to hear that she thought Justin was okay. Kids usually knew the real story about their friends, so Juliet's opinion carried weight with him. It never occurred to him that she was lying and thought she was doing Justin a favor.

Chapter 12

Two days after the Pollocks' barbecue, the moment the Wylies had dreaded and been expecting for a year finally happened. Bob was sleeping with the ragged breathing that had become familiar to Marlene. He had seen the boys for a few minutes earlier in the day. He was too weak and exhausted to speak, but he had smiled at them and touched their hands, and then he had drifted off to sleep. Marlene was sitting beside him, and saw him take his last breath half an hour later. The nurse who was in the room with them felt for a pulse and shook her head gently at Marlene when there was none. Marlene sat with him alone for an hour, and gently kissed his cheek, and then left the room and they called the doctor. He came to examine him and signed the death certificate. The funeral home came to get him two hours later after the boys had seen him, and then they took him away. Noel sobbed in his mother's arms when they took Bob, and Justin stood still and looked like he'd been hit by a bomb. The three of them sat in the kitchen afterwards and hugged each other. It was over, a year after it had started, and it had been the hardest journey they had ever been on. He had been a wonderful father and husband, and he was finally gone. He hadn't wanted to leave them, and had put up a valiant fight. But it was one he couldn't win. They had known that since the beginning, and he had held on for as long as he could.

Marlene called Anne and told her that night. "He's gone," was all she said when Anne answered, and she and Pattie went over half an hour later to sit with her and hold her hands. Justin and Noel were in their rooms, and Peter and Matt had come with their mothers. The four boys went for a walk, while their mothers talked in the kitchen.

Bob had made most of the arrangements himself months before, to make it easier for Marlene when it happened. He had always done everything hard for her. It had been his idea to come to Fishtail, to start a life of their own, away from their families, where they could lead life as they wanted. Bob had had a domineering father and an anxious mother, and Marlene's parents had been meddlers who constantly interfered in their lives. They had loved being on their own after they left Denver and settled in Montana. Bob had chosen where they would live and opened their practice. Marlene had lived and worked in his shadow for eighteen years. It had been comfortable for her and he made her feel safe, but now he was gone. She had no idea what she would do without him. He made all of their decisions for nearly twenty years.

The funeral home already had everything they needed for the service, which would be in the Immanuel Lutheran Church.

Anne thought it was a good thing that the boys would be starting school soon—Noel for his first year of high school and Justin his last.

Marlene had notified the church that afternoon, and the funeral would be in three days, with a rosary at the funeral home the night before. All of Fishtail would be there: their friends and clients, and the families of the children's friends. Everybody in town knew them. Bob had chosen an attorney who was new in town to work in the law practice with Marlene, when Bob couldn't work anymore. He was methodical and precise and had thought of everything. She had no idea who would do that now. He had told Justin to help her when he was gone, and Justin cried every time his father said it. He couldn't bear the thought of losing his dad.

He was bereft as he sat with his brother and Matt and Peter. Losing his father was worse than being lost on the mountain and faced by an angry bear ready to attack them. He had never been as frightened as he was at the prospect of going on without his father, and he knew that his mother expected him to take his father's place now, but he had no idea what that meant. He just sat and stared into space, as his friends spoke softly and talked to Noel. Justin felt paralyzed by what had happened, and overwhelmed, but didn't want to say it.

The two boys left with their mothers, and Noel went to his room to call Tim. Justin locked his door after they left, and rummaged in the bag in his closet where he kept his football cleats and shin guards. He found the small bottle of bourbon he had taken from his parents' bar, opened it, and took a long drink. He felt better after he did, and lay down on his bed, staring at the ceiling, wishing he had died on Granite Peak. Then he wouldn't have to face what was expected of him now, which he didn't understand. His father had said that he had to become a man on that day, when he died. Justin had no idea what a man was supposed to do. He felt like a lonely lost boy, and had never been so terrified in his life. He took another long drink from the bottle and put it away. He thought he should probably be with his mother, but he couldn't get his legs to stand up and carry him down the stairs. He just lay there, crying for the father he had lost, the mother he couldn't help, and his childhood, which had ended on that day with his father's last breath.

Peter called Juliet when he got home, and told her about Noel and Justin's dad. She was sad for them and didn't know what to say. She sent each of them a text saying that she was thinking of them, and how sorry she was. She told her father when she saw him a few hours later. He called Marlene and one of the hospice nurses answered. They were packing up their things and waiting for the rentals to be picked up, like the hospital bed they'd had for a year. Marlene was still sitting in the kitchen, feeling paralyzed when Tom called her. He asked if there was anything he could do for her, and she said there wasn't. She sounded like she was in a daze, and Tom felt terrible for her, but in a way, he thought it was a mercy for all of them that it was over. The end had been so hard and had taken so long. Now she could get on with her life and so could the boys. It was a hard way to look at it, and he didn't say it to her, but it seemed healthier for all of them. He was sorry he hadn't known Bob when he was at his best, since everyone spoke highly of him. He had met him twice when he first moved to Fishtail. Bob had been in a wheelchair, and Marlene had taken him out for some air. He was bald from the chemotherapy, rail thin and deathly pale, but he had kind, intelligent eyes, and had wished Tom the best in his new home. Now he was gone. It made Tom muse about the mysteries of life and death, and how strange and sad it was that interesting, lively, intelligent, good people suddenly disappeared from our lives in an instant, never to be seen again. He felt sorry for their boys, who would grow up without a father, with whatever memories they had of him as their only comfort, and their mother, who had been so brave ever since Tom had met her. He knew the days ahead would be agony for her.

"Bob did everything for the funeral himself," she told him on the phone, when he offered to help her. "He had very definite ideas about everything. I think Justin should read the eulogy, but he hates public speaking and he's afraid he won't be able to get through it, and Noel is too young." Tom had barely known him so he couldn't do it either and didn't offer. "Pitt said he'd do it," she said softly. "Will you come to the service, Tom?" she asked him.

"Of course, if you want me to," he said, as support for her.

"I'd like to know you're there." She felt like a frail, vulnerable bird, or a butterfly, whose wings had been torn off. She hadn't realized how broken she would feel and how helpless and lost, even though he'd been sick for a year. But she didn't feel prepared, no matter how much warning they had had, from the first diagnosis to the final death sentence when they stopped chemo and sent him home to die. Even then, it had taken nearly three more months for it to happen. Bob had hung on for as long as he could, for her sake and their sons'.

"I'll be there," Tom assured her, "whenever you want me."

"Thank you, it means a lot to me." Her voice was barely a whisper.

"Do you want me to have the boys come over for dinner?"

"No. I sent Justin out for food earlier. They can take care of it themselves, and Pattie and Anne are going to drop some meals off tomorrow so we don't starve." She felt incapable of cooking or doing anything else. Tom was mildly surprised by how disoriented she seemed. He had thought she was stronger than that, but she was still in shock. She had loved Bob for a long time, and relied on him. From all Tom had heard, he had been a strong, very courageous man, and he had provided well for them in every way. He'd been the most respected lawyer in their community, as was Marlene. Pitt and Bill spoke highly of them, and had used them for all their ranch legal matters for years.

"Give the boys my love," Tom said before he hung up. "And know that I'm just a phone call away, if you need me."

"Thank you, Tom," she said sadly. It sounded as though a bomb had hit her life. It had hit them a year ago, but the final explosion had come that day.

She left the kitchen and saw that the nurses had left and all the rentals had been picked up. It really was all over. She wanted to lie on her bed and scream, keening for him, but she didn't want to frighten the boys.

She saw that Justin's door was closed when she went upstairs. She knocked gently but he didn't answer, so she didn't go in. She didn't want to intrude on his privacy if he wanted to be left alone to grieve. He had a right to mourn as he needed to, and she wanted to respect that. Noel was in his own room, playing a video game to distract himself. If she had gone into Justin's room, she would have seen him out cold on his bed, with the empty bourbon bottle on the floor next to him. Justin had taken the only way out he could think of to get away from everything he felt, and all that he had no idea what to do about. He felt like he was at the bottom of a well, and had drowned at 3:17 P.M. when his father took his last breath.

Chapter 13

Bob Wylie's funeral was exactly the way he wanted it, according to all the written instructions he had left and what he had told Marlene. The music, the flowers, the seating. He hadn't told her at the time so as not to upset her, but he had picked the casket himself. It was a handsome dark mahogany, and he had paid for it, so she didn't have to do that either. The casket was closed at the rosary, which seemed suitable, given how ill he was.

Marlene had bought suits for the boys several months before, just in case, and was relieved that they still fit. She had white shirts and black ties for them, and a black suit for herself. She decided not to wear a hat since it was summer, and the one she had bought was too wintry. She didn't feel as though she needed one in Fishtail. Most funerals were informal affairs and people often wore jeans and a clean plaid shirt in a farming and ranching community. Many people didn't own suits, but Bob had worn one every day. As attorneys, he felt that they should dress the part. Marlene always wore a dress or a skirt suit for work, and never pants, although she always changed into jeans and sneakers or cowboy boots the moment she got home. She wore high heels to Bob's funeral, and looked very pretty despite the sad occasion.

Tom Marshall sat two rows behind her. He wasn't an old friend, but they were close enough, and had gotten closer when their children were missing. That whole event had made close friends of people he had scarcely known before. He sat next to Pitt. There were several rows of children farther back. Juliet was among them, between Peter and Tim. Justin and Noel were on either side of their mother in the front pew with the casket a short distance ahead of them in the center aisle. Their relatives from Denver were there, although Marlene had said that their parents had died in the last few years. But there were cousins, an aunt and uncle, some in-laws of Bob's. Tom knew all but one of the pallbearers from among their friends in town.

Bob had bought a big plot in the cemetery for himself, Marlene, the boys, and their eventual spouses, with two additional places for grandchildren, that he hoped they'd never use. He had ordered his own monument in black granite. The final dates had been added in the last two days. Everything about the service was formal and dignified, as Bob had been. He liked everything first-rate and following tradition.

Tom sang "Amazing Grace" with the congregation, and his voice rose with the others as he watched Marlene. She still looked dazed. She clung to Justin's arm when they followed the casket out of the church, and both boys looked devastated, their faces as pale as their white shirts. They were watched by the entire congregation with deep pity. Rather than having everyone go to their house afterwards for a drink and buffet in his memory, the Pollocks were doing it for Marlene, so she didn't have to think about it.

There were almost three hundred people in the church. Some had come from Billings, others from Red Sky and Big Lodge, in the neighboring communities, and all of them were handed a slip of paper on the way out by Peter and the Wylie boys' friends, inviting them to the Pollock ranch for a reception after the service. Because it was given by the Pollocks, they all came.

It was a big gathering, mostly on the patio and in their dining room and living room. The atmosphere was respectful and congenial, with old friends meeting, clients greeting Marlene, and a constant exchange of memories about Bob. Tom stayed close to Marlene. Once or twice he thought she looked as though she might faint and he spoke to her in a low voice.

"Are you okay?" She nodded and whispered thank you. He didn't see her eat all afternoon. Bob's closest friends had gone to the cemetery with the family for the interment, but Tom and Juliet had met them at the house afterwards.

All of the children were gathered outside. Their jackets had come off if they had worn one, which many hadn't, and their shirts had come loose and shirttails were flapping, ties were gone, and they were running around the Pollocks' back lawn around the pool, playing chasing games. Anne didn't stop them. They needed the relief. The ceremony had been hard for the adults and even harder for the kids. In many cases it was their first brush with death. It was a sobering experience, and the adults were buffering it with large quantities of alcohol being handed out by ranch hands at the Pollocks' bar.

There were sandwiches and sodas for the kids, and a generous buffet for the adults. Food and alcohol seemed to be the accepted antidote for grief.

Tom saw Peter and Juliet, inseparable as they had been for the past month, sipping Cokes, sitting in chairs by the pool and talking quietly. Juliet had worn the only black dress she owned, with a white collar and pleated skirt, and kitten heels and stockings. Her mother had told her on the phone that it was the right thing to wear. Tom saw Justin wandering around like a ghost, with a bottle of mineral water in his hand. Noel was downstairs in the playroom with his friends playing video games. It would have been a nice party if the reason for it weren't so sad.

He saw Justin stumble once with his cast on uneven ground on the lawn. As Justin set the water bottle down, Tom suddenly had a question in his mind. He drifted over to where Justin had left it, picked it up, and kept walking until he rounded a bend and was standing near a toolshed where no one could see him. He unscrewed the lid, sniffed it, and took a cautious sip. It was straight vodka. He wondered if it was a unique occurrence for this painful event, or if Justin had done anything like it before. He put the lid back on and dropped the bottle in a nearby trash can. He wondered if he should tell Marlene about it or speak to Justin himself. She had enough on her hands today, and he wondered too if he should let it go unless he saw it happen again. It was hard to know. It was obviously the only way Justin thought he could get through his father's funeral.

Tom's heart ached for him, and he hoped it was a singular event that wouldn't repeat itself. Justin had had a hard month, lost on the mountain, with a dying father who had finally left them. It was a heavy load for a boy of seventeen. And for Noel too, but Noel seemed to have a sturdier and more optimistic disposition. Justin was more of a brooder, and as the oldest son a lot was expected of him.

Marlene herself admitted that she was relying heavily on him. Maybe too heavily, Tom thought. He would have liked to lighten the load for all three of them, but he didn't want to be presumptuous or intrusive. He decided to just keep an eye on things for a while, especially Justin, without saying anything. Hopefully once he was back in school, he'd be busy dealing with classes, homework, and his college applications, and wouldn't have time to get into trouble. He hoped so, for Marlene's sake. It was hard enough losing her husband, without having to deal with problems with her children. Tom couldn't imagine it, and wished that he could protect her from life's blows. She seemed so frail to cope with life's storms. She was an intelligent, educated woman, but Bob had always protected her, and now he was gone. It made Tom want to rush in and help her.

After he threw the cleverly disguised bottle of vodka into the trash, he went looking for her. He found her standing alone, looking lost in the midst of a crowd of people talking loudly about everything from baseball to their summer vacations to their cattle and a new vet. He gently led her away and found a chair for her to sit on.

"Thank you. I just couldn't talk anymore," she said in a whisper. Tom looked around, but he didn't see Justin. He wondered where the boy was, but he wanted to stay with Marlene now for a while. She seemed overwhelmed, and it was slowly turning into more of a party than a funeral and she clearly wasn't up to it. Apparently neither was Justin, given what he'd brought with him.

"Do you want something to drink?" Tom offered her.

"No, I'm fine. I want to go home soon."

"Do you want me to round the boys up? I can drive you home." She smiled at him gratefully and shook her head.

"The boys want to stay here tonight. It'll be better for them. It's too sad at the house. Anne and Pitt offered to let them stay here." Tom hoped they would keep a good eye on them, particularly Justin, and he was sure they would.

"Just tell me when you're ready." He was her self-appointed guardian, but she didn't object.

"Do you think it's too rude if I go home now?" The reception at the Pollocks' had been going on for three hours and showed no sign of thinning out yet. Their parties were always excellent, and the food extremely good. They were famous for it.

"You've had a hard day, Marlene. You can do whatever you want," he told her, and she looked grateful again and stood up.

"Let's go now, then. I can't do this anymore." She felt like she'd been run over by a train, but she didn't look it. She had worn makeup, and the black dress looked good on her and showed off her figure. She was a pretty woman, even in the depths of her grief.

They said a brief goodbye to the Pollocks and quietly slipped away.

Tom led her out to the front of the house, and gave the valet the ticket for his truck. He brought it to him immediately. Marlene had come in a limousine from the funeral home, which they'd sent away once she got to the Pollocks'. Pitt said they could have her taken home, or he'd do it himself.

She got in Tom's truck and appeared to melt on the seat. She lay her head back. She felt as though all the bones in her body had dissolved. She was so tired, she couldn't even sit up as he drove her home. He glanced at her once to make sure she was all right, and she smiled at him.

"Thank you for taking me home. I just couldn't talk to anyone anymore. I should have said goodbye to the boys, I think they were downstairs."

"The boys will be fine. Just close your eyes and rest for a minute," he said gently. She did as he said and was breathing softly by the time they got to her place. He woke her by stroking her hand, and then a feather touch with one finger on her cheek.

"Thank you, Tom," she said softly, then got out of his truck, and he walked her up the front steps. She opened the front door with her key, and he followed her into the hall to make sure she got in all right.

"Will you be okay?" he asked her, but they both knew she wouldn't. She nodded with the saddest eyes he'd ever seen. "Try to get some sleep." He kissed her cheek and let himself out of the house quietly, as she began to climb the stairs to her room, looking as though she had the weight of the world on her shoulders. He hoped he could lighten the burdens for her in the coming weeks. It seemed like the least he could do for a friend.

Chapter 14

The Pollocks' annual camping trip with their closest friends was as much fun as everyone said it would be. They had reserved tents in the best section of Yellowstone Park, as they did every year. Tom and Juliet knew almost everyone there. All of Juliet's friends, the Granite Peak 7, were there, even Benjie.

Marlene had said she wasn't coming, but Pattie and Anne had talked her into it, and said it would be good for her to go, and Tom thought she looked well. It was the last hurrah of the summer, and however hard it had been for some of them, everyone seemed to forget it for three days of games, barbecue, good friends, music, and revelry.

The kids played games and swam. The adults shared meals with old friends. There was a band and a hayride, and as the Pollocks did everything, they organized it beautifully. It was the invitation everyone wanted and waited for eagerly every year. It was a totally relaxing weekend, and every time Tom saw Juliet, he saw Peter with her.

"Should we just plan the wedding now and get it over with?" Pitt teased Tom. "Don't forget, Anne and I were their age when we decided to get married. And it's worked out pretty well for us."

"Fine, have it your way. If he marries her now, will you pay for college?"

"Sure, why not?" Pitt said good-humoredly.

"It's a deal then. I'll have her bags dropped off as soon as we get home." Even though it concerned both of them to some degree, it was sweet watching their kids. They were like two puppies playing. It was the epitome of first love, and it seemed innocent so far. Tom just wanted it to stay that way for as long as possible. "How did you two manage to behave, if you started at fourteen?" Tom asked him.

"Easy. Her father told me he'd kill me if I touched her before our wedding day, and he had the biggest rifle I'd ever seen," he said, and they both laughed.

"I'm going gun shopping immediately. What kind was it?"

"Actually we held out for almost eight years—well, more like seven—but we were engaged by then. He scared the hell out of me."

"I'm not sure kids are that well behaved anymore."

"True." Pitt agreed. "Let's hope they're sensible, with a little help and guidance, and a few threats from us. I don't think we need to worry about that yet, but I've got my eye on them, and I know you do too." Tom nodded agreement as Peter and Juliet ran past them again. "The nice thing is that today kids seem to hang out in groups of friends." Tom had noticed that too, and he liked seeing it. "How do you think the Wylie boys are doing, by the way?" he asked Tom about Noel and Justin, and Tom looked serious.

"I'm not sure. I think Noel is doing pretty well. I don't know about

Justin. I think there's been a little alcohol in the mix around the time of the funeral."

"I thought that might be the case. We need to watch that. He's a good kid. Did you say anything to Marlene?"

Tom shook his head. "She's got enough on her plate. I thought I'd just keep an eye on it myself for a while before I say anything to her."

"I agree." One of the many things Tom liked about his new community was that they cared about each other, and even each other's kids. Tom couldn't imagine that happening in New York.

The weekend was everything that Tom and Juliet, and all the other guests, hoped it would be. Anne had organized games for the kids. Everyone went swimming, some went riding. The food was delicious, as it was at anything they hosted. Tom had a chance to go on some long walks with Marlene. She seemed in better spirits. Tom observed Justin, who seemed fine too. Peter and Juliet did some serious kissing, out of her father's sight, but nothing more extreme. Pitt had had a serious talk with his son about not letting things get out of hand no matter how in love with her he was.

"I'm not ready for grandchildren yet," Pitt told him, and Peter blushed to the roots of his blond hair. "Got the message?"

"Yes, Dad."

"If that happens and I don't kill you, her father will." Peter looked seriously mollified after their talk.

They all had a wonderful weekend and lots of fun. Even Marlene, who almost didn't come until Anne insisted, said she was glad she'd gone in the end. Tom was constantly attentive to her, but not oppressively so. She felt safe and protected, and she had fun with him and all her friends. She had a teary moment, talking to Anne and Pattie about Bob, but the moment passed. They had noticed how kind and caring Tom was to her, and they wondered if anything would come of it. But it was too soon to think about that, and they were sure Marlene hadn't either. She had been so in love with Bob. But it was nice of Tom to take such good care of her, and he was good to her boys.

By the time the weekend was over, they all felt like they'd had a week's vacation, and the next week, all the children in Fishtail were starting school.

Juliet was nervous about starting a new school, but she would have had to face it in New York too. High school was a big change. Peter was excited about it too.

Absarokee High School was a short seven-minute drive from Juliet's house. Her father was going to drive her on the first day. She'd take a school bus after that.

Peter had promised to meet her outside the school, so they could go in together. Matt, Tim, and Noel would be there too. She was starting with four friends on the first day, and Justin would be there as a senior. She had had endless consultations with her mother on WhatsApp about what to wear. She had settled on jeans, a pink blouse, a denim jacket, and pink Converse. She didn't expect anyone to overdress in Montana, or to compete the way they would in New York. The girls in high school in Manhattan all competed with each other if they didn't have to wear a uniform. Most schools didn't require a uniform in high school, so it was a free-for-all as to what they wore. Juliet had her long blond hair in a ponytail. She looked fresh and young and pretty, and appropriate for her age. Peter thought she looked adorable when he saw her, and she gave a last wave at her father over her shoulder as she hurried to join up with Peter so they could go in.

"Where are the others?" she asked him, looking around.

"They went in early. They wanted to hang out in the gym. We sign up for sports teams tomorrow. I'm signing up for basketball. My dad won't let me play football. He says he wants me to go to college with teeth."

"I think I'll sign up for girls' volleyball. I played it in eighth grade. Do they play field hockey here?" She saw several girls walk past them, and noticed that their hair was long down their backs. They had on makeup and were wearing short skirts, and some had on high heels.

"Do I look ridiculous?" she whispered to Peter.

"No," he whispered back. "They went to eighth grade with me. They're weird." She laughed at his description, which seemed apt. Their skirts were too short, and their sweaters were tight and a little too low cut. Juliet looked like Alice in Wonderland compared to them. They were dressed like Barbie. Some had facial piercings and tattoos. It was only a handful of girls, but they stood out.

"Is there a dress code?" she whispered again.

"Yes, but they do what they want. The rest of the girls look normal, like you, only not as pretty." He smiled at her.

"Thank you," she said with a smile. He looked nice too in a new sweatshirt, jeans, and new Nikes.

They had none of the same classes that morning, and she was in a different section, so he walked her to her classroom, and then went to find his. The school was unfamiliar to him too, but he had gone to schools like it, and navigated better than she did. She had gone to small private schools all her life, which were different. It felt intimidating on the first day, but she was sure she'd get used to it.

The classes were small, which she liked. They were roughly half female and half male. It was a geometry class, which was one of her weaker subjects, and she had to race to get to her next class. One of the girls made a comment as she sped by and referred to her as the Virgin Mary. She ignored it.

Her next class was algebra, which she didn't like either. A few of the girls in that class had pierced noses and lips, eyebrows and tongues. All she had was pierced ears, and only one earring on each. The girl in front of her had disks in her earlobes the size of a fifty-cent piece and gave her a nasty look. She saw Tim sitting in the classroom and changed her seat to be next to him. She left the class with him, and she was looking dejected.

"The first day always sucks," he reassured her. "I don't know where all the freaks come from, but they're out in force on the first day. They kind of blend in later on." She had an English Lit class that afternoon, and biology. She was beginning to wonder if she'd made the right decision. Some of the girls looked nice, others were too racy. The classes were hard, and the teachers hadn't been friendly so far. They looked overwhelmed on the first day too. Someone else had called her Goody Two-shoes in the hall. The atmosphere wasn't congenial or welcoming on her first day of high school.

Peter was waiting for her in the cafeteria. It was a big noisy room, the lines were long, and there was nothing she wanted to eat except a yogurt and a banana.

"That's all you're eating?" He looked worried. He had helped himself to a burger and fries, but they looked tired to Juliet, who was used to private school, well-balanced, appealing meals. Everything was new to her here. "How were your classes?" he asked, as they found a table and Matt and Noel found them. Tim had a different lunch break.

"They sucked," she told him. "Geometry and algebra, my two worst subjects. I didn't understand a thing."

"Tim does mine for me," he said with a grin. "He can do yours too."

"I'm going to flunk and I'll never get into college," she said glumly. The yogurt was warm and the banana was mushy.

"You won't be alive by then if you don't eat more than that," Peter commented, and Matt and Noel heaped potato chips, half a sandwich, and some cookies on her plate. "Eat!" Peter told her, and she smiled. "I hate the first day. It's always depressing. The teachers want to show you how tough they are. They shower you with homework, and all the freaks in the county show up for school. Everybody gets nice about two weeks later. What do you have this afternoon?"

"English Lit. At least I understand that." He smiled at her comment. "And biology."

"I have American History and sociology. I need a translator for those," he told her.

"I do his history," Matt volunteered. "He does my English papers. What do you do?" he asked her with interest, and she laughed.

"English. I suck at math and science." It had cheered her up to have lunch with them, and they went back into the chaos in the halls. She found her next class more easily and promised to meet Peter outside after school.

"Play nice in the sandbox!" he told her and rushed off to his own classes.

She liked the English Lit class better and had already read the book they were discussing, which made it easy. She almost cried in biology when they told her they were going to dissect a frog in the coming weeks. She nearly threw up.

She saw Peter for two minutes after school, and then had to get into her father's truck. She didn't look happy and Tom asked her cautiously how it had gone.

"Is it too soon to get my GED?" she asked, slumped down in the seat as she put on her seat belt.

"It might be. What happened?"

"I had geometry and algebra back-to-back this morning, and you know how I am at that. The teachers weren't friendly. English Lit was okay, and I know the book, and we're going to dissect a *frog* in biology! I'd rather get an F. The food was disgusting, and some of the girls in my class dressed like freaks *and* they all have piercings and I'm starving!" she said, glowering at him as he tried not to laugh. She looked the way she used to when she was five and unhappy about something.

"Other than that, how was the performance, Mrs. Lincoln?"

"It sucked," she said for emphasis. "Peter says it gets better, but I don't believe him. I had lunch with him and Matt and Noel, and they made me eat." She crossed her arms and stared out the window.

"And I looked stupid in my pink Converse. Mom thought it would look cute. It didn't. Somebody called me the Virgin Mary, and someone else called me Goody Two-shoes." Her father poured her lemonade and gave her a plate of cookies when she got home. Peter called her as soon as he got to the ranch. He commiserated with her for half an hour, and she went to her room to do her homework. She was panicked about the frog in biology and had said she'd refuse to do it.

Her mother called an hour later to see how it had gone, and she told her the same litany of woes.

"First days are always hard, give it a chance. It's a whole new experience. This is high school, in a rural public school. It's all new to you. And they can't all look like freaks."

"The girls in my classes did."

"Two weeks from now, you'll have friends, and it will all seem different."

"When are you coming out here?"

"In about two weeks. You can help me find a house, or an apartment. I have a couple of meetings and deadlines I have to take care of here first." Juliet was happy she was coming. Her mother had a way of helping her turn things around.

She wore jeans and a sweatshirt the next day, and Nikes, like Peter and many of the other kids. She signed up for the volleyball team and felt a little better. The girls on the team were nice and looked normal by her standards. By the end of the week, she had met a girl from Tulsa who had just moved to Montana and she liked her. Matt and Noel liked her too, and they had lunch together. Juliet felt better. She hung out with Peter and the others all weekend. She didn't love the school yet, but she was getting used to it. Her mother was coming out soon, and she had a psych class she loved, with a teacher she thought was terrific. Things were looking up.

When her mother arrived from New York, the first thing they did was look for a place for Beth to live. There were very few apartments so she rented a small Victorian house on the edge of town near the Wylies. Noel and Justin could walk over anytime. It had been freshly painted and nicely done, with a brand new, cheerful IKEA kitchen.

It was a cozy two-bedroom house, just big enough for the two of them. It had an upstairs playroom where she could entertain her friends, and Beth had an office downstairs. Juliet's friends could come for meals in the sunny kitchen.

They had dinner at her father's house on the first night, and after that Beth cooked at home. She didn't want to encroach on Tom or start with bad habits. It was a small town, and Beth didn't want to crowd him. He had gotten there first, and she didn't want to give him the impression that she wanted to hang out with him. She didn't.

Juliet said he'd been going to the Wylies' a lot, helping Marlene with repairs. Bob had been sick for so long that nothing had gotten done, so Tom was doing a lot of it for her. She said he did most of it in the daytime, when they were in school.

Tom's doing repairs at the Wylies' had started when Marlene had a leak in the kitchen and couldn't get a plumber to come out. Not knowing what else to do, she called Tom. He came over to fix it and realized how many other things needed to be done. The kids were back in school by then. He wasn't busy. He spoke to his investment clients by phone in the early morning hours and handled their accounts. And after that, he had ample time to help her. He offered to come over every day and get a few more things done. He estimated that it would take about four weeks to do them all, and he said he enjoyed it. He had a very professional-looking set of tools, and the week the kids started school, he showed up at nine in the morning and got to work. She made him lunch, and he went back to his house in the afternoon to return any calls from his clients.

"I can't believe you're doing this for me," she said. He was fixing things that hadn't worked in a year, because Bob was too sick to do it.

Tom even wallpapered her bedroom for her, in some English wallpaper that looked like chintz, which she found on the internet. It was by a famous designer and she loved it. He did a beautiful job, and said he loved house projects because you could see the results so quickly, unlike everything else he did. Investments took a long time to bear fruit.

"Working on houses is like magic. Instant gratification," he said to her. He arrived with his toolbox every day and got to work, and within days, everything in her kitchen was running smoothly. He had fixed shelves. He did carpentry. He was a genius at gluing things back together, brilliant with a glue gun, and was talented with wallpaper and paint. "If my business goes under, I can be a handyman, and I'll probably make more money," he said, and seemed to be thoroughly enjoying it. What he liked most was talking to Marlene while he worked. They never ran out of subjects which interested them both. She was taking a break from her law office for two months while she figured out what she wanted to do. The young lawyer they had taken into the practice when Bob got sick was handling her clients for now.

"I'm a lady of leisure for the first time in fifteen years, since I finished law school. I kind of like it," she admitted. "I was a litigator in Denver, which I enjoyed, but here we mostly get agricultural cases and they're not very exciting. Property line disputes, contracts. Bob loved practicing here, with the ranches and the farms. I was never totally convinced, and it doesn't really use my skills as an attorney. But Bob wanted to be here for the boys."

"Please don't tell me you're moving back to Denver." He looked crestfallen, and she smiled.

"I'm not moving anywhere. This is home now. I just don't know if I want to practice law here anymore or sell the practice." The lawyer filling in for her had already told her that if she decided to sell, he wanted to buy the practice, at a very decent price. Bob had invested their money wisely, and he had left her an enormous life insurance policy, which he never told her about, so she didn't have to work. "I'm not sure what I make practicing law here is worth it. Bob thought it was fun, but I didn't. Cases involving water rights and farm animals don't really thrill me." She smiled and he laughed.

"I've been thinking about writing a legal guide for laypeople. It might be a nice change."

It didn't seem like fun to practice without Bob either. She had done it for the last year, carrying his caseload and her own, and hadn't enjoyed it. In the meantime, Tom was helping her fix up her house, purely for the fun of it, and she spent every day talking to him while he did. He always asked about the boys and how they were doing. He took a real interest in them. It gave her someone to talk to, now that Bob and all the nurses were gone. She was concerned about what colleges Justin should apply to. She hardly saw the boys with all their after-school sports practices and activities. But she spent hours every day talking to Tom, and she thrived on the attention. He was good company. They laughed a lot, and she enjoyed helping him with the wallpaper and paint. She loved the results.

"Maybe we should go into business together, fixing up houses," she said, only half joking one day, and he smiled as she handed him the next piece of wallpaper. She stood there, holding it, waiting for him to take it from her, and he couldn't stop looking at her. He couldn't even remember what she had said to him. All he saw were her eyes and her hair, the curve of her neck, and the fullness of her breasts, everything he had been trying not to see for the last month of spending every day with her. Bob had been gone for six weeks, and she looked more peaceful now.

He put down his tools, took the wallpaper from her, and before he could stop himself he was kissing her, and they both felt as though a tidal wave had hit them. She hadn't realized how desperately she had wanted him, maybe even since before Bob had died. She didn't know when it had started, but they couldn't stem the tides until they were in her bed and had made wild passionate love all day. Her face was chafed, and she could hardly move by the time they stopped. She lay in bed smiling at him, and he started laughing. He'd been afraid all afternoon that she would come to her senses and either throw him out or call the police.

"Oh my God," she said, still breathless as they lay in the tangle of sheets, with their lovemaking heavy in the air. "What happened? I think we lost our minds," she said as she ran her hand over his body again and got an instant reaction. She couldn't remember ever making love the way they had all day. They were insatiable, like two starving people, which they had both been. He hadn't made love in two years, and she hadn't in a year. Her sex life with Bob had been lackluster for years, but she loved him and told herself it didn't matter. But as it turned out, maybe it did.

"Or maybe we found our minds," Tom said gently, then fondled her breasts and kissed her again. "I think we need to go to a desert island somewhere so we can make love all day all the time." But they had the perfect alibi with the house repairs he was doing, and his showing up every day with his toolbox. Their children were in school, and there was no one to disturb them. She had let her cleaning woman go with the nurses and was going to clean the house herself. Her sons never came home before six. All Tom had to do was be home for Juliet at around four o'clock, or later when she had volleyball practice. They were free, independent, single adults. The only thing that might have stopped her was the memory of Bob, and she was amazed to discover that it didn't.

"I suppose I should feel guilty," she said as they climbed into the shower together when they got up. "But I don't. We were happy together and I loved him. Our sex life was never exciting but everything else made up for it: the kids, our work. Our relationship was always more intellectual than sexual. We loved working together. He was so sick for so long, though, that our whole relationship and our life changed. I became his caregiver, but it was agony watching him die. I felt like I was dying too. And now you make me feel alive again," she said as he kissed her. He was so overwhelmed by how sensual she was that they made love in the shower before they finally got out and got dressed.

"I could hardly keep my hands off you for the last month," he confessed. "I thought you'd hate me if I reached out to you. You're the sexiest woman I've ever seen or made love to."

"How was it with Beth?" She was curious. His ex-wife was a beautiful woman. And he was a very sexual man, she had discovered.

"It was great in the beginning, but we drifted apart. And the more I hated our life, the colder she got. We stopped having sex a year before we separated, and I haven't wanted anyone since, except you. I thought I didn't care about it anymore, and I don't care about sex. What we did today is making love. That's different. Marlene, I am crazy about you."

"Me too," she whispered in a sultry voice, then stretched her body the length of his and pressed herself against him. It drove him crazy again, but he had promised to meet Juliet at home.

"What do you think we should say to people?" he asked cautiously as they both dressed. She looked panicked when he said it.

"Nothing for now. Our friends would be shocked. Bob's been gone for six weeks. We can't tell my kids for a long time either. It would be disrespectful to their father. They already love you. I don't want to spoil that."

"I agree. What do you think? Six months? A year?" He was willing to keep it a secret for as long as they had to. For a minute, he wondered if he should tell her about Justin's drinking the day of the funeral, but this wasn't the time. He seemed to be okay now. He had looked sane and sober anytime Tom saw him since then. So it might just have been a very bad day. He hoped so, for her sake. She didn't need any more worries, and he didn't want her to have any. He wanted to protect her.

They finally made it to the front door with their clothes on, and he kissed her and held her. “Thank you, Marlene . . . thank you.”

“I love you, Tom,” she whispered, and gently touched his face with her fingertips and kissed him, and he was aroused again.

“I love you too. See you tomorrow.” He slipped out the door before they could lose their heads again and waved as he drove away smiling. He could hardly wait to get back to work on her house the next day. Their days of wallpapering and carpentry were over for now. All he wanted was to be with her.

Chapter 15

What happened between Tom and Marlene felt like madness to them, but it was the sweetest madness they had ever tasted. They readily admitted that nothing like it had ever happened to either of them. He had been so love-starved during the last year of his marriage and after, and she had been so distraught watching Bob waste away and die that they came to life in each other's arms and couldn't get enough of each other. Their union was a celebration of life and everything they'd been lacking.

He arrived at her house at nine o'clock every morning, and they made passionate love all day, anywhere in the house that appealed to them. He was insatiable and obsessed with her, and she was equally mad about him. It was all the sweeter because it was a secret, and somewhat forbidden fruit as a recent widow. Marlene had to remind herself not to look too happy when she went out or saw friends, so no one would suspect what was going on. She had to look serious and down some of the time. She realized now that she had mourned Bob in the early months of his illness, and by the end, keeping him alive had felt more cruel than kind. She had never had anything with any man like what she shared with Tom. Their paths crossed socially frequently, since they got along well. The Pollocks often invited them together as their two single charity cases. Marlene and Tom laughed about it sometimes, but they were extremely circumspect when they were out in public, especially with their children.

Marlene didn't want her boys to know for a year, and Tom respected that. It was reasonable for her to want that. Then they would carefully introduce Tom into their lives, and hope that it went well. There was no reason why it shouldn't, with a respectable delay before she started dating. They weren't dating. They were having wild, passionate, unbridled sex almost all day every day. It was far more than dating, and they both knew they were in love. Even so rapidly after Bob's death, she didn't doubt that it was real.

Marlene had lunch with Pattie and Anne at the end of September, and she had to be extremely careful not to seem too cheerful. But as it turned out, Pattie wasn't feeling well, so the focus was on her, not Marlene.

"You should get that checked out," Anne scolded her. "You've been having stomach problems since this summer. I'll bet you have an ulcer." Anne looked worried about her and Pattie shook her head.

"I did get it checked out, and it's not an ulcer."

"What is it?" Anne asked her, even more concerned than she'd been before. She lowered her voice, "Is it a tumor? Is it cancer?" Pattie shook her head and smiled.

"It's actually something else. They said they can take care of it in April."

"In April?" Marlene stared at her. "They expect you to have stomach problems 'til April? What's wrong with them?" As she said it, Anne was staring at them and narrowed her eyes.

"You little shit. You scared me to death. April my ass. Pattie Brown, you bitch, are you pregnant?" Pattie nodded with a huge grin, and Anne threw her arms around her and hugged her, genuinely thrilled for her. She knew Pattie had wanted another baby but didn't have the guts to leap in.

"It was an accident. I can't even remember when it happened, and I didn't want to say anything until I knew it would be okay. I'm three months pregnant. I'm due in April. And"—she smiled even more—"it's a girl."

"You got what you wanted." Anne looked happy for her and Marlene was happy too. So she wasn't the only one in the group with a secret. But hers had to stay a secret for a year. "What did Bill say?" Anne asked her.

"He can't remember when it happened either, but he's thrilled it's a girl. He's been very sweet about it. I always wanted another baby more than he did. But since it's a girl, he's excited. I think if it were another boy, we'd have given it to you. I'm done with boys. Benjie is going to kill us. He has us up all night with his nightmares about the bear."

"Have you told the boys yet?" Anne asked her.

"Not yet. I want to wait 'til it shows. There's no point making the natives nervous before I have to." They were all happy for her, and her good news dominated lunch, which was a relief for Marlene. The subject of Tom never came up, not even in passing.

Beth had rented her new house furnished. She bought a few things, but didn't need much. She had noticed Tom occasionally going into Marlene's house, and Juliet explained to her that he was doing house repairs for her to help her out.

"That's nice," Beth said to her daughter, and then wondered if there was more to it than that. She was an attractive widow, albeit a recent one, and Tom didn't seem to be dating anyone, so why not?

She mentioned it to Juliet the next time she thought of it.

"Wouldn't it be funny if your dad ended up with, or at least dated, Marlene Wylie?"

Juliet made a face immediately. "Mom! Gross! That's awful. Her husband just died about five minutes ago." It had been a month and a half, but admittedly it wasn't long. "Daddy wouldn't go out with her now. He respects her more than that. He always says how much he admires her. That would be awful if she were dating so soon. Dad would never do that."

"Well, maybe in a year, then. I thought she was nice when I met her."

"She is nice. But she really loved her husband. They had a great marriage. The boys always say so. She probably won't date for a long time. Maybe never." Juliet was very close to Noel these days too. He helped her a lot with her homework. She was adjusting to her new school and liked it even more than she thought she would. And seeing Peter every day was terrific.

"You never know. Your father is a nice man. Stranger things have happened than a romance with a newly bereaved woman. That's not a crime," Beth reminded Juliet. Unusual things had happened in her life too.

A few days before she came back to town, Beth decided to be bold and brave, and sent Harvey Mack, the chief ranger, a text. He hadn't answered, which was slightly embarrassing, and she decided that she had misread the signs. He obviously wasn't interested. She forgot about it and had been in her new house for a week when he called her. Juliet was at her father's, and Beth had just organized her closet and was pleased. She got everything in.

"Good evening, ma'am," the distinctive deep voice greeted her. "Do you have a flock of deer in your front yard? Or a herd of bison?"

"Actually, no, I don't." She laughed at the question.

"A mountain lion? An elephant? Are your trees on fire?"

"None of the above."

"I'm very sorry to hear it, because in that case, it appears you have no need of a forest ranger." He sounded disappointed.

"Wait, I'll go and get a bison immediately and put it in the front yard. Where do I find one?"

"I'll bring one. Is ten minutes too soon?"

"Not if you bring me a bison. And by the way, you don't know where I live."

"Yes, I do. I have my spies. We're a covert branch of the FBI. Why didn't you tell me you were moving here?"

"Because it all happened very quickly, the day before I left. My daughter decided she wanted to go to school here. So, I'm going to be traveling back and forth to New York."

"And does she like it?"

"Apparently not at first. It was a big change, but she likes it better now, and is getting used to it. Do you really know where I live?"

"Yes, but only because an old friend of mine was the realtor who rented you the house. This is a very small town." They both laughed.

"Can I offer you a cup of coffee or a glass of wine?"

"Probably neither. I just thought I'd stop by to say hello, in case you'd forgotten who I am."

"I'm not the one who forgot. I sent you a text and you didn't answer."

"Oh Christ, I forgot. I'm sorry. We had an emergency and it went right out of my head. I owe you dinner for that."

"That sounds interesting. I'm still waiting for my bison." As she said it, the doorbell rang, and she answered it with the phone in her hand. It was Harvey. In full uniform. "Where's my bison?"

"I left it double parked and it got towed. I apologize for the costume. I just left the office."

"You work late, Chief Mack," she said, as she put her phone in her pocket. He looked happy to see her, and she was too.

"Welcome to Fishtail. You've just increased our population to four hundred and seventy-nine. I'll have to get the signs corrected."

"That's ridiculous. I'm from New York. There are more people in a subway car in New York."

"Fishtail is prettier." He followed her into her living room. The house suddenly looked tiny with him in it. He was huge. "I like your house." She had added some personal touches and spruced it up.

"Thank you. I do too. It's a little small, but it's cozy." She offered him coffee again and he declined. He didn't want wine either.

"So when will you have dinner with me? In exchange for the text I forgot to answer?"

"Whenever you like." Her computer was sitting on a table in the living room, and he noticed it.

"Are you working on something right now?" He had read several of her interviews since he met her, and he was impressed. He mentioned the last one he had read and liked.

"You read *The New Yorker*?" It was her turn to be impressed.

"I do now. I like your work." He had subscribed just so he could read her and wouldn't miss an article.

"Thank you." She smiled.

"I don't mean to be rude, but won't you get lonely here? Even the bison complain."

"I can see why. But it's peaceful. And my daughter is here, and she loves it. I can go to New York if I get antsy." He nodded. He thought she was a good sport to be there, and a good mother. For a woman alone, Fishtail was not an exciting place. And it would be even lonelier in winter when they got snowed in.

"Are you free tomorrow night?" he asked her.

"I would check my dance card if I had one. I think I can squeeze it in." He smiled at her, enjoying the banter between them.

"I don't know what you're doing here, Beth, but I'm glad you are. Does seven-thirty sound civilized?" She nodded with a smile. "Inviting a woman to dinner at five sounds so gauche." They both laughed. She had a feeling that he'd had a sophisticated life once upon a time, but not lately. As she had, he had taken to the mountains and made a life here. She had the impression that he'd be good to talk to. If nothing else, he was smart and fun.

They had dinner at the diner the next day, and were the last people to leave. They went to the Cowboy Bar afterwards for a glass of wine. Harvey was extremely well read, interested in many subjects, and read *The New York Times* every day, and *The Wall Street Journal* when he had time. He liked the outdoors and he cared about people. He thought Beth was the most unusual, interesting woman he'd ever met, and she thought the same about him.

"What are *you* doing here?" she asked as they finished their wine. She was curious about him.

"I think a lot of the people here, the newcomers anyway, are runaways, from a past life. I took this job because I love the outdoors. I was married when I was in the SEALs. I was young. I was gone all the time. My wife knew what to expect when we got married. But living it is something else. I was gone a lot. Too much. She died of a brain tumor. I got home three days before she died. We had three wonderful last days together, but I realized that I didn't want that life anymore. I almost missed her death. But more important, I missed her life.

"I never married again, and crazy as it sounds, Fishtail suits me. It's peaceful. I feel at home on the mountain. If I never share my life again, I'll be happy here alone. And if I do, I won't miss anything next time. I'll be home every night sitting by the fire, like Santa Claus with Mrs. Claus, waiting for Christmas." It was a sweet image. "I needed to stop running. And for some reason, I stopped running when I got here. It works for me, although that must sound very dull to you," he said simply.

"Actually, it doesn't," she said. "I think it suits me too. I didn't expect that. But I understand now why my ex-husband wanted to move here. He wasn't the right man for me to do that with. But I'm happy here on my own. I've been a warrior to get what I wanted until now. I've fought everybody and everything, including myself, to get where I wanted to be. But I don't want to fight anymore. I want to sit still for a while, and do something different." She had only realized recently that she was tired of fighting. She had understood it while Juliet was lost on the mountain. "If I need a minute of excitement, I'll go to New York. I'm not turning in my passport, just my sword."

"You make a lovely gladiator," he said, smiling at her, as they left the Cowboy Bar. "It's funny that we should meet here. There are so many other places where we could have met along the way. Destiny is strange."

"It is, and interesting too. I don't believe in chance meetings. I think we meet people for a reason, at the right time," she said, looking up at him, her eyes full of questions.

"I believe that too," he said, as they walked back to his car with the Park Service emblem on it, and his name: *Chief Mack*. He drove her home and they sat for a minute in the official car. She couldn't forget that he had brought her daughter home from the mountain. "I had a really nice time, Beth. I'm glad you came back, and that you'll be spending some time here. I'd like to do this again. Do you like to dance, by the way?" She smiled.

"Yes, I do. But I haven't had a chance to in years. I went to dancing school, and I used to dance with my father, and, it sounds ridiculous now, I was a debutante once upon a time."

He smiled broadly. "I was an escort at a debutante cotillion a million years ago. There's a place where you can dance in Billings. Kind of an old-fashioned bar with a dance floor. Would you go with me sometime?"

"I'd love it," she said, beaming. "You see, no chance meetings. Thank you for tonight." It was so perfect that long after she'd been a debutante in a forgotten world and he'd been an escort at a cotillion, they should meet in Fishtail, Montana, a town of four hundred and seventy-eight people. The symmetry of it was perfect.

She waved as she slipped into her house and he drove away.

Chapter 16

Tom and Marlene's mad passion continued all through October into November. They met every day and spent most of the day in bed, ravishing each other's bodies and touching each other's souls. He had never been as in love before, and she had loved Bob very differently. What Tom and Marlene shared was raw passion. They lay in bed talking about it one day.

"Do you really want to wait a year after Bob's death to tell the kids?" he asked her. It seemed like an eternity to him. He wanted a life with her.

"It's only nine months now," she corrected him. "And yes, I do want to wait. They wouldn't understand. And I don't want to spoil it with them."

"I hate lying to them," Tom said, and kissed her neck. "These things happen to people. They fall in love, even after they loved someone else. The boys' father is not here anymore. You are and you have a right to be loved and have someone love and take care of you.

I want to take care of you and them too. Wouldn't Bob have wanted that for you, and for them?"

"He might have, but they wouldn't. They worshipped their father. I don't want them to hate you because we rush it."

"We already have," he reminded her.

"But they don't know that. All boys think their mothers are virgins and saints."

"You may be a saint one day, but you are very definitely not a virgin, my darling, not anymore." He made love to her again after that, and proved his point. They slept in each other's arms afterwards. They didn't hear Justin let himself into the house with his key and go up to his room, where he took a bottle of rum out of an old guitar case in his closet. He had bottles stashed all over the place now, even in his car. He took a long drink and fell asleep on his bed. He had slipped out of class for just that purpose. He liked the buzz rum gave him, especially if he smoked a joint with it. He had smoked his last one on the way home from school, with a rum chaser now. He had only started drinking and smoking dope since they were lost on the mountain, and most of all since his father died. He felt as though he had failed everyone. He didn't care about college now, where he went or if he went at all. He didn't even want to fill out his applications.

The house was silent and warm, and when they woke up, Tom and Marlene went down to the kitchen naked, and she made them lunch. There was a light dusting of snow outside. Winter had unofficially arrived, and Tom could imagine them making love all through the winter. And then in the summer, they could come out of hiding and tell the world.

They were halfway through the simple lunch she had made them, when Tom wanted her again. He pulled her gently into his arms, and started making love to her, sitting in a kitchen chair. She was coming when Tom heard a gasp behind them and a shout. She opened her eyes and saw her son standing in the kitchen doorway, watching them with a look of horror on his face, and of hatred when he saw Tom. He advanced on his mother as though to strike her, and Tom grabbed his arm, with the two of them naked and Justin in a parka with tears running down his cheeks.

"You whore!" he screamed at his mother. "You bitch! How could you do that to Dad? Did you cheat on him when he was dying too?" He was sobbing and Marlene was crying, trying to explain as the two of them stood there naked and Tom was restraining Justin and telling him to calm down. Marlene ran away up the stairs then to get dressed, and Justin ran out the door. Tom couldn't run after him with no clothes on. He had noticed the distinct smell of alcohol on Justin's breath when he was restraining him, and Tom was sure Justin was drunk. He leapt in his car and drove off, as Tom closed the door on an icy blast and went to get dressed too. Marlene was sobbing hysterically on the bed, and Tom tried to console her. There was no avoiding the fact that it had been a hideous scene, her worst nightmare come true.

"Oh my God, Tom, he saw us! He saw us making love!"

"Yes, he did, and I didn't want him to see it either, but he's almost eighteen, he's not six. You're widowed, his father is not alive, you weren't cheating on his father. He shouldn't have seen what he did, and it's embarrassing for all of us, but in the real world, you didn't do anything wrong. You had sex in the kitchen, and your son saw you naked. Mortifying, but not criminal." But there was no reasoning with her. She was as hysterical as Justin had been.

"Where is he?"

"He drove away. And to be honest with you, I'm concerned about him. I smelled alcohol on his breath while I was trying to keep him from hitting you. And what was he doing home in the middle of the day? I think he'd been drinking, or he came home to drink, thinking you wouldn't be here. I saw him drinking at the Pollocks' reception the day of the funeral. He had a full bottle of vodka, masqueraded as bottled water, and he was drunk. I figured it was a bad day, but I'm worried that he's been drinking since then, and maybe before. I didn't want to worry you unless I saw him do it again. I gave it a pass the day of his father's funeral. But not today. And now he's driving. Do you know where he might go?" Tom started dressing quickly, and wanted to go and look for him, but Marlene shook her head. She had no idea where he'd go, and she didn't believe what Tom had said about Justin drinking.

"You're just trying to make us seem less guilty. He wasn't drunk, he was upset."

"I think he was both," Tom said calmly.

"And how do you know it was vodka in the water bottle?"

"I tasted it myself when he left it. It was straight vodka. Marlene, you can't ignore this." And they were both panicked at the thought of his being on the road, which was probably icy under the snow.

Tom put his clothes on and drove around the neighborhood looking for him but didn't see him anywhere, on foot or in his car. When Tom got back to the house, he and Marlene agreed that they couldn't call the police to be on the lookout for him, or they'd arrest him if he was under the influence. They had called his cellphone and he hadn't answered, it went straight to voicemail and Marlene left him a message, apologizing and begging him to come home. All they could do was wait now, for him to come home, or contact them.

Marlene called Anne and Pattie, but Justin wasn't at their homes, and they hadn't seen him. The other boys were in school.

"Is something wrong?" Anne asked her.

"We had kind of an argument," Marlene said, still in tears, and desperately worried about him.

"If he shows up here, I'll call you. I'll tell Pattie too." Marlene hung up, and she and Tom sat in her living room, waiting for Justin to return.

"Would you like to search his room?" Tom asked her as gently as he could.

"What for?" She looked panicked.

"I'd like to see if there's booze in his room. You should know too, if he has a problem." She hesitated and then nodded. But she still couldn't see how they would ever recover from her son seeing them having sex in the kitchen.

They went to his room together and looked in all the obvious hiding places. Sports bag, suitcase, guitar case, box of old clothes under the bed, chests of drawers. When they had finished, Tom had found two bottles of bourbon, a bottle of vodka, a bottle of gin, a bottle of rum, and two bottles of wine. He had enough to run a bar, and there was a small plastic bag with just a dusting of what looked like green herbs.

"What's that?" She looked at Tom.

"Marijuana. What's left of it. It's all gone. He's been smoking dope too. Maybe it all started when Bob was sick and he couldn't face it. But he can't blame you for this. This isn't because we had sex in the kitchen. It's because he has a serious problem with alcohol and substances. You need to put him in rehab," he said sternly, as they took the bottles downstairs, emptied them in the sink and threw them away.

"I'm not going to do that!" Marlene shouted at Tom. "I'm not putting him in rehab. He just lost his father, and now look what he saw today. He needs me. He needs to be at home."

"He needs to stop drinking and smoking dope, Marlene, before he gets hurt or kills someone on the road. You have to face this, and so does he."

"I won't send him away." She started crying again.

"He won't stop drinking if you don't," Tom said calmly.

They were still sitting in her living room when Noel came home from school at six o'clock, after a violin lesson, since he couldn't do contact sports because of his pump. He was dropped off by his teacher and happy to see Tom. Tom left a few minutes later to go home after telling Marlene to call him if she heard anything. He was worried about a possible terrible end to the story, if Justin was driving around somewhere drunk and out of his mind. There was absolutely nothing they could do unless they wanted to report him to the police.

Tom was restless and worried when Juliet came home after volleyball practice. One of the mothers drove four of the girls home who lived near them. Juliet was enjoying being on the team, and the girls she was meeting.

"Something wrong, Dad?" He decided to tell her at least a partial truth.

"I'm worried about Justin. I think he may have been drinking lately." Juliet was silent for a long time, and could see how concerned her father was.

"I saw him drinking this summer, at the Pollocks' barbecue. He was drinking a bottle of wine." And that was before his father died, two days before, in fact.

"Why didn't you tell me?"

"I didn't want to squeal."

"I'm just as bad. I saw him drinking vodka at the reception after the funeral. He had it in a bottle of water."

"Is he in trouble?" she asked her father.

"Not yet. But things can get out of control pretty fast. His mother is very worried about him, and so am I."

"You like her a lot, huh, Dad?" she asked, and he wanted to be honest with her, to the extent he could.

"Yes, I do. But this is a hard time for them. Especially if Justin has a serious problem. That takes precedence over everything else."

They had a quiet dinner that night, and then she went to sleep at her mother's. She liked going back and forth between them. Tom was relieved when she asked him to drop her off at Beth's. He wanted to be available in case Marlene called him for help when Justin came home, or if he didn't. He called her as soon as he got home after dropping Juliet off.

"Any news?" He sounded as tense as she felt.

"Nothing. He hasn't called me. I left him another message. I asked

Noel if he knows where he is. He said he doesn't, and I believe him. He asked if Justin is in trouble. I think he knows about the drinking too. I didn't ask him. We know enough. I don't want to put Noel on the spot."

"Do you want me to come over?" he offered.

"Why don't you wait 'til Noel goes to bed. Around nine. If Justin's been drinking all afternoon, I don't want to be alone with him when he comes home."

"Good idea." He drove to her house at nine. Noel was already asleep, and they sat on the couch waiting to hear something. They fell asleep waiting. The phone rang at midnight. Marlene answered it and her face went sheet white as she listened. Tom just prayed it wasn't the police and that Justin wasn't dead.

It was the police, and he was alive. She was choking on sobs when she told Tom. "He had a car accident and totaled his car an hour ago. He has a head injury, but he was conscious when they found him. He has some broken bones. They took him by helicopter to Saint Vincent's in Billings. He's not in critical condition, but he's very banged up. They're testing him for drugs and alcohol at the hospital." She put her coat on and wrote a hasty note to Noel, in case he woke up, that Justin had had a minor accident, he was okay, and she had gone to pick him up. And not to worry.

They were out the door in five minutes. Tom insisted on driving, and they took his truck because it was heavier. He had four-wheel drive and snow tires. Marlene cried most of the way there.

"He had an accident because he saw us," she said to Tom.

"No, he had an accident because he was drunk, even before he saw us. Although he may have drunk more after he did. But he was drunk when he left the house. I smelled it." He was determined to tell her the truth so she would face it.

It took them an hour and a half to get to Saint Vincent's, and Justin was awake when they arrived. He had a gash on his head and had had five stitches, a moderate concussion, and a broken arm. The injuries were adding up. The ER doctor recommended a few days of bed rest, and Tylenol for the pain. He was lucky he hadn't been killed. He'd hit a tree when his car slid on black ice. His license had been suspended for ninety days for driving under the influence of alcohol and marijuana. As a first offense, which was a misdemeanor, he would have a five hundred dollar fine, and would have to go to a chemical dependency education course.

They rolled him out of the hospital in a wheelchair, and he got in the back seat of Tom's truck.

"Nice of you both to put your clothes on before you picked me up," he said angrily. He was hostile and still drunk. It struck Tom how different he was now, since the summer and his father's death. He was bitter, angry, and frightened, despite the bravado and aggressive words and behavior.

"Nice of you to total your car, risk your life, get a DUI, and worry your mother to death. You're better than that, Justin." Tom didn't pull any punches.

"How would you know?" Justin shouted at him. Marlene sat in the front seat, crying with her eyes closed. It was two in the morning by then. "You're a couple of cheaters."

"I never cheated on your father," she said from the front seat.

"You are now," Justin said irrationally.

"Your mother is a widow. She's a respectable woman, she's no longer married, and I love her," Tom said in a stone-cold voice, and Justin didn't answer.

When they got to Marlene's house, Justin stumbled up the steps to his room, and lay down on his bed with his clothes on. He was still drunk and belligerent. Marlene offered to help him undress and he told her to get out of his room, which she did, and she quietly closed the door. There was no alcohol left in his room, so he couldn't get any more drunk than he already was.

"Do you want me to stay?" Tom asked her, and she shook her head.

"You'd better not. It'll only make him worse if you're here." Tom nodded, kissed her on the cheek, and left a minute later. Marlene went to her room, lay down, and waited to see what Justin would do. He didn't come out of his room again. She checked him in the morning and he was sound asleep, still dressed. She made breakfast for Noel, who looked calm.

"Did he come home last night?" he asked her. He had seen the note but hadn't heard his brother come in.

"Yes, he did." She didn't tell him in what condition or that he'd had a DUI.

"I thought he would," he said as he kissed her, grabbed his backpack, and left to catch the school bus.

Justin didn't emerge until noon, and said he had a terrible headache.

"I suspect that's the alcohol you drank, and not the concussion," she said quietly, and handed him a Tylenol. He took it and went back to bed. She walked into his room a few hours later, and sat down on his bed. He was lying there, awake. He looked at her but didn't say anything. She could see that he was sober. Noel wasn't home yet.

"Tom thinks you have a problem with alcohol. We found seven bottles and some marijuana in your room yesterday." He shot up to a sitting position and then winced and held his head.

"You had no right to go through my things!" he shouted at her.

"I had every right. I'm your mother. This is my house, and you were drunk, and driving. Tom thinks you should go to rehab. What do you think?" she asked in a gentle tone.

"I think you're a bitch, and Tom is an asshole!" he shouted at her. "And I won't go to rehab. You can't make me!" She didn't know if she could or not, but if he didn't want it, it wouldn't do him any good, and he wouldn't benefit from it. She stood up and didn't answer him. She walked out of his room and closed the door behind her. She didn't want to push it. The poor child had been through so much.

Chapter 17

Justin went back to school four days later. He had to take the school bus now, which was humiliating. The small car his parents had given him the year before was unsalvageable, and Marlene didn't intend to replace it until he stopped drinking.

He was slightly more civil to Marlene when he went back to school, but barely. She told Tom not to come by because she didn't want to provoke Justin, and she wanted things to calm down. She went to see Tom at his house on the nights that Juliet was at her mother's house, which was unpredictable, since they were no longer on a schedule, and Juliet could come and go. It was on demand, according to what Juliet wanted.

He and Marlene hadn't had sex since the scene Justin had witnessed. It just seemed safer not to until things settled down. And the whole episode had dampened their ardor a little.

* * *

Justin got drunk again that weekend, although Marlene didn't find the bottle in his room. He got dropped off at home by a friend Marlene had never seen before. When he got home, he went up to Noel's room and told him what he'd witnessed in the kitchen: their mother having sex with Juliet's father. Noel cried when Justin told him, and he asked his mother if it was true. She said it was. She said that Tom was a good person, and they loved each other. Noel asked her if she had loved his dad and, sobbing, she said she had loved him very much. She tucked him into bed that night while he cried, and for the first time in her life she hated one of her children. She hated Justin for the pain he was causing all of them, even his little brother.

She called Tom and told him what had happened. He realized how badly she needed someone to help her deal with this. Justin was out of control, and Noel couldn't cope with his brother's manipulations and shouldn't have to. Justin was playing his mother like a violin, and making her feel guilty because she had a man in her life who loved her. And she loved Tom. Justin couldn't face losing his father, the pain and grief were destroying him.

Justin slept off his latest drunken episode, while Noel went to sleep crying. Marlene lay in bed crying off and on all night. At his house, Tom fumed at how helpless he was, while Marlene tied his hands. He wanted to give Justin a piece of his mind. He wanted to protect Marlene from her own child and didn't know how. He fell asleep on his bed in his clothes at six in the morning, and an hour later, Marlene called him sobbing hysterically.

She had gone in to check on Noel in the morning, as she usually did, and found him unconscious. She didn't know if it was intentional or accidental, but his pump was out. She had a strong suspicion Noel had done it on purpose, as a feeble attempt at suicide, which wasn't so feeble. He knew what would happen if he didn't have his pump to deliver insulin to his body. He was in a coma and he was being airlifted to Saint Vincent's in a police helicopter. They were about to take off when she called Tom.

"Oh my God." He leapt out of bed and put his shoes on. "I'll be there as fast as I can get there." He grabbed his parka and ran out the door. The helicopter was already in the air.

Noel was out of the coma by the time Tom got there. He went straight to Noel's room and Marlene came out to talk to him in the hall. Noel had been given proper doses of insulin by then. He was in pediatric ICU, looking much better than he had when she found him. What she didn't know was whether the whole episode had been accidental or if Noel had wanted to kill himself because of what his brother told him. He said it was an accident, but she didn't believe him. Justin had turned into an alcoholic and was poisoning his brother's mind against Tom. It was all more complicated than she could deal with. They went to the cafeteria for coffee while Noel slept. Marlene was beside herself over what had happened and consumed with guilt.

A psychiatrist spoke to Noel that afternoon, and he confirmed that Noel said it had happened by accident. Marlene wanted to believe him, but she didn't. It was all her fault that her family was falling apart because she had fallen in love with Tom and her sons weren't willing to accept the idea that she had a right to have a man in her life after their father. It had happened quickly, but he was a good man and she loved him. They'd gotten off on the wrong foot and moved too fast for the boys, and the way Justin had discovered it was unfortunate.

Tom stayed with her all day, and they released Noel that evening when his blood sugar levels were stabilized. Tom drove them home, and he and Marlene felt like they'd been hit by a train. Their whole world had fallen apart ever since Justin had walked in on them making love in the kitchen. The fact that he was drunk seemed irrelevant to her. The real issue for her was that her sons didn't want her to have the relationship with Tom that had become so dear to her.

They rode quietly back to Fishtail as Noel dozed.

She put Noel to bed when they got home. Justin was out and hadn't left a note. She kissed Noel before he went to sleep, and he apologized for all the trouble he'd caused and promised to be more careful with his pump. He always had been before, which was why Marlene was suspicious about what had happened.

By the time she got back downstairs to Tom waiting for her in the living room, she felt like roadkill. She was crying again, but she knew what she had to do.

She spoke in a low voice so no one could hear her, but there was only Noel upstairs, drifting off to sleep quietly.

"I don't think I can see you anymore, Tom," she said sadly. "I love you very much and I want a life with you, if you want me, but we have to stop for a while, until my kids adjust to having lost their father." They'd had denial while he was dying for over a year, and it had only been three months since his death. They needed more time to adjust. They weren't being reasonable. They were acting as though his death had come as a total surprise. They wanted their mother burned on their father's funeral pyre, in some ancient barbaric rite. They seemed to think she didn't have a right to a life, or a man, in the future. She and Tom had been ready, but the boys weren't.

"Could I talk to them?" Tom asked her, and she just cried harder.

"It'll just make things worse. I need to be alone with them for a while, until they get used to their father being gone. And then we can start over, if you still want to. But for now, we can't see each other. Look what happened when Justin walked in on us. All hell broke loose. I've got one kid who's practically an alcoholic, and nearly killed himself driving drunk a few days ago, and a diabetic child who may have tried to commit suicide last night, all because of us. How can we go on seeing each other?"

"You have to put your foot down," he begged her, "and be strong with them."

"And if Justin dies, or Noel commits suicide, how will you feel then? We can't take the risk just so we can make love all day long. I don't want to see you for a few months, until our life gets sane again. Please understand. The boys are crazy right now, and they're making me crazy."

"They don't have the right to rob us of loving each other," he said.

"They can't stop me from loving you, but I can't see you right now for a while. I don't want to upset them."

"So you'd rather upset us, and deprive us?" She was sobbing as he said it, but he knew it wouldn't convince her. He bent down and kissed her gently.

"I love you. I'll be waiting when you think they're ready. Whenever that is." She looked at him longingly as he left her house. She spent the night crying and checking on Noel, who was sleeping peacefully with his insulin pump in place. Justin came home the next day as if nothing had happened. He was sober.

Juliet was worried about her father. She hadn't seen him look that rough since he and her mother had decided to separate.

"Are you okay, Dad?"

"Yeah. Sometimes life is complicated." But he didn't try to explain it to her. He kept thinking of Justin, who was an accident waiting to happen and was going to break his mother's heart, maybe sooner than later. Tom hoped not, but he couldn't see the situation with Justin turning out well. He tried not to think about Marlene, but it was impossible. He loved her.

Marlene told Anne what was happening, and Anne felt desperately sorry for her. She'd been having such a hard time with her boys ever since Bob's death. Anne talked to Pitt about it, and he said that Tom was the best thing that could happen to her, and he hoped she didn't blow it. The boys needed a firm hand to control them, particularly Justin, who was heading for disaster. He hoped that Marlene and Tom wouldn't give up.

Anne commented to Pitt that the stars must have been out of alignment, because she spoke to Pattie, and they had decided to tell Matt and Benjie about the baby they were having in April. Pattie wanted to tell them before Thanksgiving because it was starting to show, and she and Bill were so happy about it that they wanted to share it with the boys.

They had taken them out for a special lunch at their favorite restaurant and told them. Benjie burst into tears and told them he hated them, that they didn't need a baby and why were they having one, and even worse, it was going to be a girl. He had a jealous tantrum in the restaurant. Matt told them it was embarrassing, and his friends were going to think they were weird.

"Shit, Anne. We were so happy about it, and the boys are going crazy," Pattie said, disappointed and discouraged.

"They'll get over it when they see her," she reassured her friend. "And you had to tell them. You can see it. I noticed it the last time I saw you."

"I know. That's why we told them. What do I do now? Benjie said to send her back." She laughed. She hadn't lost her sense of humor. But her kids were giving them a tough time. And so were Marlene's. Pattie said that Bill was furious about the way they were behaving.

Peter and Juliet were doing fine, and were more in love than ever. They saw each other every day at school, and their other friends too, and balanced their time well. He had made the transition to a new school easier for her and came to dinner at her mother's house regularly. He liked her father too. Peter and Juliet were still behaving and trying to be good. They wanted to stay chaste for a little longer, before complicating things with adult responsibilities.

* * *

Anne talked to June a few days later. She was excited for Tim. Ted had called him from somewhere in South America, and he was coming home to see him for Thanksgiving. He'd been promising to come and see him ever since the mountain rescue. "Tim is so excited about it, he can't sleep. It's the first holiday his father will actually be here. So Tim won't be coming to Thanksgiving with me this year. I'll come alone if you don't mind." They always invited the friends who had no family and nowhere to go on Thanksgiving, June and Tim among them. She was still dating the pediatrician from St. Vincent's, and said it was going well. But he was going home to his relatives in Chicago, and their relationship was still new.

"I'm happy for Tim," Anne said quietly, hoping that Ted wouldn't break his promise this time. He had eventually stopped promising since he never came. But this time Tim had nearly lost his life on the mountain, and they really had something to be grateful for and celebrate. They all did. They had invited Harvey Mack too.

"Ted's arriving the night before Thanksgiving, and staying at a hotel with Tim in Billings," June told her. "It will be a big treat for Tim." She was happy for her son that his father was finally coming through for him. Tim had had enough disappointments from him to last a lifetime and had waited so long. Ted was finally proving himself to be a decent human being after all.

Anne was guardedly happy for them when she hung up. She still didn't trust Ted completely. His track record as a father was terrible.

* * *

The relationship that was flourishing, although Beth didn't talk about it, was Beth and Harvey's. There were no expectations on either side and no promises. They enjoyed each other's company, were fascinated by each other's histories, and were a surprisingly good though unusual match.

He took her to an old-fashioned but charming dance bar in Billings. It took them an hour to get there, but Beth loved it. The food was delicious and a small band in black tie played traditional dance music after dinner. They did the foxtrot and the waltz, and found that they could both do the tango. He was a surprisingly good dancer, and she felt like a small china doll in his arms. They were breathless when they got back to the table after a very long waltz, and Beth collapsed into the chair, laughing.

"You are the best dancer ever!" she complimented him. "I love this place. Promise me we'll come back again."

"Every night, if you like." He was beaming and pleased that she had enjoyed it so much. They ended the evening on a tender note, with a last slow dance to "Moon River," which was one of her favorite songs, and then he kissed her.

They found that they liked the same old movies, and they downloaded them on the nights that Juliet was with her father.

They were going at a slow, comfortable pace. It was turning into a sweet, old-fashioned romance. It made her feel foolish and giddy and young and optimistic about life all at once. She felt alive again, for the first time since the loss of her marriage.

He had the occasional emergency to deal with, and she found his work life interesting and varied. He loved reading what she wrote and made intelligent comments about it.

"Promise me you won't get trampled by an elk or a moose or a bison, or eaten by a bear. I'm enjoying your company. Please don't do anything to spoil it." The time she spent with him was so warm and pleasant she was increasingly afraid of something going wrong, like a helicopter crash or an avalanche—all the dangers he took for granted that worried her now.

Juliet had seen Harvey come and go ever since her mother returned to Fishtail. Beth insisted they were just friends. Juliet didn't believe her, but Beth was adamant about it. Juliet was happy for her. And she liked Harvey.

He took Beth back to their favorite dance bar the night before Thanksgiving. They had just sat down when he said he had something to tell her.

"Now is when you tell me that you have a wife and ten children you forgot to mention, or you're moving to a remote village on the Amazon or Kenya or Tanzania, and 'it's been fun, but' . . . "

"Is that what you think I'm going to do?" he asked her.

"Isn't that how life works, Harvey? You think you found the woman of your dreams, and she dies suddenly. Or the man you thought you'd spend the rest of your life with marries someone else or moves to Tokyo or Bogotá. I don't like getting attached to people anymore. I learned that with Tom. I thought we were set forever, then fifteen years later, it turns out he hated our life, and I'm at a dance bar in Montana, and I'm not even the same person anymore. People change, and happy endings don't happen very often." She believed that.

She wasn't a cynic, but she was no longer an optimist either, or very trusting. "I put all my eggs in one basket with Juliet, and one of these days, she'll wave goodbye and take off. I'm trying to brace myself for it. So, what were you going to say?" She was braced for the worst. They were so different that she fully expected him to say he didn't want to see her anymore. Nothing surprised her now. She just went along from day to day, and tried not to be shocked when the worst happened. Although losing Tom hadn't turned out to be the worst after all. She wouldn't have met Harvey if she and Tom hadn't divorced. But Harvey was fifteen years older, and maybe he wanted a twenty-year-old he could have babies with. Her reproductive equipment was still in working order, but at thirty-nine, she didn't want more children. For her, one was enough.

"You certainly are a long-winded pessimistic woman, but a fabulous dancer." He smiled at her. "That's all I wanted to tell you, and the simple fact that I've fallen in love with you, as unlikely as that is, with me, a forest ranger from Montana, and you, a successful writer from New York." They were both a great deal more than that, as they had discovered. She couldn't imagine what a future would look like with him, but maybe it didn't matter. She was smiling at what he had said, and all they needed for now was the present. It was very sweet.

"Do you suppose, Ms. Turner . . ." He had her name right now—her own, not Tom's. "Do you suppose that you would be brave enough and do me the honor of letting people know that we're dating? Or do you like the word 'courting' better? I rather like that one. It's old-fashioned but nice."

"And why would we want to do that? Tell them, I mean," she asked, looking intrigued.

"Because I'm proud to be with you, and I feel foolish hiding it. Your daughter looks like she thinks I'm going to arrest you whenever I show up."

"That shows that she's suspicious of me, not of you," Beth said with a grin. "I suppose it wouldn't hurt. Do I call you my beau or my boyfriend, if we're being old school?"

"Chief Ranger Mack," he said formally, with a grin.

"'My' Chief Ranger Mack? Or no possessive, just the title?"

"Whatever you prefer," he said, opening the car door for her, and she swept inside in the wide skirt she had worn to dance in.

She waited until they'd gotten a few miles down the highway on the way back to Fishtail. "This is where, after all the nice things you said, we get hit by a truck. We both get killed and the romance never happens."

"You watch terrible movies. I'll have to give you some homework assignments." He pulled off the road then, with the red light on the roof flashing, and turned to her. "This is where I tell you to shut up, because I love you." He kissed her then and left no doubt in her mind how he felt about her. She was smiling and breathless when he stopped.

"That was very nice. I guess we're not dead after all."

"Apparently not, and we're going to the Pollocks' for lunch tomorrow. May I escort you?"

"Yes, you may. Juliet is going with her father."

He drove up in front of her house. Juliet was at Tom's for the night and going straight to the Pollocks' from there. She had taken her dress with her.

Harvey walked Beth to the door and stood towering over her. She stepped neatly aside and smiled up at him. “Would you like to come in, Chief Ranger Mack?” she invited him, and he smiled broadly.

“Very much,” he said, walked in, and the door closed softly behind them.

Chapter 18

Tom and Marlene had survived more than a week of Marlene's self-imposed quarantine. Tom wasn't happy about it, but he had agreed to respect it. He had no idea how long she was going to impose it on them. Months probably. Maybe until the anniversary of Bob's death in August. But her children were still going to refuse to accept him. They had the upper hand now, with drunk driving accidents and a possible fumbled suicide, and he and Marlene had played right into their hands by getting caught making love in the kitchen. He still cringed when he thought about it. He missed Marlene terribly.

Juliet had just left for school. His housekeeper didn't come in on Tuesdays, so he was alone cleaning up the kitchen when the doorbell rang. At that hour, it was usually a FedEx from one of his clients. They were still amused by his new address in "Fishtail," Montana.

He opened the door with a distracted expression with his phone in one hand, juggling a stack of files in his other arm, expecting to see the FedEx man, and he found himself looking straight into Marlene's eyes. She was breathless and looked like she was about to rob a bank.

"Did something happen?" He was certain that Justin would do something bad again, it was just a question of when. "Is Noel okay? Justin?"

"They're fine. I'm not okay. Can I come in?"

"Sure." His heart beat faster just looking at her, and he tried not to let it show. Just being that close to her drove him insane. He wanted to reach out and hold her.

"I'm really not okay," she said bluntly. "I can't stand it. I miss you too much. I don't care what my kids think. I need you." She put her arms around his neck and kissed him. He was so startled, he dropped his armload of files on the floor and put his arms around her and pulled her tightly against him.

"I need you too," he said breathlessly, "like air. I love you. What are you saying to me? Are we going to have a showdown with your kids?"

"Not yet. Can't we keep it secret for a while?" she said, as he pulled her inside and closed the door.

"Whatever you want. I'll agree to anything, just so we can be together. Juliet won't be home 'til six." He grabbed her hand and raced her up to his bedroom. They flew into bed, tore off each other's clothes and made love, and then talked about how to handle the future. It was not going to be easy. Nothing was resolved, and Justin was still an accident waiting to happen, but Marlene was back in Tom's arms, and it was all he needed for now. They were addicted to each other. It was even more powerful, more flammable, and more dangerous than love.

All the usual cast of characters were coming to the Pollocks' for Thanksgiving lunch, plus a few new ones. Juliet and her parents would be there. Tom and Beth would be coming separately, but they were on good terms. June was coming without Tim, who would be spending the holiday with his father at a hotel in Billings. Her new beau was in Chicago, so she was alone but happier this year. The Browns and Matt and Benjie, who were practically family, would be there too. Marlene and her boys were coming. She had given them two options. They could stay home with her, if they couldn't stomach seeing Tom and being polite to him. Or, they could go to the Thanksgiving lunch and be courteous to him. They didn't have to be warm and fuzzy, but they had to be polite if they wanted to go to the lunch. They had opted for polite but said they wouldn't speak to him. The Pollocks had invited Harvey Mack, after his heroic rescue of their children. Including him was the least they could do. Thanks to him, they had much to be thankful for.

Anne had set a beautiful table, as she always did. Caterers had provided the traditional meal she served every year. It was everyone's favorite dinner. They had served it at lunchtime since their children were small. They were all bigger now. Benjie was the only younger child, and next year they'd have the Browns' new baby, who would be seven months old by then.

Juliet and Tom were the first to arrive, and Juliet disappeared to the playroom with Peter, supposedly to see a new video game, but in fact for a quick kiss, which their parents had figured out. Juliet was wearing a dark red velvet dress, which looked right for the season, and medium heels that her mother had allowed. Tom and Pitt were wearing suits and talking when the doorbell rang again. Pattie and Bill walked in. Her stomach had popped just in the last few weeks and she was wearing a navy wool dress which showed her baby bump. Pitt congratulated her and she beamed. Matt and Benjie were sulking visibly and disappeared to the playroom immediately. Then June appeared, with Tim, which was unexpected. He had red eyes and looked like he'd been crying.

Anne figured it out right away and hurried to tell the caterers to set another place at the table. June followed her into the kitchen to tell her what had happened, while Tim went to find the other kids.

"The sonofabitch called this morning, supposedly from Venezuela. He said he just couldn't get back in time and he was really sorry. 'Maybe' he'll make it for Christmas. I thought this year would really be different, because of the rescue. I hate that man. I hope he never calls Timmie to lie to him again."

"I'm so sorry," Anne said. "Poor Tim. Was he horribly upset?"

"He cried all morning. He didn't want to come because he was embarrassed. He told everyone he was going to Billings with his dad."

"I'm glad he came. We were sad that he wasn't going to be with us. What a terrible thing to do to a kid."

Marlene and the boys arrived after that. She was wearing an emerald green knit dress that showed off her figure. She looked nervous, and kept glancing at Noel and Justin, who avoided looking at Tom but said hello to everyone else. Marlene was praying there wouldn't be an explosion, but when she looked at Tom, she melted and there was no one else in the room for either of them. Their relationship was the worst kept secret in town. Anne had seated Tom and Marlene together. The boys were at the opposite end of the table. They'd have to get used to it someday, and they could blame Anne if they didn't like their seats.

Beth was the last guest to arrive. She stood in the doorway with Harvey looming behind her like her own private mountain that she had brought with her. It looked like they had coincidentally arrived at the same time when he walked in behind her and greeted Anne and Pitt. Everyone was happy to see her. She, too, was wearing a red dress. It looked terrific on her with its short, swirling skirt. Harvey was smiling, and he handed Anne a big bouquet of orange and yellow roses.

"From both of us," he said clearly, so everyone could hear. Tom looked surprised, and so did the Browns, but the others didn't. Marlene had seen Harvey going into Beth's house, and Juliet had been teasing her mother about him for weeks. Anne had had a feeling about it. She took the bouquet from him and thanked them both, as the children came upstairs for dinner, all looking clean and neat in blazers and gray slacks, or jackets and jeans. Harvey was wearing a dark blue suit that had been made for him.

Beth smiled at them all for an awkward moment, as Anne took the bouquet to be put in a vase.

"We're dating," Beth said. The others stared at them and smiled and she grinned up at Harvey.

"How was that? Was that good?"

"It was clear. Mine was a little more subtle."

"Should I be subtle?" she asked him. "I thought we were going to tell people."

"I think we just did. Now we can act normal and pretend like we didn't say it." The others were laughing by then, and even Tom was grinning.

"She doesn't like telling people her business," Tom explained to Harvey. "We were married for two years before she would introduce me to her friends. You're way ahead of the game."

"We're just dating," she explained. "We're not living together." Harvey was smiling at her and looked like he was going to burst he was so proud to be with her.

They all took their places and Anne said grace. She had seated Juliet next to Peter. Everyone relaxed as the meal appeared. Tim had cheered up as he heaped the delicious food on his plate and signed to his mother: *Fuck him*. She laughed and knew who he meant.

"We're having a baby," Benjie said with a look of disgust as they passed the food around. "And worse news: It's a girl." They all laughed but Matt looked mortified and rolled his eyes, looking at Peter.

They laughed and talked all through lunch. Pitt served a very fine wine. Halfway through the meal, he realized something and went to the guest powder room. Justin had left the table for a few minutes. He found him there chugging a bottle of red wine. He had splashed some on his shirt.

"I don't serve wine to minors, son." He gently took it from him.

"I'm not your son. I just turned eighteen. You can't tell me what to do."

"You're a minor 'til you're twenty-one, and in my own house I can tell you what to do. I think your dad would be disappointed right now. Your mom needs your support, Justin. Don't give her a hard time."

"My dad is dead and my mom is a whore," he said viciously. Pitt's heart ached as he listened. Justin was heading in a bad direction. He was a totally different boy now than the sweet kid he always had been.

"Let's all enjoy Thanksgiving. We'll talk about this at another time soon. I'd like to help if I can."

"You can't," Justin said. "No one can." Pitt could tell he'd already been drinking, and he had put away half a bottle of the Bordeaux. Tom was right, he decided. Justin needed to go to rehab, and he was sure he would refuse to go. They both went back to the table then, and Pitt told one of the caterers to keep close track of the wine. Marlene wondered what had happened and was worried. Tom had already guessed, and he saw the wine stains on Justin's shirt. Pitt looked as calm and unruffled as always, and he and Anne exchanged a warm look.

There were half a dozen different pies for dessert, and they had coffee in the living room. At five o'clock everyone left. Marlene went home with her sons, and Juliet went home with Tom. Harvey went to Beth's house. They watched a movie, and then he had to work that night. He always had taken the shifts on holidays, since he had no family to be with, but things had changed. Tom and Juliet were coming over, and Peter was coming too. They were all too full to eat another meal, but they wanted to be together.

"The Wylie boy, the older one, is on a bad track," Harvey commented to Beth.

"I don't think Marlene knows what to do. She's in love with my ex-husband and her boys don't want her dating anyone."

"By some people's standards, it's a little soon after Bob died, but Justin needs a leash put on him. He's going to wind up in trouble," he predicted. Beth hoped he was wrong. "Remember what I told you when I met you. Anger is just a cover for fear. You were mad as hell that night."

"I was just scared Juliet was going to die on the mountain."

"So was I, for all of them. But it didn't happen. We all got lucky, and the National Guard saved the day."

"So did you," she said. He had called them in and had organized his rangers valiantly.

"I was scared we wouldn't get them all off the mountain, and we'd lose one or two," he admitted. "But I was determined not to let that happen. That kid is scared of life without his father, of what's going to happen to them, of what his mother is going to do. I know Marlene, and I like her a lot, but she needs to rope both of those kids in—Justin anyway, to make him feel safe. She's as frightened as he is. She doesn't know what to do, and she's letting them bully her." Beth suspected that his assessment was accurate, but she wouldn't have liked to be in Marlene's shoes. She was enjoying her own these days.

"What makes you so wise?" she asked him, smiling.

"I'm old and I love you. You made a difference. I wanted to show you I could bring them home safely, and I did. Maybe I couldn't have done it if you hadn't gotten so mad at me." He kissed her then, and left for work a few minutes later. He kept a uniform in her closet.

Juliet and Tom arrived with Peter a little while later, and Anne had sent a ton of leftovers with them for that night or the next day.

"Where's Harvey?" Juliet asked, looking around.

"He went to work."

"I like him," she said to her mother.

"Me too," Beth said with a grin.

They watched one of the movies Harvey had "assigned" her that night, and ended up eating some of Anne's delicious leftovers after all.

Chapter 19

The days between Thanksgiving and Christmas rushed by in a kaleidoscope of colors. Beth was going to spend Christmas Eve dinner with Juliet at Tom's house, and on Christmas night Juliet was going back to her house for dinner. Harvey was working. The day after Christmas, Tom was taking Juliet to Aspen to ski. Everyone had their own plans for the holiday. Marlene and the boys would be spending their first Christmas without their father, and knew it would be hard.

June's doctor friend was taking her and Tim skiing. They hadn't heard from Ted again, and June wondered if they ever would. A door had closed for Tim when Ted hadn't shown up at Thanksgiving. You could only be disappointed so many times. Tim no longer wanted to play and would never believe his father again.

The Browns and Pollocks were staying home.

Marlene cooked dinner for the boys on Christmas Eve, and Justin went out after dinner. He said he was meeting friends, but didn't tell her where as usual. And he borrowed her car to do it. She and Noel watched movies on her computer. They went to bed at midnight, and left out cookies and milk for Santa, as they always did. Marlene loved their old traditions.

She was sound asleep at two A.M. when the phone rang. It was Justin. He was crying.

"Are you hurt?" she asked him.

"No, but I totaled your car, Mom." It was the only car she had, since he had already totaled his own.

"Did you hurt anyone else?"

"I don't know. I don't think so." She realized then that he was drunk. He was slurring his words.

"Where are you?"

"I'm in jail."

"What are they charging you with?"

"Drunk driving, I think. Can you come and get me?"

"Let me speak to the officer." Justin was alive and probably not hurt, or he wouldn't be calling her from jail. He'd be in the hospital if he was injured. She was strangely calm this time and asked the officer the pertinent questions. This was his second DUI, so she knew they'd be harder on him than the first time, and he was eighteen now.

They told her that he couldn't be bailed out until the judge set bail at the arraignment, and the arraignment would be the day after Christmas. Justin was going to spend Christmas in jail, and in her heart of hearts, she knew he deserved it. She explained it to him when the officer gave him back the phone.

"I can't do anything about it," she told her son.

"What about Pitt? Can't he get me out?"

"No. You're stuck there until the arraignment, and they may put you in jail this time. I can't do anything about that either." She felt sorry for him, and for Noel and herself. It was going to be a sad Christmas without him. And she was stranded now without a car.

Justin was crying when they hung up. She could hear the raucous sounds of the jail behind him, on Christmas Eve. It was a depressing way to spend Christmas. His first without his father, who would have been so upset about him.

She lay awake for a long time that night, thinking about Justin and what she was going to do.

She called Tom early the next morning and told him what had happened.

"Thank God he didn't kill himself driving drunk," he said to her. "They may send him to jail for a while this time."

"I told him the same thing. Maybe this is what he needs. It's a hell of a wakeup call." She sounded tired and disappointed. "The arraignment is tomorrow."

"I'll go with you . . . oh shit . . . I'll be in Aspen with Juliet. We leave in the morning."

"I'll manage." She'd have to rent a car until she could get a new one. And pay a lawyer for Justin. He was playing an expensive game. His father would have been livid.

"I'm so sorry, Marlene. You don't deserve this."

Tom called her again that afternoon, and he brought her Christmas present. It was a gold chain necklace with a gold heart on it. Justin hadn't called her again, and she couldn't call him. Noel had cried when she told him where Justin was.

"He's really screwed up, Mom. He's been smoking pot and drinking."

"I know."

They had a tender Christmas in spite of Justin. Marlene didn't visit him in jail. He needed to learn the lesson.

The day after Christmas, Tom came to give her a quick kiss before he and Juliet left for Aspen. She had given him a navy-blue cashmere sweater and he was wearing it.

She went to court for Justin's arraignment. She had brought him a suit for his court appearance. The judge refused to give him bail, fined him five hundred dollars, suspended his license, and sentenced him to six months in a rehab facility, or in jail, whichever he preferred. He chose the rehab. He was delivered there by the sheriff the next day. His mother had a right to visit him after the first two weeks. She couldn't see him before then. He looked pale and exhausted when she saw him in court. The rehab facility he was going to wasn't a posh one. They were known to be tough on the residents, who were under lockdown so he couldn't run away. She couldn't protect him this time, or make it easier for him. He had to face what he'd done. He wouldn't get his license back for six months. He had to attend high school classes while he was there, which he hated too. And he had to keep his grades up. Marlene was still adamant about his going to college, and fortunately his DUI was a misdemeanor again. But private colleges might not accept him with two DUI convictions. He might go to a state college.

She did a lot of thinking while Tom was in Aspen, and she finally knew what she had to do. It wasn't what she wanted, and things weren't turning out the way she had hoped. But Bob was gone, and she needed a change. She couldn't just switch horses and hope that someone else would take care of her. It wasn't fair to Tom, no matter how crazy he was about her, and she was about him. She was using him, and now she realized it. She had to stand on her own two feet, at least for a while, no matter how much it scared her.

She told Tom when he got back. She had already made the arrangements and spoken to the lawyer in her office. She was selling him their law practice, and putting their house up for sale. She needed a fresh start. And she had to get out of Fishtail.

"I'm going back to Denver," she explained to Tom. "I have family there, even though my parents are gone. I can get a job in a law firm or start my own practice. Bob wanted to come here, I didn't. I always let him decide everything for me. Now I have to get my kids in control. Justin will be in rehab until the end of June. I'm moving the day after New Year's. I have to get Noel enrolled in school. Denver will be better for us. At least for a time. I don't want to go and I'm sad to leave you, but if I stay here, I'm just going to hang all over you and Justin will run wild. You don't deserve to have the burden of two kids who think they hate you and will give you a hard time. I have to solve my own problems now. And they need time to get over their father's death. Maybe we can make this work later, but not now. It really was too soon."

Tom had been thinking about it too, and he knew she was right. He was crazy about her, but crazy was the operative word. He needed peace in his life now, not insanity. He couldn't inherit all of her problems and two angry boys. Marlene had to clean up her own mess and get back on her feet, on her own this time. He knew he couldn't do it for her, no matter how much he wanted to.

She told Anne and Pattie that she was leaving, and wished Pattie luck with the baby. She promised to stay in touch and tell them where she was living.

She had told Justin they were moving to Denver, and he didn't like it, but that was too bad. He had to pay the consequences for what he'd done. It could have been a lot worse. He could have killed someone or himself.

All the boys came to say goodbye to Noel, and he promised to come and visit, or have them visit him. When she sold the house in Fishtail, she could buy one in Denver, and until then they'd be living in an apartment.

They drove out of Fishtail the day after New Year's, in the van she had rented. The rest of her things were coming later. She felt like a grown-up for the first time in a long time, and she was scared. She could see that Noel was too. He was facing the unknown and so was she. They were both sad to leave Fishtail and their friends. And she was sad to leave Tom.

"It's okay to be scared," she told Noel, "just as long as you're honest with yourself. We're all scared sometimes. You were scared on the mountain, I'll bet. But you came through it. That's the challenge. You win by seeing it through. We'll get through this together. And Justin will too. You survived three days lost on a mountain. Compared to that, this is a piece of cake."

Tom had come to say goodbye before they left. They had started a fire that had turned into a blaze. It was bigger than both of them and had gotten out of control, like the fire on Granite Peak. It was contained now, but still smoldering. Tom didn't kiss her goodbye. He knew that if he did, the obsession would start all over again. And for now it had to stop, for both of them. He was still watching as the car drove away. And he knew he'd miss her terribly.

She smiled at her son and he turned the radio on, as they drove away, and headed for Denver. It was a new life. A new day. For both of them.

Chapter 20

By the end of March, Pattie could hardly move. The baby was a girl but it felt twice the size of her boys when she carried them. She felt like a beached whale, and she still had three weeks to go. Benjie had finally started to get excited about the baby, even though it was a girl. Matt still acted like she was stealing a beach ball under her dress when he went out with her. The whole idea that his mother was having a baby at her age, which wasn't very old, when he was a teenager, was mortifying. He tried to pretend he didn't know her at the grocery store.

Bill had been busier this time than he'd been when she'd had the boys. She hardly saw him. She had lunch with Anne and June whenever they had time. She couldn't wait to have the baby so she'd have something to do.

She was putting the breakfast dishes in the dishwasher when she saw that Bill had forgotten his phone. She was going to call and tell him but decided to walk over to his office and take it to him. She needed the exercise, and it was a sunny day. It had finally stopped snowing and was starting to feel like spring. She picked the phone up to put it in her purse, and it came alive in her hand. He had a text coming in, and by pure reflex, she opened it. He never locked his phone. She thought at first that it was some kind of spam, one of those sex messages that pop up and belong in junk mail or the trash.

"Time for a quickie before lunch? I'll be naked waiting for you in the conference room. Guess what? I'm for lunch!" She read it again and made a face. It was from someone named Kitty. The only Kitty she knew was the new bookkeeper at the ranch office, whom she hadn't met yet. She was twenty-two years old, supposedly with breasts the size of melons, according to Bill's secretary. She realized then that this wasn't spam. It was a real message to Bill. She stopped walking and responded to see what would happen. "Love to. What time?"

She responded quickly. "Same as always, Big Boy. Anytime you want to come in my mouth." She felt sick as she read it. Bill was having sex at the office with the bookkeeper he'd recently hired. And then a random text: "Can you get out tonight?"

"Sure. Your place?" Pattie texted rapidly, not even feeling guilty. She wanted to kill him. What had he been doing, and how long had it been going on? And how many other Kittys had there been?

Kitty responded, "Of course. You've got the key. Use it. See ya at noon. Conference room." She dropped the phone like it was on fire and burning her hand. She wasn't sure if she should ignore it, confront him, hire a detective, call a lawyer, or just sit down and cry. She felt as though there was a white hot blaze raging inside her that she couldn't put out. She was too angry and too hurt. She was carrying his baby and he was screwing around.

Afterwards she didn't know how she'd had the guts to do it, but she picked up the phone, went back to the house, waited until a few minutes after noon, then went to the office, counting on the chance that no one knew about their rendezvous except the two of them. At ten after twelve, she found one of the assistants in his office, put on her sweetest Mrs.-Brown-I'm-a-mommy face, and told her she had accidently locked her purse in the conference room. Without hesitating, the girl handed her the key. She walked to the conference room, unlocked the door and walked in. The twenty-two-year-old bookkeeper was lying on the conference table with her legs as far apart as she could get them, and Bill was slamming into her and moaning. The room was soundproofed, so he knew no one would hear them. Pattie had closed the door silently behind her and stood staring at her husband.

"Having fun?" she said loud enough for them both to hear her. He opened his eyes and looked like he was going to have a heart attack. The girl looked annoyed, as he pulled out of her, and she spun around like a gymnast.

"Who's that?" she said in a loud angry voice. And then, "Oh fuck, is that her?" She had seen the belly and knew instantly, although she hadn't met Pattie yet. But she knew the boss's wife was pregnant. She'd only been working there for two months and Pattie rarely went to the office and she'd been busy at home.

"Yes, it is," Pattie answered. She wasn't even embarrassed. She was too angry to be. "Nice lunches you have here," she said, then threw the keys at him and walked out of the room. He came after her as fast as he could get his pants up and run.

"What the hell are you doing?" he said to her in a loud whisper, his voice and face contorted with unfinished sex and rage.

She stopped and wanted to hit him. "What am I doing? Are you kidding? *What am I doing?* What the hell are *you* doing while I carry your baby?"

"The baby was your idea," he said, grabbing her by the arm.

"I'll tell you what I'm doing. I'm calling a lawyer. And you're packing and getting out of my house."

"Our house," he raged at her, as people at their desks started to stare.

"It's not our house anymore. It's mine. I want a divorce. You're a lying, cheating sonofabitch." She had kept his phone to show her lawyer, if she needed evidence. As much as she had loved him before, she hated him now. She walked straight out of the building, got in her car, drove to the Pollocks', and told Anne what had happened. She was shaking when she told her.

"You'd better calm down or you'll have the baby right now," Anne warned her, and handed her a glass of water. She took a sip.

"I'm a nurse. I'll deliver it myself," Pattie said. "Shit, I can't believe this. How long has he been doing it? He's a complete asshole." Anne wondered if Pattie would ever forgive him. She wasn't sure she would have. Pattie stayed for half an hour, calmed down a little, and went home to call a lawyer.

She told him what had happened. They had no prenup and Montana was an equitable distribution state, so half of everything Bill had was hers, even though she hadn't worked. "I want a divorce," she told the lawyer.

"Why don't we slow down for a minute. Don't you want to have a conversation with Mr. Brown?"

"About what? Sex in the office? Their lunch menu?"

"Why don't we talk in the morning? I've got a meeting in ten minutes."

"Fine. Start the ball rolling. Call me tomorrow at nine-thirty." She was mad at the world and hated her husband. Bill was home half an hour later.

"I don't call that a quickie," she said when she saw him. "You took an hour."

"What the hell happened?" He had no idea how she'd found out.

"You left your phone on the breakfast table."

"You read my texts?" He was furious but didn't have a leg to stand on.

"Yes, I did. You can read mine anytime. She wanted you to come in her mouth. Did you?"

"What is wrong with you?"

"What's wrong with *me*? You're asking me that? You're a miserable, cheating sonofabitch. And don't come to the hospital to see the baby, which was apparently my idea. I don't want to see you, and you're not welcome to see the baby. The only place I want to see you is in court after this." She slammed into her dressing room and closed and locked the door. She came out an hour later, and hoping that he had packed and left. He was still standing there when she opened the door.

"I want my phone." He looked ashen, and she saw a suitcase standing next to him.

"I'm sending it to my lawyer as evidence. Get another one, while you can still afford to." She was going to take him for every penny she could get. He decided that the best course of action was to leave and negotiate later, when she had calmed down.

She never did. She went into labor four days later, two weeks before her due date. Anne went to the hospital with her. It was an easy delivery and Pattie only stayed in the hospital for two days. She called her lawyer two hours after the delivery. She was serious. She wanted a divorce and nothing Bill tried to say to her made a difference. He had betrayed her and their sixteen-year marriage.

"Hell hath no fury like . . ." his lawyer had warned him. "You cheat and get caught, it's going to cost you."

"That's ridiculous. I own the ranch."

"You married young and had no prenup. We're an equitable state. She owns half of it. Half of *all* of what you have. And she's out for blood." Her lawyer had already called him and told him her terms.

"She won't let me see the baby," Bill complained. He wasn't that excited about it, but she was his child too.

Pattie refused to speak to him, and she demanded a full appraisal of the ranch. It would take months to give it to her. Her lawyers were relentless and they had forensic accountants. Bill was in shock. She was actually going through with it.

Anne and Pitt felt sorry for the kids. Matt and Benjie were upset that their parents were getting divorced. She had named the new baby Penny, and she was three months old the first time Bill saw her, with two armed bodyguards present to ensure that Bill didn't abduct her since she was so young. Anne didn't trust him, and she had good reason not to. Matt didn't understand why his mother was so mad at his father. Benjie had supervised visits with his father. At fifteen, Matt could express his wishes, and wanted to see his father two weekends a month and occasionally for dinner. Penny was too young for visitation.

Privately, Bill told the Pollocks that Pattie had gone insane, maybe from the pregnancy. But they knew the whole story. They thought Pattie was going to extremes, but Pitt suspected that this wasn't the first time he had cheated on her. Bill had hinted at his exploits before and Pitt hadn't taken him seriously then. Now he did. They felt as though they had lost members of their family. Pitt still saw Bill for lunch, but Anne had taken Pattie's side. It was a bloody battle, and their court appearances and depositions were scheduled to start in July. They'd be doing that for the rest of the year and maybe longer.

The one thing Pattie hated most was a cheater. Her father had been one. She had suspected Bill of cheating on her before but he denied it. Now she knew it was true. She'd seen it. And in retrospect she realized he had cheated the other times too.

Bill rented a house in town and lived there while he came to work every day to run the ranch. Pattie had a court order forbidding him from entering the house, and his lawyer advised him to obey it, or she'd enforce it and put him in jail. She wasn't kidding.

He had fired Kitty immediately, also on advice of counsel, and saw her occasionally at his house in town, as well as a waitress from the diner, or other pretty young girls he met around town.

Pattie's goal, once she settled the terms of the divorce, was to stay in Fishtail for the next three years, so as not to disrupt her kids, and then move to L.A. when Matt left for college. She was ready for a bigger life, and she was planning to take the children and half of Bill's money with her.

Pitt and Anne were crushed to see what had happened, but Bill turned out not to be the man they thought he was. People around town were talking and he'd had casual affairs with many women.

Tom was thinking of buying the Browns' house when Pattie left, and Bill said he would sell the ranch to Pitt to expand his operation. He needed the land for his horses, and Bill was talking about moving to Texas and starting over with the money he'd have left.

Tom wanted to put down roots in Fishtail. It had been the right move for him. And he loved the idea of buying the Browns' big, beautiful house, even in three years. He wanted a real home there. He intended to stay.

Beth's divided life between New York and Fishtail was working and so was her relationship with Harvey. He had been to New York with her twice and loved it. He loved all the cultural options there, and enjoyed them all, theater, opera, symphony, ballet, museums.

With his parents' bitter divorce, Matt was closer than ever to the Pollocks, and went there all the time. Noel came back from Denver every chance he got, so Matt, Peter, Tim, Noel, and Juliet were still the closest friends. The bond they'd formed on Granite Peak would last forever.

In July, it was the anniversary of the day the kids got lost on the mountain. Beth remembered it all vividly. A year later, so many things had changed. The parents who had shared the agony had dispersed.

Anne and Pitt were still there. Pattie and Bill were at war and intended to move away. Bob Wylie had died, and Marlene was living in Denver with Noel and trying to find her way. Justin had gotten out of rehab in June, and had done well. He was sober and starting at the University of Montana in September, and was excited about it. He had a summer job at a dude ranch in Wyoming, and had grown up a lot. Tom was still recovering from Marlene, and had to fight himself not to follow her to Denver, but it was still too complicated for now. She had been an obsession at the wrong time for both of them. But maybe in time things would be different. They had rushed it too soon after Bob's death. He recognized that now. They spoke on the phone from time to time. And Noel and Justin had calmed down about him. Their moving to Denver had been the right decision for now. Tom had been love-starved after Beth, and Marlene had dazzled him, and she needed him. Beth didn't. June was still dating the pediatrician from Billings. They were talking about getting married and Tim loved him. He was like a father to him, and the doctor wanted to adopt him.

Beth and Harvey had been dating for nine months. It wasn't an eternity, but it was a longish time. He had saved their children, and he and Beth were still discovering each other: the stories, their histories, the hidden facets, their childhoods, their fears, the things that made them happy. Their relationship was based on admiration and joy. They loved doing things together, in Montana and New York. They enhanced each other's lives. A year later, she was happy living in Fishtail and going to New York less frequently, but often enough to keep life interesting. Juliet loved living and going to school in Fishtail. She liked Harvey, and she was still in love with Peter, with his parents as their role models.

Beth wondered if the real challenge had been the mountain or just life, or were they one and the same? She hadn't figured it out yet. Maybe she never would. Life was like the mountain. Ever challenging, frightening at times, dangerous, exciting, deceptive, alluring, with hidden crevasses and ravines. And then at last, you went home, with the memories and the victory that you had survived it.

"What are you thinking?" Harvey asked her, as she stared at Granite Peak, which had been their nightmare a year ago and seemed so peaceful now.

"I was thinking that you changed everything when you saved the children. Life would be so different now if you hadn't."

"I was lucky," he said modestly.

"So was I." She smiled at him. The mountain had been treacherous, the ultimate challenge, and he was the unexpected gift, the surprise after they won. It was the sweet spot that you never knew what life had in store. Some had lost, some had won, some had gone home with the prize, some were gone. But for now, she and Harvey were happy. She was grateful for that and for him every day. And for her daughter. And she and Tom were friends now.

"Do you want to go dancing tonight?" Harvey asked her, and she smiled.

"Yes, I do." They had much to celebrate, and she hoped they would continue to for a long time.

"So do I," he said, and they walked down the path hand in hand, to the same spot where the children had left the mountain and had been saved a year before. It was holy land.

About the Author

DANIELLE STEEL has been hailed as one of the world's bestselling authors, with a billion copies of her novels sold. Her many international bestsellers include *The Wedding Planner, Worthy Opponents, Without a Trace, The Whittiers, The High Notes, The Challenge, Suspects, Beautiful,* and other highly acclaimed novels. She is also the author of *His Bright Light,* the story of her son Nick Traina's life and death; *A Gift of Hope,* a memoir of her work with the homeless; *Expect a Miracle,* a book of her favorite quotations for inspiration and comfort; *Pure Joy,* about the dogs she and her family have loved; and the children's books *Pretty Minnie in Paris* and *Pretty Minnie in Hollywood.*

daniellesteel.com
Facebook.com/DanielleSteelOfficial
Twitter: @daniellesteel
Instagram: @officialdaniellesteel

Look for

Palazzo

coming soon in hardcover

A stirring novel about the legacies families inherit, create, and carry on, from #1 *New York Times* bestselling author Danielle Steel.

Chapter 1

Cosima Saverio sat on the terrace of her penthouse apartment in Rome, looking out over the familiar monuments and rooftops of the city as the sun came up. In the distance, she could see Saint Peter's Basilica and Vatican City, the dome of the San Carlo al Corso Basilica, and to the north, the Villa Medici and the Borghese Gardens. It was a view she never tired of. It was her favorite time of day, before the city sprang to life. It was already warm and would be hot by midmorning. As she stood at the rail of the balcony a few minutes later, she could see below the Piazza di Spagna, the Spanish Steps, the Fontana della Barcaccia, and the Trinità dei Monti church.

The apartment was conveniently located on the top floor of the store, which was her family business. The Saverios made the finest leather goods in all of Italy, or all of Europe, rivaled only by Hermès, which was a worldwide enterprise. Saverio leathers were sold only in their two stores, one in Venice, the other in Rome.

Like all of her ancestors, Cosima had been born in Venice, to an illustrious family that traced its history back to the fifteenth century. The Palazzo Saverio in Venice still belonged to them, although her father had moved the family to Rome shortly after her younger sister, Allegra, was born, and Cosima had lived in the same apartment with her parents and brother and sister on the top floor over the store almost all her life. Her younger brother, Luca, had his own villa now on the Via Appia Antica, and her sister lived in a smaller apartment on the floor below her, with a design studio. It was more convenient for Allegra because it had an elevator, which didn't go to the top floor. Cosima lived in solitary splendor in the same apartment she had grown up in. She reached the penthouse apartment by a narrow staircase, and the terrace gave her a three-hundred-and-sixty-degree view of the city she considered her home. Venice was their history, but Rome was where she lived and worked, and ran the family business she had inherited fifteen years before, at twenty-three.

As a young girl, it had never been her plan to run the business or even work there. When they were children, her father intended to have her younger brother, Luca, run it one day, and step into his shoes. Luca had never shown any interest in it, even as a boy. His friends had been the spoiled, indulged sons of other Italian noblemen, and he had a passion for fast cars and beautiful women at an early age. He didn't have his father's interest in business, or his grandfather's talent for creating beauty as a remarkable artisan. Ottavio Saverio had designed each piece for his shop in Venice, whether a saddle or an alligator handbag or an exquisite pair of custom-made shoes. People who were familiar with the finest of everything could recognize a piece created by Saverio anywhere.

Ottavio Saverio had been the eighth child and only son of a respected banker in Venice. He had inherited the palazzo in Venice by default when each of his sisters married and moved away to Florence, Rome, and other cities in Europe. None of them wished to be burdened by the palazzo where they'd grown up. It was four centuries old and troublesome and expensive to maintain. Ottavio had used his inheritance to buy all of his sisters' shares of the palazzo. He had used what was left to establish the store in one of the narrow streets off the Piazza San Marco where he created his magnificent leather pieces, and gained a reputation throughout Italy, and eventually Europe, for the exquisite work he did. Each piece was a masterpiece of beauty and luxury, made of the finest leathers and exotic skins. Every creation was unique at first. He filled the orders quickly and the business grew into an astonishing success in less than a decade. For all the years that he ran it, he was the master craftsman and genius behind the name. Saverio products were sold only at the store in Venice. Women waited a year or even two for their orders to be filled and were never disappointed by the results. Ottavio's list of clients included royals, famous women, movie stars, and wealthy people from all over the world.

His son and only child, Alberto, never became a craftsman like his father, although Ottavio made him study as an apprentice for two years so he would understand the products they were selling and how they were made. But Alberto was more interested in the business side of the store. Once he inherited the company, Alberto maintained his father's tradition that Saverio products were sold only in their own store and nowhere else.

When his father died, Alberto kept the store in Venice, and moved his wife, Tizianna, and their three children to Rome. He bought the building that still housed their store, and built the apartment that had previously been home to their whole family and where Cosima lived alone now on the top floor. She had designed Allegra's apartment on the floor below, when she was old enough to live alone, so they each had privacy. Luca had already moved out by then, when he turned twenty-one and Allegra was still only seventeen.

When their father opened the store in Rome, it was spectacular and increased the business exponentially. Alberto had groomed his son to run the business ever since he was a little boy, but he had never succeeded in capturing Luca's interest. Luca neither understood nor cared about the magic of what they made.

What Alberto had wanted was to have their business grow without giving up any of his father's traditions. It was a fine line between the two, and Alberto had grandiose plans that were always just slightly more expensive to implement than he'd anticipated, so the business wasn't as profitable as it should have been. He had a flawless eye for quality and beauty and was an extremely elegant man himself. He and Tizianna were among the social leaders of both Venice and Rome and exuded an aura of elegance and style.

Cosima inherited some of that, but she had a more retiring nature than her parents and loved her studies. She'd always been relieved that she would never have to run the business. She worked at the store in Rome for a month every summer to please her father. She was a dutiful daughter. Luca managed to escape that because he was five years younger than Cosima, and Allegra was still a child.

In July and August the family went to their other home in Sardinia. They spent two months on the family's boats and entertaining the friends they invited to stay with them. Invitations to their home were greatly sought after. Alberto and Tizianna were fabulous hosts, and were invited everywhere in return, or by new friends in the hopes of being invited to stay in their home. They were generous with their hospitality and lavish with their guests. Cosima still remembered the extravagant parties her parents gave, both in their apartment in Rome and at the palazzo in Venice, where they held grand balls.

After lengthy discussions with her father, Cosima had chosen a career in the law. She went to university in Rome and lived at home. She loved her years at university, her studies, and the friends she made. Her father teased her that she would be the attorney for the business one day. He never expected her to practice law, but he thought it would be useful for her in business, if she didn't marry first. Her mother had never worked, and he didn't expect his daughters to.

Allegra, the youngest of the three children, had inherited her grandfather's talent and had a passion for design. She was always sketching a dress or a bag or a shoe on a scrap of paper. She had a bright, happy nature and enjoyed living on the fringe of her parents' busy social life even when she was very young. They would let her stay at their parties for a short time, and she always wished she could stay for the entire evening. Cosima was less interested in their parties but always had a flock of suitors among the sons of their friends, even though Allegra was far more flirtatious than her older sister by nature. Cosima always had a more serious, studious side, much more so than her younger brother and sister.

Luca was five years younger than Cosima and Allegra was nine years younger than her older sister, four years younger than Luca, and hated being treated like a baby. She couldn't wait to grow up and discover a broader world. Luca hated spending time with his family and preferred to be with his own friends. He had a wild side in his teens. His parents struggled to curb it with little success.

At twenty-three, Cosima had one year of law school in Rome left to complete. She arrived at the family home in Sardinia after working at the store for a month during her school holiday, as she always did. She worked in the administrative offices, not with the customers, and won high praise every year for her efficiency. She had the precise mind of a future lawyer, and also her mother's blond beauty. Allegra and Luca had their father's dark hair, and Cosima and Allegra both had their mother's deep blue eyes. Tizianna was from Florence, and Cosima had her typically Florentine fine-featured beauty. Luca and his father had classic aristocratic faces that belonged on a Roman coin.

The summer before Cosima's final year in law school, she arrived in Sardinia just as her parents were about to leave for a weekend in Portofino with friends who had a home there and had just bought a new speedboat. Luca was supposed to go with them, but a party in Porto Rotondo given by friends of his changed his mind at the last minute and he decided to stay in Sardinia. Cosima stayed in Sardinia with him. She was tired after having worked six days a week at the store for the last month. So her parents left for the weekend and took fourteen-year-old Allegra with them, since their hosts had a daughter the same age. They had a son close to Luca's age too, but Luca found him dull and was happy to escape the weekend in Portofino. Even the lure of the new speedboat didn't sway him.

The house was quiet after they left. Luca disappeared immediately with his friends, and Cosima relaxed and lay in the sun and was happy to have some time alone. She knew they were expecting a house full of guests the following weekend and her parents would expect her to help entertain them, so she was happy to have time to read and take it easy before they came back.

The weekend in Portofino ended in disaster. The hosts allowed their exuberant, reckless nineteen-year-old son to drive them all in the new speedboat. He collided with another boat at full speed, going dangerously fast in the new boat he wasn't familiar with. The two boats crashed and exploded in midair. Both sets of parents were killed instantly, as were the son of the hosts who had been driving the boat and their daughter. The only survivor was Allegra, badly burned on much of her body and with a spinal cord injury so severe that she had to be airlifted to Rome for surgery.

Cosima got the call on Saturday afternoon. She came into the house from the pool to answer the phone. Twenty minutes later, she was dressed and waiting for a cab to take her to the airport to fly to Rome to be with Allegra. Her parents were dead, and she was in shock, unable to believe what had happened. She was torn between grief for her parents and terror for her sister after the accident. Everything rested on her now, and the responsibility for her brother too. She was suddenly faced with adult decisions. She couldn't reach Luca, who was on the family's boat in Porto Rotondo, before she left.

She had to leave him a note with the terrible news. He called her crying when she got to Rome and they sobbed together about their parents and Allegra.

Cosima spent the next weeks at her sister's side as Allegra recovered from surgery and was kept in a medical coma while she healed from the burns. It gave Cosima much time to think and grieve for her parents. After the surgery, the doctors told Cosima that Allegra would never walk again. Her spinal cord had been severed. It was yet another terrible blow after losing their parents.

Cosima left Allegra only long enough to plan and attend her parents' funeral in Venice and returned to her sister at the hospital in Rome as quickly as she could. She let Luca return to Sardinia after the funeral, as he wished, since she had no time to spend with him while Allegra was in the hospital, and he didn't want to spend the rest of the summer in Rome.

Luca was greatly subdued and in deep grief over his parents at first. But as he began to feel better, he returned to his old ways and by the end of the summer was going wild with his friends, who came from all over Italy to visit him with no supervision. Cosima was in Rome, couldn't control her brother, and didn't want to leave Allegra alone. She was struggling with the loss of her parents too, and the use of her legs. Cosima left her only for very brief periods of time to go to her father's office and attempt to understand what she needed to know. Her father's assistant and the family attorney, Gian Battista di San Martino, were both very helpful, trying to impart as much information as they could in a short time. They brought papers to the hospital almost daily for Cosima to sign. And Gian Battista was a constant presence and strong support for Cosima to rely on. He took her out to dinner sometimes just so she would get a change of scene from the hospital.

It was two months later, in September, when she got Luca back into some semblance of control, and back to Rome. He refused to return to the university where he'd been studying, and insisted he needed time to "mourn" their parents, which in his case meant going to every party in the city, being out every night, and consuming large amounts of alcohol. But he was back at their apartment, and she got him to check in with her several times a day, so she at least knew where he was, although he often stayed out all night and came home in the morning. She suggested that he work at the store, which he refused to do, and with no set activity, he did whatever he wanted. He stayed out late, slept half the day. She didn't have time to force the issue with him. She was busy with Allegra. And Luca became harder and harder to control. He was enjoying having no parental supervision at eighteen, and paid little attention to Cosima and her rules.

Allegra's progress was slow but steady. She'd had several skin grafts and painful surgeries, but she was surprisingly brave, and philosophical about her injuries. She was quieter than before, after the loss of her parents. But unlike her older brother, she was back in school by Christmas, with a remarkably positive attitude. She would be in a wheelchair forever, but Cosima nursed her as lovingly as any mother, and without parents, the two sisters were even closer than before. Cosima had hired a man to carry Allegra up the staircase to their apartment. Luca was almost never there to help them.

Within six months, Cosima was more serious than ever, still mourning their parents, and had been catapulted into full adulthood. She was running the business, learning as she went. It was the hardest year of her life, and once Allegra was out of the hospital, Cosima went to Venice as often as she could to oversee the store there. Sometimes Gian Battista went with her when he had the time. When he didn't, the palazzo in Venice, where they had spent holidays and family time, seemed achingly empty. It was painful to remember how vibrant it had been when her parents were alive, and how sad it seemed now. Cosima had no time to see her friends or do anything except work at the stores and take care of her sister. Gian Battista was the only source of support in her life.

Allegra was determined to be as independent as she could be once she came home from the hospital. She still talked about designing for the store one day, as though to confirm she had an active future ahead of her. Their longtime housekeeper, Flavia, helped Allegra when Cosima was at work. When she wasn't working or with Allegra, Cosima was chasing Luca down and trying to help him find a sense of direction. He took full advantage of the lack of parental control and fought Cosima on every point.

Their parents' estate was divided equally among them, and Cosima rapidly discovered that her father had spent more than the business had made, on their lifestyle, constant entertaining, several homes, luxurious boats and cars, and extravagant improvements to the store. She was constantly trying to rein in expenses, to pay the bills and her parents' debts, and fighting to keep the business afloat. She couldn't let it go under. She wanted to honor her father, which was a mammoth task for a girl then twenty-four. Her own studies fell by the wayside. She had more important tasks at hand while running the business, taking care of Allegra, and trying to keep Luca in control.

Her father had bought another, bigger building in Rome before he died, on the Via Condotti. He was hoping to enlarge the store into something even more grand. Cosima sold it as soon as she was able to, before construction was started. She sold it at a loss, but they needed the money, and she poured it back into the business. Their production was so meticulous and so slow that she wasn't able to increase their income immediately, and had to find money from other sources, just to keep the business going and meet their expenses and payroll.

They had a huge staff, particularly in Rome, of very fine and well-paid artisans, and a large sales staff with a limited amount to sell. Many of the long-term employees resented her ownership at her age, and the direction she was taking, with her constant concern about cutting costs. She kept a much more watchful eye on their cash flow than her father had. It didn't sit well with the employees, so she had a battle on her hands getting them to follow the new guidelines, directions, and boundaries she gave them. It was an intolerably hard time for her, with life-and-death struggles every day that made her miss her parents all the more, although she was aware now that some of their financial struggles were her father's fault.

A year after her parents' deaths, Cosima put the house in Sardinia on the market. Luca objected strenuously, but she told him point-blank that they were short of money, and since he had no solutions to offer, and didn't want to work himself, he finally gave her his permission to sell their summer home. She was able to sell it at the end of August at a fair price, along with their boats, and the sale gave her much-needed cash to pay her parents' remaining debts and use for the business, and for the family personally. When she gave Luca his share, he spent it within months on new cars, and on the entourage of unsavory people he had collected around him, who preyed on him for money and what he could provide for them. She couldn't stop him, although she tried valiantly to convince him to be more prudent and more selective about his friends. He laughed at her.

She was forced to concentrate on the business, so she could pull it out of the slump her father had created and keep it running. It took another year of dedicated hard work and focus, but she finally increased their profits, and within another year, she could breathe again.

Five years after her parents' deaths, business was booming in both stores, Rome and Venice. Cosima had increased their production speed by adding more artisans and trimming off the fat elsewhere, despite grumbling from the old-timers, which she steadfastly ignored. Allegra was attending design school by then, and very efficient at leading her life from her wheelchair. Luca had taken a showy apartment in Milan and was dating models. He was twenty-three years old and had become a well-known playboy in Rome and Milan, and constantly asked Cosima for money. He had blown through most of his inheritance by then, and had developed a penchant for gambling, in Venice, San Remo, and Monte Carlo. Cosima had done nothing but work for the last five years, but it had borne fruit, and the business was safe for now.

* * *

It had now been fifteen years since her parents' deaths, as she watched the sun come up over Rome from her terrace. She no longer took two months of vacation in the summer, only a few weeks with Allegra, while remaining in frequent contact with her office. The days of extravagance and extreme luxury were over. She had worked hard for the last fifteen years and now Allegra did too. She took Allegra to more modestly priced beach resorts for their holidays, places where they could manage her wheelchair. Allegra was very independent and confident. She had finished design school and Cosima allowed her to introduce small leather items of her own design. Allegra dreamed of designing handbags for the store one day, with a more youthful look, but Cosima had stuck with their traditional models and didn't want to risk losing business with extreme innovations or excessively modern designs. They had their set, ultrareliable, loyal client base, and Cosima didn't want to lose that, so she kept Allegra on a very tight leash as to what she would allow her to design, none of which used her talent or challenged her, which was frustrating for Allegra. Cosima took no risks with the business and stuck with what had always worked.

Allegra rarely went to Venice now. The palazzo was too complicated for her in her wheelchair, and so was the city. Luca stayed at the palazzo occasionally and gave wild parties there, which Cosima scolded him for, and he always reminded her that he was part owner of the palazzo and the business, his share was equal to hers, and she couldn't tell him what to do. They had two old caretakers to watch over the palazzo. And all she could do now was coexist with Luca, knowing that she would wind up picking up the pieces of his messes later, and lending him money. He acted like the son of a rich man, with unlimited funds at his disposal, all of it provided by Cosima to keep the peace and keep him out of trouble. She paid him a substantial allowance every month, which seemed like more than he deserved, since he always wasted it and gambled more than he admitted. He spent as little time as possible with her and told everyone that his older sister was a tyrant and a bore who didn't want him to have a good time and drove him crazy. Cosima felt as though she spent her life cleaning up after him and keeping him from spending as much as he wanted. As a result, he avoided her whenever possible, and tried to poison Allegra against her. He was painfully transparent in his manipulations, and called Cosima shamelessly for money, which she wouldn't give him. He even borrowed money from Allegra at times. She was far more careful with her money than he was, and always had some stashed away. He was totally without conscience or embarrassment about who he borrowed money from. He hadn't become someone Cosima was proud of. He was one of the burdens she managed and endured. She attempted to limit the damage as much as possible, which was all she could do. He couldn't be stopped, only reined in a little, like a wild young stallion.

But as the day dawned over Rome, for once she wasn't worrying about the business, or thinking about her brother, or even Allegra's future, which she worried about too. She was simply enjoying the view from her terrace of the elegant shops on the Via Condotti, the familiar area around the Piazza di Spagna, and the irresistible beauty and magic of Rome before she got swept up in the day and the decisions she would have to make all day at her desk.

She had recently rented out the Palazzo Saverio in Venice. She was determined never to sell it, and to preserve the family history. But renting it was one way to stop Luca from abusing the privilege of owning it. Renting it saved them money, since she hardly used it, and Allegra not at all now because it was on so many levels and had no elevator for her chair, which made it impossible for her without construction for accommodations. For the past six months, since renting the palazzo, Cosima had stayed in a small hotel when she was in Venice, which she was becoming accustomed to. She had rented the palazzo to an enormously wealthy American couple who owned a chain of department stores.

The Johnsons, Bill and Sally, were Texans, very pleasant people who would have loved to carry Saverio leather goods in their stores, but Cosima had explained it wasn't possible. It was against the family philosophy of keeping their goods exclusive to their own stores, a tradition she had upheld to honor her grandfather. Sally and Bill were gracious about it, and had brought in a decorator to transform the palazzo into Texan luxury. Cosima had agreed to it provided the Johnsons made no permanent structural alterations.

They were giving a housewarming party that weekend, which Cosima had agreed to attend, although she never went to big parties. She thought it would be rude not to accept the invitation, and she was curious to see what they'd done to the palazzo. But she was apprehensive too. She was sure it would be vulgar and nothing like the interior during her parents' lifetime, but she had to be practical now. She had rented the palazzo for an enormous amount, so she wouldn't have to sell it. And the Johnsons had agreed to the price without hesitating or complaining. They loved Venice, spent two months there every year, and were thrilled to have the palazzo. Sally had told Cosima that people would be flying in from all over the States and Europe for their party.

Despite how effusive the Johnsons were, and how larger than life, Cosima liked them. They had grown children she'd never met, and interesting taste, and it was always possible that they had done the palazzo beautifully, although the famous decorator they'd used had a reputation for over-the-top excess. He'd done a château in France, and Cosima had cringed when she saw the photographs. She hoped that the Johnsons hadn't gone too overboard in their décor at Palazzo Saverio, even though it was more than likely they had. But they hadn't bought it, and how far could they go in a rented house? She was about to find out.

She had important meetings that week before the party. She had the entire new fall line of designs to approve, and she worked closely with the designers. They'd added a line of silk and cashmere clothes for men and women five years before. It was doing extremely well and had turned out to be a real moneymaker. They had also added a line of hunting clothes for men. They were very popular, along with their other equestrian items, which had been inspired by the saddles her grandfather had made.

Saverio's only real competition was Hermès, and even her grandfather had said that there was room in the world for both of them. Each house had its own distinctive style, and their clients were loyal. Both houses followed many of the same old-fashioned rules to protect their exclusivity and brand. Many of the Saverio customers loved having to come to Italy to buy from them.

Cosima entertained her biggest customers when they came to

Rome, and invited them to dinner at her apartment, or their favorite restaurants, and even let them wander peacefully through the store after hours, noticing items they might not have seen otherwise, and she had her selling staff bring them some of the very latest items directly from their workrooms. Their signature handbag, the Tizianna, named after her mother, had been made famous by Sophia Loren. Grace Kelly had ordered three of them and wore them alternately with her Hermès Kellys. There was even a smaller one, for evening, named the Adria bag, which her grandfather had named for her grandmother when he created it. Cosima had the Tizianna in every color and wore them daily. It was a perfect work bag.

Luca objected vehemently to the signature bags, and said they were just one more old-fashioned element that kept them out of step with the modern world. He thought everything about Saverio was antiquated, and he had no respect for tradition. Allegra had designed a bag she named the Cosima, which she was dying to have made, but Cosima wouldn't let the workroom produce it. She thought it was too avant-garde and fashion-forward for their line. She insisted that Saverio wasn't dictated by passing fashion trends. It was about timeless elegance and style. Their products were classic. At twenty-nine, Allegra was hungry to move forward as a young designer, but Cosima kept her within the boundaries of their brand and history.

Luca was bored by all of it, except that their profits paid his bills. He was more interested in buying fast horses and gambling, or in almost anything for a profit. Whatever brought in fast, easy money, Luca liked. He considered their own products ancient history and predicted that one day Saverio would be viewed as the dinosaur of the industry. He dismissed his sister's success at keeping their stores relevant and alive as one of the most respected brands in the world, no matter how limited their distribution. That was part of the magic of Saverio products. Being hard to get created a high level of demand for them, none of which Luca understood or appreciated. History was of no interest to him, only easy money, which he was able to spend even faster than they could make it.

Cosima left the terrace to shower and dress, and she would stop for a cup of coffee with Allegra before she went to her office. She liked to be at her desk by eight o'clock. She would have a slew of emails to answer from suppliers and important customers, people who appreciated Saverio and couldn't get enough of them, many with famous names, and new customers begging to own one. The business was already far more successful than it had been in her father's day. It was still a struggle at times, but she had big dreams, and maybe one day she'd no longer have to worry about money. Until then, she was honoring the name, and carrying on the traditions, just as her grandfather and father would have wanted. It had been a long, hard climb for fifteen years to grow the business, selling only in the two cities her father and grandfather approved of, and she respected their wishes.

At thirty-eight, she felt as though she had only just started. They still had far to go, but she was sure that they would get there. She was thinking of opening a pop-up store for two weeks for Fashion Week in Milan, trying to keep the brand current and in full view in another city at a busy time, which would attract attention. She still had new ideas for the brand. Considering where she had started at twenty-three, unprepared to run the business, she had done a very good job. And there was always so much more to do. Every day there were new challenges for her to face. She could hardly wait to get to her desk each morning. She loved the business and all it represented. It was the epitome of elegance and style.

It was a new day, and a beautiful morning. She brushed her long blond hair and twisted it into a knot without looking. Even after fifteen years of running the business, she was still excited about what lay ahead, as she stepped into the shower and began her day. She was grateful for how far they'd come. Her love of the business was the driving force in her life. She knew she had single-handedly kept it alive for the past fifteen years, and she had saved and improved the company she had inherited, with love and hard work.

Her family and their business were her life.